THE LAST MORIARTY

THE LAST MORIARTY

CHARLES VELEY

THOMAS & MERCER

Text copyright © 2015 Charles Veley
All rights reserved.

Published by Thomas & Mercer, Seattle

www.apub.com

Amazon, the Amazon logo, and Thomas & Mercer are trademarks of Amazon.com, Inc., or its affiliates.

ISBN-13: 9781477829721
ISBN-10: 1477829725

Cover design by Todd Alan Johnson

Library of Congress Control Number: 2014957572

Printed in the United States of America

For Pam

TABLE OF CONTENTS

PART FOUR: NEVER FORGOT

Remember, remember the Fifth of November,
The Gunpowder Treason and Plot,
I see no reason why Gunpowder Treason
Should ever be forgot.

Anonymous poem

PREFACE

These papers describe certain events that occurred during a period of five days in early November of last year. For reasons that will be obvious, I have sworn faithfully to Mr. Sherlock Holmes that this account will never be published during my lifetime, and that I will not even mention the existence of two of the principal characters in any of my other chronicles. I have therefore instructed my executors to delay publication of these papers until the twenty-first century. In that far-distant future, I trust, readers who love Sherlock Holmes will want to learn even more about this most brilliant and honorable man.

John H. Watson, MD
London, 5 April, 1896

PART ONE

REMEMBER, REMEMBER

1. INSOMNIA, INTERRUPTED

My story begins before dawn on Friday the first of November, 1895, All Souls Day. Nearly three years had elapsed since my beloved wife, Mary, had departed this life. Nearly two years had gone by since I had returned to the lodgings I had shared with Sherlock Holmes at 221B Baker Street.

Holmes never explained why he had asked me to come back, but I believe that he wanted me close at hand, where I would be readily available to employ my medical skills. Only a very few clients and senior government officials knew that he had survived his fateful confrontation with the evil Professor James Moriarty at the Reichenbach Falls four years before. Yet he had been busier than ever, immersing himself in his work in a manner that I could see was taxing even his strong constitution. Of course he ignored my repeated warnings. I believe that some inner guide told him that one day he might go too far, however, and that my immediate help might then be urgently required. I should also like to believe that Holmes at least equally valued my friendship and concern, and that I filled a need for emotional support, even in one who presented himself to the public as purely an impersonal, calculating, machinelike intellect.

Holmes had slept fitfully that night, as I knew from being awakened intermittently by the sounds of him moving about amid the customary clutter in our sitting room and his laboratory space. I had not had to endure this disquiet when Holmes and I had shared our Baker Street lodgings prior to my marriage, but since my return, his wakefulness had occurred almost nightly. Accordingly I was convinced that the cause of Holmes's insomnia was somehow connected with the ordeal he had suffered at Reichenbach with Moriarty and his ruthless associate, Colonel Sebastian Moran, and that he had not told me the whole story of that fearsome encounter.

I also felt there was some connection with this event and his refusal to let me publish any account of his return, or tell the public of the many singular triumphs he had attained during the past four years. Further, although Holmes continued to perform brilliantly during his waking hours, I sensed a growing frustration in his manner, as if he felt that the cases that occupied his time were somehow lacking in significance, and that there was some other, greater problem that he felt unwilling to share with me. Each time I woke and heard him rustling his papers or rattling his lab equipment below my sleeping quarters, I tried to fathom the cause of his distress. To calm my spirits and return to sleep, I comforted myself with the vow that in some manner, someday, I would help him with whatever afflictions might be troubling him.

My wakeful thoughts were running along these lines before dawn on that November 1, when they were interrupted by the sound of footsteps ascending the stairs that led from Baker Street up to our rooms.

Concentrating, I realized the steps were heavier than Mrs. Hudson's, and slower, and were those of one individual rather than a group. From the firmness and regularity of the sounds, it was plain that the intruder was making no effort to conceal his presence. I sat up in the darkness, recalling that my service revolver lay unloaded in the top drawer of my dressing cabinet.

The footsteps stopped as they reached the hallway outside our door. Our rooms had been set ablaze by the Moriarty gang four years ago, and shot at by Colonel Moran from across the street eighteen months previously. Were we now to be invaded? But Colonel Moran was behind bars, and Professor Moriarty, the leader of the gang, was dead. Many of his former associates had been arrested and tried, and were now in prison. The gang had in all likelihood withered away and would no longer be a criminal force to be reckoned with. I chided myself for such a foolish fear.

Still, as quietly as I could, I got out of bed and hurried into my robe, neglecting to put on my slippers. I went to my dressing cabinet, my wakeful mind filled with the vague notion that if I were wrong and there really was danger, a show of my service revolver might be useful even if it was not loaded. Below me I heard Holmes's rapid footfalls on our sitting room floorboards. The steps softened as he crossed our Oriental rug, and then slowed and stopped as the latch in our entry door clicked open. Then I heard Holmes's voice:

"Mycroft. Do come in."

I felt immediate relief, but nonetheless my heartbeat quickened as I heard the name. Whatever had brought Mycroft Holmes to Baker Street would be momentous. Only the most extreme national peril would induce Holmes's brother to leave his familiar, well-protected universe in Whitehall.

I opened my bedroom door and, coming down the small flight of stairs that led from my room to our sitting room, I saw the faint glow of the street lanterns below our bow window, along with another light at the entrance to our chambers. There, Holmes's older and magnificently corpulent brother stood patiently just inside our doorway, holding a brass candleholder with a lit candle.

In the yellow-gold candlelight, Mycroft's round face shone beneath his top hat and above the cape that enfolded his body. His facial expressions conveyed concern, embarrassment, and a sense of crisis.

Holmes was clad in his dressing gown. He said, "You were too overwrought to notice the switches to our electric lamps."

"The matter is urgent, as you have deduced."

"What time is it?"

"5:40. I did not want to wake Mrs. Hudson. Where is Watson?"

"I am here," I said from my stairway.

"Ah. Watson, good morning. Sherlock, get dressed."

"Tell me why."

"The Prime Minister is waiting. Lansdowne and Goschen are with him."

I recognized the names of the Secretary of State for War and the First Lord of the Admiralty.

"Where?"

"St. Thomas Hospital."

"So there is a body. Whose?"

"I have a carriage outside. At the hospital you will learn all about the case."

And with that, Mycroft withdrew, carefully maneuvering the candleholder as he closed our door.

We heard Mycroft descending the stairs. And my heart surged with a familiar feeling of anticipation as Holmes said, "I take it you will come?"

2. A BODY IS EXAMINED

In the glow of the streetlamp, wisps of yellow fog greeted us as we emerged from 221B Baker Street. Mycroft's carriage awaited us at the curb just outside our doorway. I noticed a black four-wheeler cab drawn by a powerful bay horse waiting for someone not far down the street. As our carriage pulled away from the curb, the cab moved out to follow us.

Holmes and Mycroft were both silent during the carriage ride. Traffic at that hour was light, and soon we had driven past Parliament and crossed over Westminster Bridge to where we could see the hospital, a sprawling chain of brick buildings newly constructed in the Gothic style. As we approached Lambeth Palace Road the huge structures loomed darkly above us, their pointed rooftops silhouetted against the first showings of the sunrise in the eastern sky.

We came to a stop behind the last of four well-appointed carriages, all waiting in a line along the curb in front of the hospital entrance. A cluster of uniformed drivers and footmen stood beside the first carriage, smoking and chatting among themselves.

Dismounting from our carriage, I noticed the same black cab had stopped about twenty feet behind ours, on the far side of the hospital entrance. I pointed this out to Holmes.

"Thank you, Watson" was his only reply.

Inspector Lestrade was waiting on the curb. The Scotland Yard man looked nervous, his sharp features paler and his small black eyes even more worried than usual.

Holmes indicated the cab, visible at the edge of the yellow fog. He asked Lestrade, "Is that yours?"

"Should it be?"

"If you intended to provide us protection with it, then yes. It followed us from Baker Street."

"Maybe it's the Commissioner's doing." Lestrade shook his head and turned away from the cab. "I'm to escort you."

The four of us passed through the entrance hall with its statue of the Queen seated on her throne in full ceremonial robes, and soon entered the hospital's operating theater, a spacious area behind the entry lobby. The room had been specially constructed for medical school instruction and demonstration, with soaring walls and steeply raked seating that could accommodate nearly one hundred onlookers. Today there was a mortuary gurney positioned at the center of the lower level, draped in a water-stained olive-drab blanket. The blanket covered a human shape. Small rivulets of water seeped from brown towels placed on the floor beside the gurney wheels. Light came from a skylight high overhead, supplemented by electric lamps placed strategically at the head and foot of the gurney. The lamps would illuminate its contents without disturbing the view of the five very important gentlemen who, we saw, were to be Holmes's audience.

These leaders of England sat on the wooden benches above us, their shoes at our eye level as we stood beside the gurney. I recognized the Prime Minister, Lord Salisbury, perched uncomfortably in the front row, his face a mask behind the spreading curls of his magnificent black beard. To his right was George Goschen, now First Lord of the Admiralty, a bluff, hearty gray-haired former businessman who, in his previous role as Chancellor of the Exchequer, had been grateful for Holmes's assistance on several occasions. Beside him sat Baron Halsbury, Lord Chancellor of Her Majesty's courts. Holmes and I knew of him, of course, though none of Holmes's cases had come before him. The papers were fond of caricaturing him in the form of a toad, for his face was corpulent and pouting, and he sat hunched over, as if prepared to spring up at any moment. Behind Goschen was a younger man I did not recognize. Slender and flaxen-haired, the young man wore a steel-rimmed monocle in his left eye, along with a haughty expression, possibly, I thought, to compensate for his junior status.

Sir Edward Bradford, Commissioner of the Metropolitan Police, sat at the young man's side. Also an admirer of Holmes's work, Sir Edward was normally the very essence of urbane white-haired aristocracy. Today I thought I detected a tremor in his wide white mustache and a note of anxiety in his greeting.

"Thank you for coming, Mr. Holmes. I hope you are prepared to help us. And thank you as well, Dr. Watson."

"I will do what I can, Commissioner." Holmes was already circling the gurney. I merely nodded. Clearly the stage was Holmes's and the august personages in this audience had no interest in whatever response I might make.

Mycroft had hauled himself up the steep stairs to the first level of seats and settled beside the young flaxen-haired man. I quickly joined him. Mycroft leaned forward to speak, but the younger man spoke first.

"I am Henry Clevering, chief of staff for Lord Lansdowne, who I believe you know is Secretary of State for War. He unfortunately could not be with us this morning. I am authorized to represent him."

Holmes nodded.

"Your task, Mr. Holmes, is to discover why the unfortunate American gentleman on the gurney there chose to commit suicide last night by leaping from the Westminster Bridge and drowning himself."

Taking his cue, Lestrade drew back the blanket from the gurney, revealing the body of a clean-shaven middle-aged male Caucasian in water-soaked evening dress. The formal white shirt-front and white bow tie were stained yellow-gray, presumably from the waters of the Thames.

The dull brown eyes held no clues for me as they stared vacantly upward at the skylight.

"Who is he?" asked Holmes.

As if in answer, Lestrade removed the wool blanket completely. At the foot of the gurney was a soggy black wool cape lined with black silk. Positioned as I was in the front row, and close to that end of the gurney, I was able to discern next to the cape a man's black leather wallet, opened to reveal possibly a dozen five- and ten-pound notes, and a silver card case. Beside the wallet was a large brass key attached to a round brass key tag. Holmes turned it over and said, "On one side of this key tag is engraved the number 404. On the other side is the word *Savoy*."

Holmes picked up the wallet and glanced at its contents. "Mr. Frederick Foster, of 21 Riverside Drive, New York, New York. Has anyone here seen Mr. Foster before?"

Mycroft, Goschen, and Clevering all nodded.

"Why is he so important?"

"We have not yet decided whether to disclose that." Clevering glanced at the Prime Minister for confirmation, but Lord Salisbury remained impassive.

From inside the silver case Holmes withdrew and held up several identical business cards, each presumably with Foster's name. "Perhaps I should ask Mr. Rockefeller how he would like the investigation to proceed?"

"No!"

This from Goschen, who went on, "The matter is entirely too sensitive."

Clevering turned accusingly to Mycroft. "Sir! What have you told your brother?"

"He has told me nothing," Holmes said. "These cards identify this man's employer as the Standard Oil Corporation, and a child could deduce that a man carrying Standard Oil business cards is Mr. Rockefeller's employee. Now, why is this man's death important enough to bring three leaders of Her Majesty's government to St. Thomas Hospital at an hour when the sun has barely come up?"

While the four officials and Mycroft conferred quietly, I watched as Holmes walked around the body. He removed the man's right shoe and placed it beside the cloak. At the other end of the cart he carefully lifted the head and knelt to observe the neck. He placed both of his hands on the soft, wet shirtfront and pressed down, putting his weight behind the movement. Then he did so once more.

He looked up to his audience. "Mr. Clevering. I cannot fulfill the task you have assigned me."

The young man gaped in surprised indignation. "Then you are dismissed. We shall have to find someone else."

"No one can do what you have asked me to do."

"Mr. Holmes, I have heard of your high opinion of yourself, but this is hardly—"

"Oh, do shut up, Clevering." Commissioner Bradford raised a hand. "Mr. Holmes. Please explain what you have learned from your examination of Mr. Foster's body."

"He was murdered," said Holmes.

The Commissioner frowned. "How?"

Holmes turned to Lestrade. "First, did anyone witness Mr. Foster's fall from the Westminster Bridge?"

"A constable was on duty on the other side of the bridge, making his rounds from Parliament. He heard a loud splash."

"Any others on the bridge?"

"No one. It was just after midnight."

"And what did the constable do?"

"He ran up to the center of the bridge and looked down."

"And he saw no one on the bridge?"

"No one. Well, he did say there was a carriage. It was at the far end of the bridge, and going away. It was too far away to identify in the fog."

"What did the constable do then?"

"He ran to the base of the bridge and untethered a small rowboat that is kept there for such emergencies. He rowed as quickly as he could, and found Mr. Foster's body floating on the surface. Facedown."

"Did he notice anything else in the water? Perhaps a sponge, or a towel? A cloth of some kind?"

"No, nothing else. He brought the body to shore on this side of the river and called for help from a constable there to move it to the patrolman's outpost."

"And, upon seeing Mr. Foster's wallet and realizing that he was the subject of an urgent lookout notice from Scotland Yard—"

Clevering interrupted, indignant once more. "How can you possibly know that?"

"He was important—since otherwise you would not be here—so his absence would have been noticed and urgent attempts made to find him. Such attempts would include Scotland Yard."

"Quite right," said Commissioner Bradford. "Now, Mr. Holmes, you say he was murdered?"

"No water was expelled from his lungs when I put my weight on his chest, so he did not drown. Chloroform fumes, however, were expelled, so sudden inhalation of chloroform was the cause of death. His chin and upper lip are slightly bruised, and no pad or towel was seen in the water or on the bridge, so he did not inhale the chloroform voluntarily. He was murdered."

The Commissioner nodded. "Inspector Lestrade, did you notice the odor of chloroform?"

"Just now, yes, sir. We had not thought of pressing on Mr. Foster's chest."

"Have you anything to add, Mr. Holmes?"

"Mr. Foster was not killed in an ordinary robbery, since his wallet was full. He was probably lured to his death somewhere on this side of the river, in a building with a fine-gravel carriage path where carpentry work was taking place. One of his attackers was known to him and was likely a woman."

His audience stared at Holmes in astonishment. Clevering said, "I am sure we all marvel at your clairvoyant powers, Mr. Holmes. Now if you will be so good as to explain this incredible chain of suppositions—"

The Prime Minister interrupted, standing and making a polite show of glancing at his pocket watch. "Mr. Holmes. Will you promise me your assistance?"

"If I am in full possession of the facts."

"We do not condone murder," said the Prime Minister. "However, an unsupervised investigation could have consequences adverse to the national interest. We cannot have this case brought into the papers."

"I have no desire for public recognition. But I shall need access to room 404 at the Savoy."

"The police have inspected it and found nothing to indicate foul play."

"They may have missed something."

"The room has already been cleaned and made available for rental, since it was apparent that Mr. Foster had committed suicide."

"If it was so apparent, and you wished to conceal the matter, then why did you summon me here?"

An awkward silence ensued.

Holmes nodded, "Now I understand. When Mr. Rockefeller asks, I shall tell him my conclusion as to the death of his employee."

"Why would Mr. Rockefeller want to ask you anything?"

"Since we were all called here at dawn, someone of importance wanted me to investigate. Since clearly you gentlemen wish me *not* to investigate, none of you is that important someone. You were therefore coerced into sending for me. Mr. Rockefeller coerced you."

The Prime Minister had descended the steps of the amphitheater and was walking toward the door. The others were following him.

"You cannot run away from this," said Holmes. "Mr. Rockefeller is not known for his patience or his credulity. He will want the truth, and he will want to hear it from me."

The Prime Minister stopped for a moment, turned, and inclined his head in a nod toward Mycroft.

Mycroft said, "The Prime Minister would like you to assist us. I will explain."

But just at that moment from the direction of the hospital lobby came a deafening thunderclap that shook the walls all around us. From the skylight, broken glass began to fall.

3. A YOUNG AMERICAN

Two hours later, our eyes still smarted from the smoke and dust at the hospital entrance. In my memory I could hear the agonized cries of the horses and see the mangled form of one of them as it writhed, horribly wounded, on the pavement beside the remnants of what had been the Prime Minister's carriage, first in the procession and now demolished.

Holmes and I sat with Mycroft and Commissioner Bradford in the Diogenes Club, in one of the upstairs rooms where talking was permitted. The curtains were drawn, but electric wall sconces were lit, and fresh coals now glowed in the wrought iron grate of the oak-paneled fireplace. The stout oak door had been shut to ensure our conversation would remain confidential.

The PM, Clevering, and Goschen were no longer with us, having been spirited away to their offices in Downing Street and Westminster by Lestrade and the Commissioner's men. Mycroft had poured a restorative snifter of brandy for each of us. I gratefully sipped mine, inhaling the warm bouquet as I tried to identify what possible motive anyone might have had for causing such an outrage. Holmes left his brandy untouched. He had wanted to stay at the scene, but the Prime Minister had insisted that we all depart at once from what he referred to as the zone of danger.

The coachmen and footmen had seen what had happened. An old ragpicker had come shambling out of the wooded area at the fringe of Archbishop's Park, pulling a cart piled high with the bundles of refuse that were his stock in trade. He had come nearly halfway across the road when some of the men noticed that he was apparently heading for the Prime Minister's carriage. Naturally they called for the ragpicker to turn back and stay away from the carriages, whereupon the man took to his heels and ran back into the park, leaving his cart behind. The blast came moments later, a great flash of light and a concussive report that rendered the men temporarily blind and deaf.

They had described the ragpicker as tall, gray-bearded, and stooped, dressed in a porkpie hat and dirty long black coat. No, they could not recall anything else about him, other than their impression that from the way he ran he was not a young man, though they could not be certain due to the shock they had received.

"We know one thing, however," said the Commissioner. "The bomb was detonated by a timing device that made use of electricity, similar to the one in this drawing." He showed us a penciled sketch of a bundle of cigar-shaped tubes, a cube-like object with wires, a geared clockwork mechanism, and two conical objects. "It would have been about the size of a loaf of bread." Then he held out his palm, on which rested two white ceramic conical objects that matched those in the drawing. Each was about an inch and a half in length. "These are ceramic insulating connectors. They are used to connect electrical wires. One of Lestrade's men found them amid the remnants of the ragpicker's cart."

"Deductions, Sherlock?" asked Mycroft.

At this moment the door opened and we saw a young man, tall and ruggedly handsome, in a tweed suit of American style, peering at us through rimless spectacles. He was the picture of American confidence, apparently well accustomed to influence far greater than that of most men of his age. Coming up breathlessly behind him was one of the club's gray-haired attendants.

"I do apologize, Mr. Holmes. Young Mr. Rockefeller would not wait for me to announce him."

"But you have done so nonetheless," said Mycroft, unperturbed. "Thank you, my good man. Please join us, Mr. Rockefeller."

Young Rockefeller came in as the attendant withdrew. "I'm John D. Rockefeller Jr.," he said, shaking hands with each of us in turn. "Johnny to my friends." As he came to Holmes his face lit up in an eager smile. "I guess the Prime Minister got my father's telegram. And wow, what a thundering big explosion there at the hospital. As soon as it happened I told my driver to skedaddle! Then I thought better of it and waited around till you came out and got into your carriage, and we followed you here."

Holmes said, "It was you in the cab?"

"Yep. I came to your place on Baker Street and followed you. My father wanted to be sure you were on the case. He wants the best."

Holmes nodded somberly. "Please take a seat, Mr. Rockefeller."

"Johnny, please." He joined us at the table, sitting across from Holmes.

"Johnny, then. Now, what does your father want me to investigate?"

"He wants you to find out what happened to Foster, our security man, who disappeared last night. Father is with my mother on their steamship in Southampton. They plan to sail up the Thames and arrive here Monday. But Father wired the Prime Minister that if you weren't put on the case immediately he would go back to New York."

"I have taken the case."

"Was Foster in that hospital?"

"Mr. Foster's body was in the hospital. His death had been officially ruled a suicide," said Holmes with a glance at the Commissioner. "However, a further examination of the body leads to a different conclusion."

"Murder?"

Holmes nodded.

"Poor old Foster. What did he get himself into?"

"I would be happy to share the details with you or your father at another time. I will also find the murderer."

"You're hired," said Johnny.

Mycroft said, "The Prime Minister would also like to retain your services, though in another capacity. I was about to explain that when the explosion interrupted us."

"Is there any reason why I should not pursue both matters at once?"

"Mr. Rockefeller's and the Prime Minister's interests are aligned," replied Mycroft.

Holmes was jotting a name on a notepad. He tore off the sheet and handed it to the Commissioner. "Then would you please have your men compile a list of any reported thefts of dynamite occurring within the past year? Knowing the quantities that are missing would be particularly important. Also I should like to have a conversation with this gentleman at the earliest possible opportunity. Would you please have your men arrange for me to visit him in his prison cell?"

"There is a telephone outside," Mycroft told the Commissioner, who left the room, closing the door securely behind him.

Holmes then turned to his brother. "Now, Mycroft, will you please explain why the Prime Minister was testing my integrity, and what that has to do with the Admiralty's impending meeting with Mr. Rockefeller?"

4. A REQUEST FOR ASSISTANCE

Mycroft did not seem at all surprised at what to me were two astonishing assertions on Holmes's part. His tone was very matter-of-fact. "Lord Salisbury wanted to see for himself that you still retained your deductive powers and your independent spirit. There is a meeting to be held between certain cabinet officials, Mr. Rockefeller, and two equally prominent Americans. There will be enormous official pressure to proceed with the meeting and to ignore any obstacles that may arise. The Prime Minister feels it is imperative to have your assistance."

"How am I to assist?"

"You are to find Mr. Foster's killer or killers, discover whether or not the security arrangements for the meeting have been compromised, and if so, devise alternative arrangements and insist that they be followed."

"Was Clevering aware of the PM's view?"

"He was not. Lord Salisbury kept his own counsel, except for confiding in Mr. Rockefeller, and in me. He telephoned Mr. Rockefeller in Southampton after Foster had gone missing, and asked him to send the wire insisting on your involvement."

"I am pleased to have his support. Will he enforce my recommendations?"

"He hopes your persuasive powers will obviate the need for that."

"I see." Holmes gave one of his wry smiles and turned to young Mr. Rockefeller. "Now, Johnny, what else can you tell us of Mr. Foster?"

"Foster was with the Pinkertons before Father hired him. We all came over to Southampton, and Father sent me ahead with Mr. Foster to London. He thought it would be good experience—that's why he let me take time off from college."

"When was the last time you saw Mr. Foster?"

"Yesterday morning at breakfast. He said he had an appointment with a little old lady."

"Did he say where?"

"He said she lived on Threadneedle Street. He said it as though it was funny."

Holmes nodded at Mycroft. "So the meeting is to be held at the Bank of England."

"The Bank is sometimes referred to as 'the old lady of Threadneedle Street,'" I explained to Johnny.

Holmes continued, "Were you and Mr. Foster both staying at the Savoy?"

"It's been about a week now."

"And have you noticed anything unusual during your stay?"

Johnny blushed. "No, not really."

"Please describe it nonetheless."

"Well, someone slid a theater program under the door of my room."

"Was there anything unusual about the program?"

"It was for the show playing at the Savoy Theatre—that's just next to the hotel. The unusual thing was that someone had drawn a circle around the name of one of the women in the chorus, and it was the name of a young woman I had met back home. I asked Mr. Foster if he knew anything about it and he said he'd check around."

"A young American lady in the Savoy Theatre chorus?"

Johnny shrugged. "Is that so unusual? She's very talented. We sang together in a concert. The girls from her school and the boys from mine got together in our campus chapel in Providence. That's in Rhode Island. And I'd corresponded with her a bit after that. Brilliant girl. Her name is Lucy James. But I can't figure out how anyone here would have known that I'd even met her."

"Clearly someone wants you to see her and renew your acquaintance."

"I bought a ticket for tonight's performance."

"Use it, then, by all means. Write her a note and ask her to meet with you. Learn what you can. But be exceedingly careful."

"You think there is danger?"

"There is an organization at work here, Johnny. Someone murdered Mr. Foster and took care that we should learn that he had been killed when they could easily have hidden his body or removed the wallet and the room key that identified him. Their confederates waited until the body had been discovered and followed to where the body was taken. Then they observed the parade of official carriages, and then they set off a bomb. Their capabilities have been demonstrated, and their message is clear."

"What message?"

"'Mr. Rockefeller, go home. Mr. Prime Minister, do not hold your meeting. If you do, you may expect us to cause you harm.' This is what we have been told this morning, Johnny."

"My father is not a coward. He receives threats against his life every day of the year."

"No one is doubting his bravery. But please consider the consequences if your father and his associates were to be harmed here, after having come to England at the invitation of Her Majesty's government."

He was about to continue when we were interrupted by the return of the Commissioner. Ashen-faced, Sir Edward handed Holmes the sheet from the notepad. He said, "We cannot arrange for you to meet Colonel Sebastian Moran. Three nights ago, Moran escaped from Dartmoor Prison."

"Who is Colonel Moran?" asked Johnny.

"He is an assassin," said Holmes. "He was formerly employed by the Moriarty gang, once the most powerful criminal organization in England."

5. A DELIGHTFUL PERFORMANCE

One of the more remarkable qualities possessed by Holmes is his ability to focus his mind on what he chooses, rather than being distracted by each of the urgent matters that press upon him and that would, for persons of a different emotional makeup, be all-consuming. I was marveling at this ability of his that evening as we sat together in our mezzanine box at the Savoy Theatre. After the disturbing news of Colonel Moran's escape, we had spent a fruitless several hours at the Savoy Hotel and much of the afternoon at the Bank of England inspecting its entrances, exits, and conference rooms. I was wondering why Holmes had decided to pause in the investigation, and, moreover, why he would choose to appear in a public venue without a disguise for the first time since his return from Reichenbach. I had even questioned him on these points, but his only response had been a shrug and an enigmatic "Because someone obviously wants Johnny Rockefeller to meet with someone named Lucy James at the Savoy Theatre. Because Mr. Foster was killed after he promised to check on Lucy James. And because life is short."

We were watching the revival of what I consider to be Gilbert and Sullivan's masterpiece, *The Mikado*, from the same seats we had occupied for the original performance ten years earlier, thanks to Mycroft having kept up the payments for the box during Holmes's three-year absence from London. As the first act unfolded, I sometimes imagined that I had gone back in the time machine of Mr. Wells's novel, to those days when I had yet to meet my beloved Mary and when our all-too-brief years of married happiness were still before us. After I thought of the perils that lay ahead, I tried to anticipate how I could assist Holmes, scanning the audience from time to time for any sign of Moran's presence. But each time I caught my attention wandering backward or forward in this fashion, I reminded myself that I should emulate Holmes's example and appreciate the beauty of the performance that we had come to the theater to enjoy.

Our box was on the second upper level, very near to the right side of the stage. While these seats were not the best to appreciate the symmetry of the colorful Japanese setting, they did allow us to hear Mr. Gilbert's witty lyrics and spoken dialogue with remarkable clarity. The view from this angle also enabled us to see the facial expressions of the conductor and several of the violinists in the orchestra pit. Glancing at Holmes after the frequent moments of humor during the performance, I had been puzzled to see that he had apparently not been paying attention to the actors at all, but rather looking at the conductor and the musicians.

Attempting to discern what in particular had merited Holmes's attention, I took up the opera glasses that were provided by the management for long-preferred customers such as Holmes. Through the glasses, I scanned the faces below us, trying to identify some distinguishing expression or trait.

At first I could see nothing of apparent interest. All were engrossed in their sheet music. From time to time, the conductor would glance up from his music stand to stay in time with the actors, and the musicians would glance up from their music stands to stay in time with the conductor.

But then the aristocratic loveliness of one of the violinists caught my attention. Graceful as a swan, but with the large dark eyes of an Egyptian princess, she seemed to embrace her violin with a lover's passion as she moved with the music. Then, as the song she accompanied came to an end, she lowered her instrument and leaned forward, like the other musicians, to prepare her sheet music for the next orchestral entrance.

Unlike the others, she did not sit back and wait disinterestedly while the actors spoke their lines. Rather, she looked upward at the stage to view what she could of the scene, exhibiting the keenest interest and appreciation as she did so. I was unable to guess whether she was attempting to observe any one actor, but I remember thinking at the time that if one man was indeed the object of her attention, then he was a lucky fellow indeed.

At that moment, however, something inexplicable occurred. She seemed to become aware of my speculation, for she glanced up in my direction, and then stared for a time that seemed like an eternity. She was looking directly at me, her dark eyes and lovely mouth widening in astonishment, as if to say, "How dare you, sir, to intrude upon my private thoughts!" Through my opera glasses, I even thought that I detected a blush suffusing her pale cheeks with a bright pink. I lowered my glasses with acute embarrassment, but I could not keep my eyes from her.

She dropped her gaze and, in what I thought was a very marked manner, reached out to adjust her music. She then sat back with her instrument held primly on her lap, waiting impassively, just like the others around her.

I puzzled over this for a few moments, but could not account for it. When the music resumed, the lovely violinist was once again engrossed as she performed with her companions.

"Holmes," I said quietly, without turning my head, "did you see the first violinist a few moments ago? She seemed to be looking directly at us."

There was no reply. I turned and saw that Holmes was not in his seat.

I looked around to the entrance to our box and saw his retreating form as it passed through the maroon entry curtains. Quickly I followed, passing a black-uniformed usher who stared at me with disapproval, and found myself in the upper lobby.

I saw Inspector Lestrade standing at the refreshment bar in his black overcoat, holding his fedora hat as he waited for Holmes. As I caught up to Holmes I noticed a white note card in his hand. No doubt Lestrade had given the note card to the usher I had just seen, with a message asking Holmes to join him.

Soon the three of us were together beneath a glittering chandelier that commanded the center of the lobby.

Lestrade's sharp eyes darted around the room. "Mr. Holmes, further interviews with the hotel staff indicate Foster purchased a ticket for last night's performance at this theater. But he did not pick it up from the box office. However, he was seen backstage yesterday afternoon."

"Where, precisely?"

"In the workshop."

"By whom?"

"By the set supervisor."

"The set supervisor remembered Mr. Foster's name?"

"Evidently. We have arranged with the manager of the theater company to interview the fellow after tonight's performance."

"If you please, Lestrade," said Holmes. "After we interview that gentlemen, I would appreciate a few moments with the actress named Lucy James."

"I'll see to it, Mr. Holmes."

"And now, if you will excuse me, unless there is something else that is immediately pressing, Watson and I will return to our seats. With Colonel Moran at large, we will take care not to miss those few delights that present themselves for us to experience."

6. AN EFFUSIVE IMPRESARIO

After the performance Lestrade took us into the recesses of the theater behind the glittering white marble lobby. We walked through a narrow corridor lined by colorful but fading posters of past productions at the Savoy. Soon we found ourselves at the door to the office of Richard D'Oyly Carte, a principal owner of both the Savoy Theatre and the adjacent Savoy Hotel.

Lestrade opened the door. "Mr. Carte, these are the gentlemen I told you about. To interview the set supervisor and the actress."

Carte nodded absently, barely glancing up from behind a desk loaded with stacks of papers. Though he was in his fifties, his smooth, handsome features had retained a youthful firmness beneath his close-cropped beard and mustache, as if he were somehow protected from the ravages of worry and time. "He'll be in the theater for the cleanup," he said. "She'll be in her dressing room."

"I'll fetch the supervisor first," said Lestrade. He motioned for us to enter, and then left, closing the door behind us.

For a long moment Carte continued serenely to inspect the paper he was holding. His mild dark eyes appeared capable of facing any crisis with calm, even with friendliness. At the time it struck me that this attitude was likely the source of his still-youthful appearance, and that it would be very helpful to him in his dealings, not only with hardheaded tradesmen and financiers, but with the emotional artistic sensibilities of the theatrical troupers in his employ.

Then Carte looked up and saw us. His face registered frank and open amazement, and he moved quickly from behind the desk toward Holmes as if to embrace him. "Why, it's Mr. Holmes, and in evening dress just as always! My dear fellow! Inspector Lestrade said there would be two gentlemen, but he did not say who—why, I can't tell you how delighted, how *astonished* I am to see you! When I read Dr. Watson's report—what was it called? Oh, yes, 'The Final Problem'—I was deeply moved! Deeply! And so were we all! Barrington and Lely—you saw them tonight as the Mikado and Nanki-Poo, of course—both were hardly able to speak of it, and Jesse Bond, well, Jesse actually wept! By the way, did you like the way she handled the tea set in the second act? That was a new addition—"

Here he broke off, for he had come close to Holmes, who, I suspected to avoid an embrace, had put out his hand. Carte clasped it, shook it vigorously, and then held it for longer than the customary time, looking into Holmes's eyes. "And you are real, indeed, flesh and bone, solid, solid flesh! Oh, my dear fellow! What a relief!"

He caught sight of me. "And look, here is Dr. Watson, whose narrative has caused me—caused all of us—such a feeling of, well, *loss*! Doctor, hello, and can you please explain yourself?"

His emotion robbed me of any ability to dissemble. "I didn't know at the time" was all I could manage to say.

"But of course, you must have had some reason to keep the facts from the public now."

"I—"

"Don't tell me! Of course, you cannot tell me! Other forces must be working in opposition to you, Mr. Holmes, I quite understand that, and we ordinary citizens should generally be left to go on in our own little worlds without knowledge of what would no doubt distress and distract us—"

Holmes spoke with his customary restraint. "Yes, thank you. We are indeed here on a case of some importance and would appreciate your assistance."

"Of course. Anything I can do. Anything!" He blushed. "Please forgive my effusiveness. Pass it off to the emotional shock, to my relief at seeing you again—"

Here he broke off, and looked into Holmes's eyes once more with a deep and sympathetic gaze. "But how difficult it must be for you, Mr. Holmes, to move about in anonymity, unable to share the affections and admiration of the hundreds and thousands of people who love and appreciate all that you do to keep us safe. Please allow at least one of us to express heartfelt thanks."

"You are most welcome."

"May I tell Barrington and the others?"

"Please do not. Perhaps one day it will be safe for Dr. Watson to publish an account of my return. But for the moment it is best that I remain—how did Mr. Gilbert express it in tonight's performance?—'a disembodied spirit.'"

Carte's face lit up in a wide smile. "Oh, you are perfect, Mr. Holmes. And you have not lost any of your wit, I'll be bound! You have my word. Or should I say, 'The word for my guidance is *mum*'?"

Carte waited expectantly for Holmes to acknowledge the quick-witted reference to another line we had heard from the actors this evening, which Holmes did, politely, but briefly. Then his expression turned serious once more, and we proceeded to the business that had brought us to Carte's office.

7. A SURLY SET SUPERVISOR

The first person we interviewed was the set supervisor. He was tall and looked to be extremely fit, with a chest and upper arms that bulged beneath his black uniform coat. His face, dark-browed and shadowed with a stubble of black beard, seemed set in a perpetual scowl.

"I found him outside your door," said Lestrade as they came in. The two men stood at the side of Carte's desk.

"Thank you, Inspector," said Carte. Then to the set supervisor, "What did you hear of our conversation?"

"Nothing" was the abrupt reply. Then, glancing quickly at Carte and then away, as if recollecting his place and the politeness owed to his employer, he added, "Sir."

"Then will you please state your name for these gentlemen and answer whatever questions they may put to you."

"Blake."

"Is that your surname?" asked Holmes.

"What?"

Carte interjected, "His name is James Blake."

"Well, then, Mr. James Blake," Holmes continued affably, "we are looking for a missing person, a Mr. Foster, of New York City in America. We understand that you saw Mr. Foster recently."

"Yes."

"Could you tell us when that happened?"

"Thursday afternoon."

"And where?"

"Why, 'ere, of course. In the theater."

"Where, precisely, in the theater?"

"Where I was workin', of course. In the shop."

"It's all right, Blake," Carte said. He nodded toward the one empty chair that remained before his desk. "Please take a seat and just tell us what happened, there's a good chap."

The man sat and seemed to relax a bit. "I don't want no trouble."

"So, where were you and what did you hear?" Holmes asked patiently.

"I was puttin' some reinforcements into the stand for Ko-Ko's garden, and this man comes in. And I said, 'What do you want?' and 'e said, 'My name is Foster, and I'm just making an inspection for Mr. Carte.' And then 'e walked around the shop and then 'e left."

"And what did he look at?"

"Nothin' in particular. You might say 'e just nosed around the props. Looked under the platform once. I didn't think nothin' of it."

Holmes nodded. "Please describe his attitude, Mr. Blake. Did you get the impression he was in a hurry?"

"Might have been."

"Might have? Did he seem suspicious of anything in the shop?"

"Might have been."

"Of what, specifically?"

The man shook his head resignedly. "I thought you'd be askin' me that, but no, I don't remember nothin' special. I did think 'e was a copper, though," he added, looking up at Holmes.

8. AN ATTRACTIVE ACTRESS

A few moments later Lestrade had ushered Blake from the office and returned with Lucy James. I recognized her as the young actress we had seen earlier that evening in the role of Yum-Yum. This puzzled me, as Yum-Yum was one of the leading characters in the operetta, and I recalled Johnny saying that Lucy James was in the chorus.

She had changed from her Japanese costume, of course, into a perfectly ordinary white blouse and long dark skirt. Her abundant dark hair was swept up severely into a bun. There were no earrings on her small delicate earlobes, and she wore no rings or necklaces or bracelets. I thought the plainness of her attire was unusual for someone in the world of the theater. Yet one glance showed her to be far from ordinary. Slender and small-boned, she moved with a determined energy, yet with feline grace. At first impression she appeared haughty, due to her high-arched eyebrows, but it seemed to me that her lovely green eyes looked frightened. As she moved to her chair, the electric wall sconces behind Carte's desk revealed the deep blue undertones in her eyes, reminding me of the brilliant spots that distinguish a male peacock's feathers. What a shame, I thought, that the Savoy audiences were too far from the stage to appreciate those eyes!

She sat before Carte and looked at him expectantly, her lips pressed thin as though she anticipated trouble.

"Miss James," Carte began, "let me first compliment you on your performance this evening."

Holmes added, "Your solo at the beginning of the second act was quite exceptional. Your tone, your expression, your clarity— all were very moving. You have a gift, Miss James."

"Hear, hear," I chimed in, not wishing her to think that I in any way disagreed with this praise, for I had been fascinated and delighted.

She continued to sit stiffly upright, but she conveyed her appreciation with a polite smile. "Thank you, gentlemen. But Mr. Carte, may I know who these men are and why you have brought me to your office?"

"Of course, Miss James." Carte caught Holmes's warning look and went on, "This is Inspector Lestrade, of the London Metropolitan Police. These other two gentlemen are . . . consulting with the force in the matter of a missing person."

Holmes added, "The person is of some importance and we would very much appreciate your telling us anything you may know of him. He is an American from New York City. His name is Mr. Frederick Foster."

She looked puzzled, then amused. "America is a pretty big country, sir. And though I am an American, I've never been to New York, except for last month when I sailed from there on the White Star *Britannic*. That was right after I got the telegram from Mr. Carte asking me to come and understudy for Yum-Yum. Which I was just pleased as punch to do, of course."

"You did not meet Mr. Foster here in London?"

"Never heard that name before."

"He was staying at the Savoy Hotel, adjacent to this theater."

Her eyes narrowed and hardened. "And so am I, temporarily." She sat up even straighter, clenching her hands into fists, lifting her chin abruptly. "But who do you think you are, to be making insinuations that I'd go meeting with a strange man? I'm a graduate of Miss Porter's School, in Farmington, Connecticut, and I got straight A's in deportment all four years I was there, and I don't take kindly to some irresponsible smart aleck—"

"Here, now," cut in Lestrade, "you can't talk that way to Mr. Holmes!"

She stared, wide-eyed in disbelief, and then more closely. "Are you Mr. *Sherlock* Holmes?"

Lestrade grimaced and gave Holmes a look of apology.

Holmes merely nodded and said, "Yes, Miss James. That is correct."

Her look of shock turned into a glad smile, and then, in the next moment, a puzzled frown. "But you were killed! *The Strand Magazine* said so! And I cried my eyes out!"

Then, still talking, and before Holmes could interrupt the flow of her excitement, she was up from her chair and standing before him. "And look at you, you're just like Dr. Watson said, and just like those pictures of Mr. Paget's! Your nose *is* like a hawk's and your eyes *are* close-set, and dark, and just glittering! I do declare! And how perfectly noble you look, in your wing collar and white bow tie. I have to tell you, Mr. Holmes, I worshipped you when I was growing up. You were my inspiration—" She broke off, suddenly looking at me. "And you must be Dr. Watson! Sir, why did you write that Mr. Holmes had died? Why did you make us all grieve so?"

As she stood before me she seemed the embodiment of righteous indignation, but also she seemed endearingly vulnerable, filled with the fragile hope and expectation of youth. Coming as it did after Carte's equally passionate reaction, her outburst reminded me of my duty to be truthful in my accounts of Holmes. I felt the magnitude of my responsibility with a force of particularly strong emotion. I was also struck by the realization that if my Mary and I had been blessed with a child, and that child a girl, I would have been proud to see her grow up to be such a one as Lucy James. I tried to reply, but my sentiments at that moment overcame me.

Holmes was speaking, quietly and patiently. "Dr. Watson did not know I was alive. At the time of my return, it was necessary that no one know. Since then, I have resumed my work for a limited circle of clients. But there are still reasons why I should remain out of the view of the public."

"And yet you go about openly!" she broke in. "I saw you tonight in the second-level box stage left, the second one in, and for some reason you stood out from the others in the audience and for a moment I imagined you were, well, 'you,' and I was so distracted I nearly forgot my next line!"

Holmes sat forward and took her hand. "Miss James. I sincerely regret the distress you have undergone. But we are caught up in a matter of some urgency and danger. Will you help us?"

Her eyes softened and a smile gradually suffused her lovely face. "I would be proud to help you, Mr. Holmes." Her hand went to her blouse, just above her heart. "In my dormitory at school I have dreamed of—" Then she cleared her throat, moved gracefully to the empty chair, and sat, hands clasped primly in her lap. "How may I be of assistance?"

"Please tell us about your family."

This was to my mind a very strange question for Holmes to be asking, but Miss James seemed to take it in a perfectly ordinary way. She replied, "I have none."

"You have left them behind in America?"

"No, I never had a family, even though I have wished for one for as long as I can remember. All my life I have lived in institutions or boarding schools."

"Who pays your tuition and expenses?"

"There is a trust, and a trustee I have never met. He communicates with me only through correspondence, delivered by school officials."

"And you reply through the same channel?"

"Yes. I've told him about my classes, my singing, who my friends are, that kind of thing."

"Did he know you were coming to London to perform with the Savoy troupe?"

"Oh, yes, he sent a telegraph message to congratulate me, and he made the arrangements for me to stay at the Savoy."

"His name?"

"I have often asked, but to no avail. I am sure he paid the school officials to keep me uninformed."

"Has he told you the name of your parents?"

Her face flushed. "No. Only that my father is dead."

"Very well. Now, I am most curious to learn how a young lady recently graduated from a school in America comes to appear in a leading singing role at London's Savoy Theatre."

She gave a wry smile. "As are many of the ladies in the chorus, I can tell you. But all I know is that I had a telegram from Mr. Carte asking me to come. As an understudy. Miss Perry is the lead, but she took sick, so I went on tonight. I think they liked me all right."

This was an understatement, of course. At the end of the performance she had received prolonged and enthusiastic applause.

"Mr. Carte?" Holmes turned toward him, expectantly.

Carte turned up an empty palm. "In truth, I was unaware of her singing talent when I sent the telegram. She was strongly recommended by one of my principal investors. He had heard her sing in America."

"Did he say where?"

"It must have been in Providence, Rhode Island," she replied. "Our school had a joint concert there with the Brown University glee club. We were very well received."

Holmes nodded. "Mr. Carte. Can you tell us the name of the investor?"

"I regret that he has asked me to keep his name in confidence."

"Do you have any idea who this investor might have been, Miss James?"

"Haven't the foggiest. There's only one person I remember from that concert, and he was one of the boys in the glee club. The two of us sang a duet from *The Magic Flute*. The one at the end, where we both are stuttering. On purpose, of course."

"His name?"

"Johnny Rockefeller."

Holmes did not react, merely asking, "He has a singing talent?"

"He's pretty good. I don't think they gave him the part just because he's wealthy, if that's what you're getting at. There are lots of wealthy boys at Brown."

"Have you seen him since you've been here?"

"Not yet. We're to have supper tonight at the hotel restaurant. He sent me a note during tonight's performance."

"And he—cares for you?"

She shook her head, dismissing the notion. "It's been a long time since that concert, and other than a few brief letters, this is the first I've heard from him."

"How did he know you were here?"

"His note said he'd recognized me on the stage from the way I sang, and then he noticed my name in the program."

"Can you think of anyone who would have told Mr. Rockefeller to come to this performance and see you?"

She shook her head. "Nary a soul. Why should there be? And why should you care?"

"Your relationship with young Mr. Rockefeller may be of some consequence to us. His father has important business here that could be affected by . . . the matters we are investigating."

"Well then. I'd better tell you that I'm not all that much interested in Johnny Rockefeller, or being accepted into his social circle. I've spent vacations visiting the homes of other girls at school. I've seen their mothers."

"You do not wish to emulate them?"

She smiled ruefully. "Have you read Mr. Thoreau, Mr. Holmes? But no, of course you haven't, for he is an American philosopher and Dr. Watson says your knowledge of philosophy is 'nil.' But anyway, Mr. Thoreau says that the masses of men lead lives of quiet desperation and that happiness does not arise from the trappings of success. I don't know whether he is right about the masses of men, but I can tell you that the lives of several married women at the heads of several very wealthy households look to me to be pretty darned desperate."

I was a bit confused at this point, for I did not see what the writings of an American philosopher had to do with the matters that occupied our concern. Moreover, I continued to be baffled as to why Holmes had adopted this line of questioning with Miss James. She seemed totally irrelevant to our case, and her personal aspirations would be even less relevant. Yet Holmes continued to draw her out on what I considered to be her private and subjective opinions.

"How are these ladies desperate?" he asked.

"When I see them at their unguarded moments, they're always looking over their shoulders, as if they are in fear of disapproval."

"Disapproval of what?"

"Come, Mr. Holmes. You have visited the royal houses of Europe. Surely you know what I'm talking about. They have families, but they're afraid they're not measuring up."

"But we are all judged, are we not? Even you, when you are on the stage?"

"But on the stage I feel—I don't quite know how to say it. When I sing, it is as natural as breathing, and at that moment I have no care at all what others may think. And I forget that I have no family, because I'm wrapped up in my work. I bet you know what that feels like, to be all wrapped up in your work."

"I do indeed," said Holmes. "It is the only reward one can be sure of."

Holmes's remark seemed cryptic to me, but Miss James nodded as though she understood.

"We don't always get applause afterward, do we?" she replied.

At that moment I, too, understood, for I had seen how many of our cases ended in anger or despair as Holmes brought the wrongdoer to justice, and how infrequently Holmes received any credit or expression of gratitude from the police. Yet I felt puzzled at how easily the conversation seemed to flow between this young lady and Holmes, as though they had been longtime friends. I also felt a moment's pride, since Miss James, though barely more than a schoolgirl, had clearly been able to reach this state of familiarity while relying on only what she had read in my accounts of Holmes's and my adventures.

Then the door to Carte's office flew open.

Two tall figures stood at the entrance, their outlines, at first glance, nearly identical. At the front was a tall ruddy-faced man in a black cape. Behind him was the set supervisor, Blake, looking abashed.

"He couldn't wait, Mr. Carte," Blake said.

"Never mind that," said the other man and pushed Blake further behind him. "Carte, you and I have business to discuss."

I stared, astonished at the man's rudeness. He looked respectable enough, attired in evening dress like the rest of us, and even distinguished, with a luxurious growth of perfectly groomed gray hair, though his right shoulder slumped downward several inches lower than the other, thrusting the left shoulder forward and giving him an oddly twisted, misshapen air. Further, his protruding square jaw, framed by graying muttonchop whiskers, his cold blue eyes, and his lofty, dismissive bearing as he surveyed us in evident appraisal—these all were the marks of a man who cared little for the niceties of social politeness.

"This is Mr. Adam Worth," said Carte, nodding at the intruder and speaking smoothly, though I detected a hint of embarrassment. "He is one of my principal investors."

"Here, now—" began Lestrade.

But Holmes interrupted, speaking with ease and perfect equanimity as he stood up. "I completely understand the urgency of business matters. We thank you very much for your time, Mr. Carte."

9. A MUSICIAN'S APPEAL

We all got up then, following Holmes's lead. Once outside Carte's office the four of us walked quickly and in silence back along the corridor to the theater lobby, which by now was nearly in darkness. The once-brilliant chandelier hung in shadows above us, only vaguely outlined by two small wall sconces, one on either side of the doorway. The lobby was deserted. Through the windows of the exit doors I could see two ushers standing outside to bar entry from that direction.

Miss James was talking as if to herself. "I didn't like that man one bit. I'll just go get my coat from my dressing room and then go straight to the restaurant to meet Mr. Rockefeller. The ladies' dressing rooms are this way."

We followed her gaze down one of two corridors, leading to the backstage part of the theater on the eastern side. Coming toward us in the corridor was a shadowy figure in woman's dress with a shawl over her head, carrying a violin case. As we four looked in her direction, the woman paused, evidently not wanting to intrude on our conversation.

"Watson," said Holmes quickly, "would you kindly wait here for Miss James and then escort her to the Savoy restaurant? Lestrade and I must go to our clients. I fear the meeting will not be a pleasant one and we do not want to keep them waiting any longer than absolutely necessary. Please join us there when you can."

"Of course," I said, feeling some pride in the responsibility, but Holmes did not acknowledge my acceptance. He was already moving toward the exit door, Lestrade at his heels.

Miss James called after him, "Mr. Holmes, when will I see you again?"

But Holmes was already outside the building and the door was closing behind Lestrade.

"He is distracted," I said to Miss James by way of apology for Holmes's abrupt departure.

"I know. He's on a case. Now, the restaurant is just next door, and I can take care of myself." She gave me a little smile and patted her reticule. "You don't have to wait for me."

"Nevertheless, I shall."

"Then I'll just be a minute."

She turned away, striding confidently down the corridor, her white blouse and dark hair clearly visible in the electric light against the drab dun color of the painted walls. The other woman waited, turning away from the light, her figure shadowed. I watched carefully as Miss James moved past her without incident.

Then I saw the woman pick up her violin case. She was looking at me. In a moment she was walking quickly and purposefully in my direction.

"Dr. Watson!" she said.

I waited, astonished to hear her call me by name. Then she stopped before me, drew back the shawl from her lovely face, and I recognized the violinist whom I had observed through my opera glasses during the performance.

Up close she was even more strikingly beautiful than from a distance. I judged her to be about forty years old. She appeared to be in radiant health, possibly due to the beneficial effects of frequent exposure to music. Her dark green eyes fixed me with an intensity that demanded respect. She spoke rapidly, urgently. "I know who you are. I saw you with Sherlock at numerous performances here years ago, sitting in your usual box seats, and you were in your seats again tonight. And just now, before he ran away from me, he called you by name. I have read your accounts of your adventures with him, so I know that your nature is to be truthful. I beg that you will be truthful with me."

I stood silent, transfixed by the deeply emotional tone of her appeal. I felt both relieved that she had not come to accuse me of spying on her during the performance, and bewildered that she had thought Holmes would be running away from her. All I could manage to say was "I will."

"My name is Zoe Rosario. You may tell Sherlock—Mr. Holmes—of my inquiry if you wish, but I must warn you that it will cause him some distress, and so I would urge you not to discuss our encounter with him or with anyone."

"You have my word—Miss Rosario."

She gave a wry smile at the name, and I wondered if indeed it was really hers.

"Thank you, Dr. Watson. Now I have one question for you. One fact that I must know. Your account of Mr. Holmes's death. Clearly that was false, for he was just here. And others know it was false, for the young American actress called his name as he left. But—"

She pursed her lips, drew in her breath and held it, trying to bring her evident distress under control. "But what of the—the other man? I cannot bring myself to say his name. Is he, too, alive?"

I replied without hesitation. "Professor James Moriarty fell to his certain death in the way I described it. I have the account directly from Mr. Holmes, and there is another who witnessed the Professor's death and tried to avenge him." I shuddered inwardly at the knowledge that the murderous Colonel Moran was now at large. "Mr. Holmes escaped death through a combination of agility, training, and good fortune. Someday I will be free to publish the truth, but at this time I cannot."

Her eyes held mine for a long moment. Then she gave a deep sigh and the anxiety in her expression changed to relief. I saw a blush suffuse her cheeks as she leaned forward, touching my arm for support. "I believe you, Dr. Watson."

She seemed lost in thought. Then, as though she had only now become aware of her hand on my forearm, she drew back slightly. "I cannot tell you the reason for my urgency in this matter. I must collect my thoughts and decide on my course of action."

She stopped suddenly, as the sound of a door opening came to us from the direction of Carte's office and, with it, the voices of Carte and Worth. She paled, drew in her breath, and picked up her violin case, holding it close to her. "I must go," she whispered.

She turned and walked quickly back down the dun-colored corridor, leaving me to wonder just what could be troubling her and how Holmes could be of assistance. Even more baffling was her assertion that Holmes had run away from her.

As I puzzled over these matters I kept an eye on the beautiful but bewildering Miss Rosario. She had nearly reached the end of the corridor when she stopped and turned.

Then I realized that Worth was coming my way from Carte's office. He strode rapidly, his dark cape billowing behind him. "You're still here," he said curtly, but he did not slow down as he passed me and pushed through the exit door to the street.

I looked back for Miss Rosario, but she was no longer there. A moment later, I saw Miss James coming around the corner.

"Did you see anyone?" I asked Miss James when she stood before me.

"One of the violinists passed me. We haven't been introduced yet." As I pushed open the lobby door and we felt the chill November air she added, "But I'm expecting to make friends with everyone in the company."

Moments later, Miss James and I entered the Savoy Hotel. Almost immediately I saw young Mr. Rockefeller waiting for her just inside the entry area to the fashionable hotel restaurant.

His alert gaze found Miss James and me, and his face lit up in an eager smile. I had already cautioned Miss James not to mention my name or that of Sherlock Holmes, and now I held a finger to my lips, indicating that young Rockefeller should not disclose our previous acquaintance. He nodded, and I withdrew.

10. POLITICAL CONSIDERATIONS

After a brisk walk along the well-lit Strand and a short turn onto Pall Mall, I soon reached the Diogenes Club, where I found Holmes and Lestrade waiting on a settee in the third-floor lobby. "You are not late, Watson," said Holmes. "We are waiting to be granted an audience by those who have summoned us. Mycroft has told us they have some important preliminary decisions to make." He nodded in the direction of a heavy oaken double door through which came the sounds of muffled discussion.

"What has happened?"

"Probably nothing."

Lestrade smiled wryly at Holmes and then looked gloomily at the oaken doors. "And they'll do as they please no matter what we say, and if it all goes wrong they'll have us to blame. That's what we police are for. And now they'll drag you into it, too, Mr. Holmes."

At that moment the oaken doors opened and Mycroft stood waiting. His formal nod indicated we were to enter.

The room was relatively small, with a table only large enough for eight chairs, three on each side, with the Prime Minister at the head. The others from this morning were there, as well, and their expressions of concern had only become more pronounced in the hours that had passed. Clevering, at the Prime Minister's right, beckoned Holmes to the opposite end of the table and its single empty chair. No one took any notice of Lestrade or me. Fortunately there were smaller chairs available along the sides of the room, so the two of us were not required to stand throughout the meeting.

"Are you quite comfortable, Mr. Holmes?" asked Clevering. "I trust no bomb makers have followed you this time?"

Holmes nodded, politely.

"Have you caught the bomber? Can you assure us that our meeting with the Americans can take place without incident?"

"Had the bomber been caught, all of you would have already been informed by the Commissioner. As to your final question, I will not dignify it with an answer."

Clevering brandished his monocle, outraged. "How dare you, sir!" The others around the table looked uncomfortable. None spoke in support of Clevering.

"But I have a question for you, Mr. Clevering," Holmes went on affably. "On this occasion, a late-evening meeting attended by our Prime Minister and three members of his cabinet, why does your minister send you? Why does he not attend himself?"

"He is indisposed. A digestive ailment."

"You visited him today?"

"I did. And I assure you that I have his full authorization to represent him and to take any action that he would be authorized to take."

"And these more senior gentlemen have elected you as their spokesman this evening?"

"You have cheek, sir! This is a war office matter!"

The Prime Minister intervened then, putting Clevering into his place with a cold stare and an upraised palm. "We are interested in Mr. Holmes's opinions here, Clevering."

Holmes replied, "Thank you, Prime Minister. Now, it would be most helpful to me to know more of the meeting being planned with the Americans. I believe the subject of the meeting to be the conversion of the Royal Navy from coal to oil, and the construction of suitable oil-fueling equipment to be installed throughout our fleet's domestic and international network of coaling stations. This would be an enormous investment, and would greatly strengthen our nation's military capability, so therefore the arrangements must be held in absolute secrecy for political as well as military reasons. That conclusion occurred to me the moment I saw Mr. Foster's business card, given the unusual interest of both the Secretary of War and the First Lord of the Admiralty in the death of a missing American."

"I thought you would see that," said the Prime Minister.

"And now you have confirmed it. So we can proceed to identify the other American participants at the meeting. I shall name two names, and you may respond as you see fit. First, Mr. Andrew Carnegie, since the construction of the seaport fueling facilities will require enormous quantities of steel and since several of the port locations are likely to lie in his native Scotland."

The Prime Minister shrugged. Holmes nodded.

"And Mr. J. P. Morgan, since enormous sums will be required, and since Mr. Morgan has wide experience in financial dealings between our two nations. By the way, I would expect that you, Prime Minister, and President Cleveland have agreed that this current project is the *quid pro quo* for the Morgan bank's bond issue this past spring. As I recall from the newspaper accounts, the bank's bonds saved the American dollar through the backing of our British gold reserves, and generated no small amount of political controversy on both sides of the Atlantic."

The Prime Minister shrugged again, but there was a gleam of approval in his eye.

"Now. Do you or your colleagues have questions for me?"

"We jolly well do," said Clevering. "About the case you claimed to be a murder. What about this woman you spoke of? Did you find her, or is she just a figment of your imagination?"

"She is a deduction, not a figment. I deduced her presence from my inspection of the body of the unfortunate Mr. Foster."

The Prime Minister leaned forward before Clevering could speak. "Please continue, Mr. Holmes."

"The body showed no signs that Mr. Foster had been bound or struggled, so the attack took him by surprise, which indicates someone took him from behind while the other kept his attention. An attractive woman would be most suitable for that task. A woman might also be excused from the physical exertion of carrying the body. Had both attackers been men, they would most likely have carried the body by the shoulders and feet, rather than dragging it."

The Commissioner asked, "How do you know that the body was dragged?"

"Mr. Foster's dress shoes were new, the soles and heels barely worn. Yet the glossy black patent leather above both heels was deeply scratched, and the bottoms of his trousers were frayed, indicating that the body was dragged across a hard, rough surface." He looked at the expectant faces around the table and continued, "This morning I also mentioned that the scene of the crime was near carpentry work and a gravel carriage path. Those I deduced from the particles of sawdust and fine silvery gravel embedded in Mr. Foster's socks and inside his shoes."

"You also mentioned the death occurred on the other side of the river?"

"Since the constable did not see anyone approach the bridge from the Parliament side, it follows that the carriage came from the other side to the center point of the river and turned around. Then, seeing no witnesses, the occupants of the carriage disposed of Mr. Foster's body by throwing it into the water."

"Most ingenious," said Clevering. "What do you intend to do next?"

"I propose to return to my home and go to bed. It has been a long day for all of us."

"That is not what I meant."

"I also propose to speak briefly and privately with the Commissioner, Inspector Lestrade, and my brother, Mycroft. And Dr. Watson, of course."

"You will not take the leaders of Her Majesty's government into your confidence?" Clevering shook his head. "You continue to outrage us, Mr. Holmes."

11. OUR MOST OBVIOUS DIFFICULTY

In a short time Lestrade and I were sitting at the table with Holmes, Mycroft, and Commissioner Edward Bradford.

As I have mentioned, Sir Edward was an ally. He had expressed his gratitude for Holmes's brilliant work in preventing the underground robbery of an enormous amount of gold bullion from the Bank of England, which would have been a disastrous start to his first year as Commissioner. His military bearing bore witness to his thirty years' service in Persia and the Indian subcontinent. The empty left sleeve of his well-tailored coat, neatly stitched and folded at his side, attested to his bravery during an encounter with a tigress in the Guna province. I knew that he was well respected by Lestrade and the forty thousand other Metropolitan Police Department employees who were in his charge.

"What now, Mr. Holmes?" Sir Edward asked, the hint of an ironic smile beneath the wide expanse of his white mustache.

Holmes's features tightened. "There are a number of individuals whom we should investigate. First there is Mr. Clevering, whose attitude appears so inappropriately and inexplicably arrogant and uncooperative. I should like to know why. Then there is Blake, the set supervisor at the theater, who so very helpfully provided us with his recollection of Mr. Foster's visit to the prop room the afternoon before his murder. Also there is Mr. Worth, Carte's investor. Watson and Lestrade no doubt observed, as did I, that Mr. Worth did not so much as glance in the direction of Miss James when we were all together in Mr. Carte's office earlier this evening. For a man of his age, such behavior is highly unusual, given her attractive appearance. I would ask you also to learn what you can of Mr. Worth, in particular of his finances. Where has his wealth come from? Who are his associates? Where do his funds go, and for what purposes?"

Lestrade, Sir Edward, and Mycroft exchanged glances. Then Mycroft said, "I shall initiate inquiries on an urgent basis."

The Commissioner said, "I shall do the same, and we shall learn what we can." He hesitated and then pressed on. "But there is something else. We have the report you requested regarding recent thefts of dynamite."

"Have you told the Prime Minister?"

"Not as yet."

"Then the news is not good."

The Commissioner said, "There have been two incidents. The first was in March, at the Senghenydd Colliery near Cardiff. Two crates, each containing three dozen nine-inch cartridges, were reported missing the morning of March 18."

"And the second?"

"That incident occurred the night of June 20, on the Glasgow and South Western Railway line somewhere between the Nobel Explosives factory in Ardeer, where a train was loaded, and Newcastle, where it was unloaded."

"The quantity stolen?"

"Four freight cars filled with dynamite left Ardeer. In Newcastle, one of the freight cars was found to have lost nearly one third of its cargo."

"That is an appalling piece of news."

"Taken with the incident at St. Thomas this morning, it is indeed appalling. That amount of dynamite would produce an explosion several hundred times greater than the one outside the hospital. Thousands would die."

"Have there been any arrests? Are there any suspects? Has any of the dynamite reappeared?"

The Commissioner shook his head. His tone was grim. "And four months have elapsed, so the trail has gone cold."

12. BREAKFAST AT 221B BAKER STREET

On awakening in our Baker Street rooms the following morning, I dressed and descended my stairway to find Mrs. Hudson, our esteemed landlady, setting out a hearty breakfast from a heavily laden tray. A warm smile wreathed her middle-aged features when she saw me. Then she gave a dubious glance at Holmes, who sat cross-legged on the carpet in his morning coat, surrounded by piles of papers and books, and a folded copy of the morning's *Times*. He had a sheaf of notes and envelopes on his lap and was sorting these into three piles, while puffing a lit pipe filled with his customary strong-smelling shag tobacco.

Mrs. Hudson spoke in her usual brisk fashion. "There's ham and sausages, a nice white pudding, some white-bread toast and some fresh creamery butter for it, along with some of that Dundee marmalade you're fond of, Doctor," she said. "And fresh coffee, of course. There's more than enough for both of you, if you take my meaning," she said, with another disapproving look at Holmes.

I knew Mrs. Hudson was well accustomed to Holmes's neglect of sustenance, other than tobacco, when he was immersed in a case, but she never gave up her attempts to nourish him with proper fare. I felt a kinship with her on this point. Though I had long since despaired of successfully changing Holmes's eccentric and medically unsound habits, I, too, frequently chided him, if only to appease my own conscience.

Today, however, Holmes surprised both of us. "Excellent, Mrs. Hudson! You have brought us a breakfast fit for a famished Yorkshire countryman—two of them, in fact. I shall attend to my share in due course. Watson, please do not wait for me."

These words he spoke in his most cordial tone, though without once taking his eyes from his work. Then he fell silent once more, glancing at each item and placing it onto one of the three stacks as one would deal out a hand of cards, all the while sending up great blue-gray clouds of tobacco smoke. Mrs. Hudson and I exchanged looks of resignation as she withdrew and I sat down to the table.

I finished my meal in silence, Holmes remaining on the floor with his pipe and papers. These, I had come to realize, were associated with the other cases with which Holmes was currently occupied. I wondered how he could be even thinking of his other work, given the magnitude of the task the Prime Minister had assigned him. Or was this the result of his compulsion to continually occupy his mind, to meet the challenge of every case that might interest him? If so, I feared for the worst, for I knew his constitution had its limits, and if he placed too much strain on faculties that were, though extraordinary, subject to mortal frailty, after all, a breakdown of some sort would someday be inevitable. Then I could bear my apprehension no longer. I asked, "Holmes, what are you doing?"

"Sorting, Watson." He gave me a placid, understanding look. "I am sorting these cases according to their level of urgency. If I succeed in helping the Prime Minister and Mr. Rockefeller, I will be ready to resume my other activity in an efficient manner. If I fail—"

"Surely not, Holmes!" I could not help but interrupt.

"Nevertheless, there is a possibility that Colonel Moran may be the winner in this current encounter. If such an event occurs and I am unable to continue, I ask that you will be so good as to turn these papers over to Lestrade."

"I will do as you ask, of course. But you have defeated Colonel Moran once before."

Holmes gave an ironic smile. "On that occasion, the Moriarty organization had been broken up. The Colonel had little or no assistance. Now, matters are different."

"I do not follow you, Holmes."

"No one escapes from a fortress such as Dartmoor without careful planning and assistance from others. Just as no one steals more than a ton of dynamite without similar planning and assistance. Now, the trail to the dynamite theft has grown cold. But Colonel Moran escaped four days ago and there may still be clues for us. So let us examine this problem. Three questions then arise. Whose organization assisted Colonel Moran, for what purpose, and why now?"

He drew a clump of papers from the top of one of the three piles. "During the past several months, there have been indications—without the name of Moriarty appearing even once, of course—that the old patterns and methods were beginning to reassert themselves once more." He held up a page or two at a time and then replaced it in the pile as he continued, "A robbery, so cunningly planned that the theft is not noticed for days. An attack, with the victim too terrified to disclose what might possibly be the motive to cause him harm. An insignificant thief who barely has funds to feed and clothe himself is caught and imprisoned, and then suddenly a solicitor and a bail bondsman appear to procure his freedom. The actions chronicled in these papers show all the hallmarks of Moriarty's operations."

"Possibly someone eluded you from the old Moriarty organization, and that person has formed a new one."

"Let us take that as our assumption. We may further assume that this someone, this organization, has extracted Moran from his imprisonment. But why has the escape come now? Moran has been languishing in Dartmoor more than a year."

"Perhaps the resources to manage his escape have only recently become available."

"Perhaps. But I think it more likely that an opportunity for the organization has arisen that requires Moran's particular skills. Now ask yourself what that opportunity might be."

"The meeting with Mr. Rockefeller and the others."

"A meeting that would increase our nation's naval power, and which therefore other nations would pay handsomely to stop. Now, ask yourself how the organization learned of the proposed meeting."

"Possibly Mr. Foster let something slip. Or someone may have recognized young Johnny."

"But they arrived in this country only a week ago. And Moran escaped four days ago. That leaves three days, which is not nearly enough time to plan and execute an escape from Dartmoor." Holmes nodded. "If our chain of reasoning is correct, the knowledge of Rockefeller's visit would have had to come to the organization weeks or perhaps months earlier. And the only persons aware of the visit at that time were within the Prime Minister's inner circle."

"So there is a traitor." I struggled to contain my consternation. "Holmes, this gets worse and worse! And we have no evidence! We have no evidence against anyone."

"Then we must test our suppositions, and be guided by the results of our test."

Before I could even imagine what he meant by this pronouncement, we heard the voices of Mrs. Hudson and another woman below, and their footsteps ascending our stairs.

13. MISS JAMES NEEDS HELP

Soon Mrs. Hudson was with us once again, announcing our visitor. "Miss Lucy James. She says she met both of you at the Savoy."

"Please come in, Miss James," said Holmes, looking up from his papers.

Wrapped tightly in a maroon-colored wool cloak, Miss James was nonetheless shivering as she stepped into the room. Her cheeks were not pink from the morning chill as I would have expected, but rather pale and drawn, and her lovely eyes appeared fearful.

Holmes's voice became gentle. "Will you not take breakfast with us? See, there is a place already set for you. Mrs. Hudson, will you please bring some fresh coffee for our guest?"

I rose to greet Miss James and escort her to our table as Mrs. Hudson withdrew, but she did not sit. Instead she moved around the room, looking at her surroundings with a kind of reverence, and clutching her reticule with both hands as if fearful of losing it. She paused but once, to trace her fingers lightly over some of the bullet holes that still formed the initials *VR* in our wall.

Finally she spoke. "Thank you for your kind hospitality, Mr. Holmes, but I couldn't eat. I've had something of a shock and I need your help."

"Then you had better sit down," said Holmes. "Take that seat by the fire." He quickly got to his feet and stepped lightly over the clutter, taking her cloak and helping her into my chair. He then took his usual position in the other chair.

I drew a chair from the dining table to a position where I could observe them and then I went back to the dining table and poured coffee for Miss James. I noted that today she again wore a plain white blouse and dark wool skirt, again with no jewelry. "Here is hot coffee," I said, bringing the cup to where she sat, hunched over and staring into the glowing coals. "You appear chilled. We have brandy as well—"

"No, no, please. I don't drink brandy or any other ardent spirits." Her lip trembled as she sipped at the coffee. Then she looked up, her green eyes wide in frightened appeal. "Mr. Holmes, I need you to find my true parents. I quite realize that you are occupied with other matters"—she gestured at the heap of newspapers and books still strewn untidily on our floor—"but I have no one else to turn to. Until now I have relied solely on my trustee, whom I have never seen until, well, until last night and this morning."

"Last night?"

"Yes. In Mr. Carte's office. I did not know his identity then, of course, but he presented himself to me this morning at the Savoy as I came into the restaurant. He was very overbearing. He made it plain that if I do not obey his direction he will no longer pay my bills and I shall be thrown penniless into the street."

Holmes spoke gently. "And your hope is that your real parents will help you?"

"It seems foolish, I know, after twenty-one years. Yet they did care enough to establish the trust."

"In all likelihood they are not living together as husband and wife. And as I recall, your trustee told you that your father was dead."

"I realize that. But my hope is that he was not being truthful, or that at least my mother may take an interest in me. And I must try, for I know I cannot continue in a state of dependency on a man such as Mr. Adam Worth."

"The same man who interrupted us last night in Mr. Carte's office? He is your trustee?"

"Yes. Please excuse me for not explaining this clearly. Yes, the man last night in Mr. Carte's office. The man who interrupted us. A horrible man."

"And you are certain that he is your trustee?"

"This morning he showed me the paid receipts for my tuition over the past three years, and for my passage from New York on the *Britannic*, and for my room and meals at the Savoy Hotel."

"Did he leave any of those receipts with you?"

She shook her head.

"Did you notice an address on any of the receipts?"

"He did not let me examine them, but I did see the first one clearly, one from Miss Porter's School. It was addressed to him at The Western Lodge, Clapham Common. I have no idea where that might be."

Holmes gave an approving nod. "I credit your powers of observation, Miss James."

I saw a faint blush appear on her cheek. "I brought one of his letters." She opened her reticule and handed a cream-colored envelope to Holmes. "You see the envelope is addressed simply 'Miss Lucy James,' and there is no postmark or return address."

Holmes looked briefly at the letter. "He signs himself as simply 'your trustee.' Now, you mentioned a direction of Mr. Worth's that he requires you to obey?"

"He wants me to 'cultivate a relationship,' as he put it, with Johnny Rockefeller. When I told him—told Mr. Worth what I told you yesterday, about not being interested in all that high-society life—well, that's when he threatened me. He says he'll have Mr. Carte dismiss me from the company. He said he can fix it so that none of the other theaters will hire me. He says singing talents like mine are a dime a dozen."

"And what does he hope to accomplish by putting you together with Johnny?"

"I don't really know. But he seemed . . . inspired by the idea, somehow. Like he'd dreamed about it. If that kind of man can dream about anything."

"Did you point out that Johnny may not have a romantic relationship with you in mind?"

"I did. He said he knew I had a superior intellect that could accomplish difficult tasks. I remember thinking how preposterous that sounded."

"Preposterous?"

"As if romance was an intellectual problem. As if love was something that could be swayed by reason. All that stuff that everybody writes about."

"Everybody?"

"I was thinking of Shakespeare, actually, but there are lots more. Didn't you read Shakespeare when you were in school?"

"I did."

She nodded. "But now you don't clutter up your mind with such things."

Holmes smiled briefly. "Does Mr. Worth require anything else of you?"

"He asked about Johnny's father."

"What about him?"

"About his coming to London Monday. Johnny says Mr. Rockefeller—Johnny calls him 'Senior'—has chartered a steam-liner—one of the fastest, Johnny says. There's a big meeting here, with very important people. Johnny told me when we had supper at the restaurant last night."

I stared, shocked at her casual tone. Here was a meeting whose very existence we were bound by the harshest penalties of the law to keep secret, and Miss James spoke of it as though it were a holiday dance or some other perfectly ordinary social gathering.

Holmes remained calm. "Did he say where the meeting was to be held?"

She shook her head. "That was what Mr. Worth wanted to know, too."

"He knew about the meeting?"

She nodded. "He knew Johnny's father was coming and that J. P. Morgan would be there. When I couldn't say where it was, he said I should try to find out from Johnny and then tell him. I think that's wrong, so I told him I wouldn't and that's when he said those awful things about making me a homeless pauper. I must get free of that man, Mr. Holmes."

14. THE IRREGULARS

Holmes stood up abruptly and went to our front window. Parting the curtain, he gazed intently at the street below. Then he drew the shade down to the windowsill and returned to his chair. "How did Mr. Worth say you were to communicate with him?"

"I'm to leave a message at the front desk of the hotel telling him when I can meet him in the lobby."

"And when will you meet young Mr. Rockefeller again?"

"Later this afternoon. He wants to take me shopping and then to tea. I can stay out with him until our six o'clock call—before tonight's performance." Her eyes clouded and she shook her head. "But that's not important." Her voice caught and her next words came nearly in a whisper. "Will you help me find my parents, Mr. Holmes? Will you help me?"

Holmes leaned forward in his chair to meet her gaze. "Do you know the date and place of your birth?"

"I don't. Not for sure. But according to my school records I will be twenty-one this January seventh, and I have received a gold sovereign as a birthday present from my trustee the first week of every January that I can remember."

"I will look into the matter."

Her face lit up. "Oh, thank you!"

His voice took on a cautionary tone. "But I believe you are in danger, Miss James."

As if to underscore Holmes's words, there came from below the sound of our front door knocker, soon followed by Mrs. Hudson's voice.

Holmes went on, "Moreover, I cannot tell you the reasons for my belief. You will have to trust me."

"It's because Mr. Rockefeller and J. P. Morgan are coming here, though. Isn't it?"

Holmes remained silent, but I thought I detected a hint of an approving nod as he got up from his chair.

From the stairs came light, rapid footfalls.

"I have arranged to have you watched. For your protection."

Our entry door opened, and a small, ragged boy burst into the room and stood before us. The boy drew himself up to attention and said, "I saw the shade come down, sir."

Fear and delight mingled on Miss James's lovely face as she saw the new arrival. She whispered, "The Irregulars!"

After Holmes made the appropriate introductions, he instructed Flynn, for that was the name of the boy, as to the procedure he was to follow and the terms of employment that he was to offer to the other Irregulars, who were always in need of money and eager to assist Holmes.

"A shilling a day to each, through this coming Wednesday and possibly later," said Holmes. "But take care to remain unobserved, both when following Miss James and watching the entrances to the Savoy. That is extremely important. It is imperative that you not reveal yourselves, for you may otherwise be in serious danger."

Young Flynn shrugged his frail shoulders and nodded at this warning with the offhand courage of youth and the bravery of one accustomed to scratching a living each day from whatever opportunities he could find in the streets of London. Holmes then said good-bye to Miss James, taking both her hands in his and looking directly into her eyes while urging her to remain on her guard and, if she met Worth again, to claim she had learned nothing more from Johnny about the impending conference. I escorted her down the stairs. Before we went outside I saw to it that she draped her head in a shawl borrowed from Mrs. Hudson. When we were on the sidewalk I hailed a hansom cab for her, taking care not to select the first or the second that offered itself. The driver looked surprised when Flynn scrambled up onto the seat beside Miss James, but a shilling pressed into his palm immediately changed his attitude. "The Savoy Hotel," I told him. As the cab pulled away, I noted with approval that Miss James had closed the curtain.

I turned back to our doorway. To my surprise, Holmes was coming out, pulling on his tweed cap and wearing his brown tweed ulster. "Quickly, Watson. Another cab!"

I hailed a hansom and it pulled over. "Bank of England, Threadneedle Street," Holmes told the driver. As we got in he added, "But with a stop at Somerset House." Then he remained silent.

15. SOMERSET HOUSE

After two chilly miles in the hansom we arrived at Somerset House on the Strand. Holmes asked me to wait in the cab. I did so with some impatience, for he had not told me the reason for his stopping there, nor how long he expected to be occupied, and the uncertainty made the minutes crawl by.

I watched hundreds of Saturday strollers walk along the shops of the Strand and through the tall arched passageway from the north wing of Somerset House that led to the magnificent, spacious courtyard. As I waited I scanned the faces of those who passed, wondering what Holmes could be doing, or if he had emerged in disguise and one of the faces now before me might be concealing his own. However, at last I saw him coming toward me. His face was set in that expressionless manner he adopts when his mind is occupied by a problem that is particularly perplexing.

He climbed in and sat beside me. I remarked, "You did not meet with success?"

"On the contrary. I have found important evidence in the matter of our most recent client."

"Mr. Rockefeller?"

"Miss Lucy James. I have found her name in the registrar general's index of births and deaths. She was born Lucy James in Linton Hill, county of Kent, January seventh, 1875, weighing eight pounds, seven ounces. I have applied for a copy of the birth certificate. It should be available in two weeks' time."

"So she is a British citizen. I wonder why she was educated in America."

"As her trustee, Mr. Worth would know. But we are hardly in a position to ask him."

"Did the index show the names of her parents?"

"Both the father and mother are listed as 'person unknown.' The name of the witness is listed as 'Mr. Adam Worth.'"

16. THREADNEEDLE STREET

For the remainder of the ride, about a mile and a half along Fleet Street, Holmes remained silent. We arrived at Threadneedle Street and mounted the wide, expansive steps to the main entrance of the Bank of England. I drew in my breath as I glanced up at the soaring columns and Grecian-temple facade. I took comfort in the silent architectural message that the Bank, like the classical roots of our civilization, would endure for many centuries after our own generation had concluded its mortal struggles and given way to the next.

Llewellen Perkins, chief clerk, gave us an apprehensive glance when, having been alerted by the guard, he came to the doorway. He was a small, officious, and tidy man, with a well-trimmed, waxed black mustache and pomaded black hair. His small dark eyes moved rapidly from me to Holmes as he spoke.

"I received your message, Mr. Holmes. I regret that pressing matters of business prevented Chancellor Hicks Beach from joining us. He has interested himself in your inquiry and would have been glad to assist you in person. Of course, any inquiry in which the Chancellor of the Exchequer takes an interest is also of interest to the Bank. Please come to my office, both of you. Mr. Holmes, your brother awaits us there with a policeman. I believe the police-man's name is Lestrade."

We walked through the magnificent front entry hall amid its gilded Greco-Roman columns, and then down a long corridor where clerks hurried along with their bundles of papers. From one room a constantly clicking din of machinery emanated, and as we passed I glanced in the partially open door to see five tall black boxes, each with a crank being turned by a clerk at a slow pace. Since we were late, however, I did not take time to ask what bank-ing activity was being performed but rather continued along with the group until we had reached Perkins's office.

There we found Mycroft and Lestrade, who, while awaiting our arrival, had sent out for roast beef sandwiches. Two remained. I gratefully picked one up and Holmes declined the other.

Lestrade nodded solemnly. "We have some news for you."

"I think that should wait," Mycroft interposed, "until we have finished our business with Mr. Perkins, if you have no objections, Inspector Lestrade. We have already imposed on his hospitality longer than he expected."

"Most appreciative, I'm sure," said Mr. Perkins, beaming effu-sively. "Well, Mr. Holmes. And you, Mr. Holmes—the younger Mr. Holmes, of course. I, too, have a bit of news about the subjects, the gentlemen, that I was requested to pursue. Pursue figuratively, of course. Yes, I have not been entirely unsuccessful. Would you like me to begin with Mr. Carte? Very well. I have been able to ascertain that his theater has not been as profitable as in the past, and that he has indeed received financial backing from a syndicate headed by Mr. Adam Worth as recently as last year."

"So he was telling the truth about Worth," said Holmes.

"Not entirely, Mr. Holmes!" Perkins preened with satisfac-tion as he continued, "For Mr. Carte is now quietly seeking new financial backing—in order to buy out the interest of Mr. Worth! It seems that their relationship is not amicable!"

"Reflects well on Carte," said Mycroft. "Now, what can you tell us about Adam Worth?"

Perkins opened an oxblood-colored calfskin folder and extracted a sheaf of notes. "We have done a bit of research, as you can see," he told Mycroft proudly. "We had expected the Chancellor to be present and we wanted to be as thorough—"

"Most industrious, I'm sure. Now, what do you have there?"

Savoring his moment, Perkins lifted a lorgnette to his eyes and fluttered the papers. "Let me see. He came from America. Served in the Union Army in the American Civil War, during which he was wounded in the shoulder. He banks at the Union, County, and Westminster banks—that we know of, you understand. There may be more that we do not. His income is sporadic, consisting of deposits of cash from time to time in various currencies. The sums have been substantial, but by no means immense. He has been suspected of coming by these funds dishonestly. Nothing has been proven. He is not known to be a gambler and is not a member of any club—that we know of, of course."

"When was his most recent deposit?" asked Holmes.

"Two hundred pounds in the Union Bank, October 16." Squinting at one of the papers, Perkins added, "A Wednesday."

"Is that significant?" Holmes asked.

"You gentlemen must judge that for yourselves. I merely mention it for the sake of completeness."

Holmes nodded. "How long has Worth been in London?"

"Since at least January 1888, when he rented what is known as The Western Lodge, a respectable estate on the west corner of Clapham Common. It is a curious fact, however, that he has never lived there in the usual sense, for according to our information the house is nearly bereft of furnishings and servants. He spends most of his time in a flat that he rents in Westminster. I do not know the address."

Holmes nodded. "So he rents a flat and an estate. Have you found any other significant expenditures?"

"There is a yacht."

"Indeed?" I could tell Holmes's interest was aroused. "Where?"

Another quite maddening flutter through the papers ensued. Then, "The Isle of Dogs. He has an arrangement with the West India Company."

"And did he purchase the yacht?"

"He leases it through a subsidiary company. We had a bit of difficulty making the connection, but it is virtually certain that the company is wholly owned by Worth, for he personally guaranteed the lease. Since late September of this year."

Mycroft said thoughtfully, "A large empty house and a yacht, not far from one another. A criminal organization might meet quietly in either or both locations."

"Oh, dear," said Perkins.

"We do not mean to alarm you," said Holmes. "Your information is very helpful. But I should like to understand one thing. If Mr. Worth were to come into possession of a substantially large sum of money—say, hundreds of thousands of pounds, or more likely the equivalent in a foreign currency—would you have a way to know it?"

"We have a reliable network among our banking fraternity," said Perkins. "So if Mr. Worth were to deposit a cash sum of such magnitude in one of his accounts, I am quite sure I would be able to learn of the circumstances." His face clouded. "However, such a large amount of cash is generally bulky, and for that reason rarely found in a personal transaction. Might I ask if you could tell me the type of transaction you are, dare I say, expecting?"

"Let us say a foreign power wishes to send a substantial payment to Mr. Worth for a substantial service."

Perkins blinked rapidly. "Then that payment could be sent via diplomatic channels. But as I noted, the cash form would be bulky and therefore inconvenient. It is more likely that payment would be sent in the form of a bearer bond."

"Why?"

"A bearer bond is as anonymous as cash, but as easy to transport as a single piece of paper. The Americans invented them when they needed investment funds to rebuild their cities after their civil war. A bond of one million pounds could be carried in an envelope in a gentleman's inside pocket. Mr. Worth could take that with him to whatever country he chose and be assured of payment at virtually any bank, without having to show any identification."

"And a London bank, as well? He could proceed with anonymity?"

"Provided he did not want to create an account to deposit the bond—or the cash, as it would become, of course. If he was not known to the bank when he went in, he would remain anonymous when he went out."

Perkins's small dark eyes took on an imaginative gleam as he continued, "Worth could carry an inconspicuous satchel, have it filled with hundred-pound notes at the bank, and then go to that empty estate house of his, or that yacht, and parcel out the cash to his accomplices, and no one would know. You would have to follow him, or post watchmen every day at each of the city's three-hundred-odd banks, in order to have an inkling of such a transaction, and even then he might simply travel to Manchester, or to Leeds, or anywhere else to cash in his bond."

Holmes shut his eyes briefly in a gesture I was sure indicated his exasperation. Then he stood. "Mr. Perkins, you have been most helpful. We will intrude upon your patience no longer."

As we left, we passed the room where the clerks still stood, cranking away at their tall black boxes. My curiosity prevailed and I asked Perkins what they were doing. "They are weighing gold sovereigns," came the reply. "Each machine can process thirty-three sovereigns in one minute, separating out those of short weight from those with full value. Every month nearly one million sovereigns are judged by these machines, and nearly a third, being found short, are sent to the furnaces to be melted and recast."

He gave a brief, pious smile. "Each time I pass this room I think of the judgment day that will come to each of us, and pray that my soul will not be found wanting and sent to the furnaces when it is weighed in the balance by our Maker."

"A most worthy sentiment, Mr. Perkins," said Holmes. "By the way," he said as we stopped beneath the soaring high ceiling domes of the magnificent front hall, "you are no doubt aware that I am engaged by Mr. Rockefeller?"

"I believe Chancellor Hicks Beach mentioned it."

"Mr. Rockefeller is considering a large transaction that would require financing here in London. Several days ago he sent his American agent, one Mr. Foster, to determine a suitable location in which the necessary negotiations might be conducted."

Perkins's gaze flickered momentarily upward and over Holmes's shoulder, in the direction of the imposing cantilever staircase. "I do not recall meeting that gentleman."

"Would you be able to arrange a suitable meeting room here at the bank? One where a group of, let us say, twelve gentlemen might confer, and with three or four adjacent smaller rooms, where each of the principals might confer with his own staff and advisors?"

"Such arrangements are made by a different department here. But I would be happy to make the introductions, and to help in any way I possibly can."

"Your cooperation is much appreciated," said Holmes, and we took our leave.

When we four were all outside, Mycroft said, "It was as well that Chancellor Hicks Beach did not attend. We should otherwise have been subjected to even more of Perkins's sycophantic ardor."

Holmes nodded. "Though I think he did provide some useful information."

"He knows the location of Mr. Rockefeller's meeting." As I struggled to understand, Mycroft continued, "Have you seen Moran, Sherlock?"

"No. But I would not expect him to show himself in my presence."

"You should stay away from Baker Street. I have made arrangements for you and Watson to stay at the Diogenes Club. There are rooms available on the top floor."

"Watson and I are grateful."

Holmes turned to Lestrade. "Now, what was the news you spoke of?"

"Oh, yes, Mr. Holmes. This morning we at Scotland Yard also learned of Mr. Worth's estate in Clapham Common. I had one of my men take a look. In the carriage drive he found silver sand."

17. A TRAP IS BAITED

At the Diogenes Club shortly thereafter, the Prime Minister, the Commissioner, and Clevering sat with Baron Halsbury, Lord Goschen, Mycroft, and Lestrade around the great walnut table in the south library as Holmes and I entered. Shelves surrounded us, filled to the thirty-foot-high ceiling and representing the wisdom and dreams of thousands of our predecessors.

"You have been to the Bank of England." Clevering's tone was polite, but guarded. "We should like to know who you spoke with at the Bank and what you may have learned."

Holmes looked toward the Prime Minister, and at that gentleman's nod, replied, "The chief clerk indicated that the bank might be the location of a meeting with Mr. Rockefeller next week. You must change the location."

"Why?" asked the Prime Minister.

"I have three reasons for the recommendation. First, because an assassin formerly employed by the Moriarty gang has escaped, undoubtedly with the help of a criminal organization similar to the late Professor's. Second, because Mr. Foster, Mr. Rockefeller's man in charge of security, visited the bank less than twenty-four hours before he was murdered. And third, because I believe that a man named Adam Worth is connected with both the escape of the assassin and the murder of Mr. Foster."

"Who is this assassin?"

"Colonel Sebastian Moran. I was responsible for placing him in the dock."

"Are you in danger?" asked Clevering.

"I have left my rooms on Baker Street and shall be staying elsewhere."

I wondered briefly at this statement, because I knew that we had not left our rooms.

"Have you any evidence to support a connection between Mr. Foster and this Mr. Worth?"

"Inspector Lestrade has unearthed what I believe to be a valuable clue. I propose to follow it up, either tonight or early tomorrow morning."

"What clue?" asked Clevering.

Holmes nodded to Lestrade, who said, "We found silver sand in the driveway of a house belonging to Mr. Worth."

"What bearing does that have?"

Holmes spoke patiently, as though to a child. "You may recall when we met last evening, I mentioned that silver sand had been discovered on the socks and inside the shoes of Mr. Foster."

"Do not patronize me," said Clevering. "And as for changing the location, remember we are dealing with Americans of the highest station and enormous influence, each of whom possesses several grand estates and cannot be expected to take direction from a consulting detective who lives in a rented flat."

"Mind your tongue, Clevering," said the Prime Minister. "It is imperative that Mr. Rockefeller be able to conduct business in safety whenever he is on British soil."

Baron Halsbury rapped his knuckles hard upon the table, as though calling for order in his courtroom. "Speaking of our

American friends, I think we must also inform Mr. Holmes of the evening's entertainment we have arranged to inaugurate the meeting. Mr. Morgan has offered the use of the *Corsair*, his personal yacht, and will provide a sumptuous banquet for the occasion. Mr. Carnegie has kindly offered to pay all the expenses for the entertainers. The performance is certain to please our guests, because its subject matter already enjoys great popularity in America."

The others nodded their assent. Holmes asked, "And who are the entertainers?"

"They are an established British cultural institution that represents our leadership in the world, including our sense of humor as well as our appreciation for beauty. I am sure you have heard of them, Mr. Holmes. We shall all be entertained—I might even say captivated—by Mr. D'Oyly Carte's Savoy Theatre opera troupe."

"And where will the *Corsair* be located for the troupe's performance?"

"West India Docks. Conveniently close to Mr. Rockefeller's *White Star.*" Baron Halsbury gave a benevolent smile. "Do not worry, Mr. Holmes. All manner of security arrangements will be employed. Everyone will be perfectly safe."

18. A CONFRONTATION WITH A LADY

Less than an hour later we were at the Savoy Theatre. Holmes had used the telephone at the Diogenes Club to call Mr. Carte's office, and the usher stationed beside the door was expecting us. We went first to the rehearsal room. Some of the musicians had already begun to gather, chatting and tuning their various instruments. Holmes took in the scene briefly, and then we returned to the stage door entrance.

We waited inside the doorway with the usher. Soon the door opened and Miss Rosario arrived, carrying her violin case. I wondered briefly whether I ought to have broken my promise and told Holmes of our meeting Friday night.

Her lovely face paled when she saw Holmes. Her green eyes met mine in what I felt was an indignant accusation. I shook my head, hoping she would realize that I had kept my word.

Holmes's face took on a studied impassiveness as he addressed her.

"Miss Rosario."

"Sherlock."

"You have my apologies for this unannounced visit. Is there a place where we could speak privately?"

"There is not." She walked with us to the end of the passageway, where the usher could no longer hear us. "I shall be late for my rehearsal. Why are you here?"

Holmes said, "Because of what happened in the county of Kent near the village of Linton Hill, on the seventh of January, 1875."

Miss Rosario's features turned scarlet. She pushed past us and entered the rehearsal room, closing the door behind her in a marked manner.

19. A DISCOVERY AT CLAPHAM COMMON

Holmes did not discuss Miss Rosario's reaction. Nor would he discuss the added complication represented by the entertainment proposed for the *Corsair*, other than to say that smuggling more than a ton of dynamite onto Mr. Morgan's private yacht would be a task too difficult for even the Moriarty gang to attempt. From the Savoy we returned to Baker Street for a light supper and a few hours of fitful sleep.

Half past three the next morning found us in a hansom cab, driving south on Regent Street. The driver was well known to Holmes. The approaching day was of course a Sunday, so at that hour Regent Street was nearly deserted and a goodly portion of the working populace was home enjoying the beginning of a once-weekly day of rest.

I envied them.

Despite our precautions Holmes's features were grave as he scanned the shadowy streets around us. We crossed Westminster Bridge to the Albert Embankment. Then we drove southwest on Wandsworth Road to Lavender Hill. The cab stopped. We climbed out and stood on the pavement amid dark rows of dark houses.

Gas lamps were few and far between in this part of the city, but our surroundings were somewhat illuminated by a pale moon.

After Holmes gave instructions to the driver, we walked briskly due south on the Elspeth Road, taking care to keep clear of shadowy store entrances and alleyways. We wore our evening garments; in white tie, thin-soled shoes, and top hats we would appear to be two gentlemen returning from a very late Saturday evening. Holmes carried a small satchel. There was no fog and no wind, but the chill in the November air cut deeply.

I wrapped my thin evening cloak closer around me as we came within sight of the dark and far-reaching expanse of Clapham Common. By day the Common was more than 220 open acres of grassland, lake, and shrubbery available to the public. At this hour the Common was a vast, nearly stygian void, almost impenetrable to the eye. My watch put the time at just past five a.m. It would be more than an hour until the sky above that murky panorama began to lighten with the sunrise. By then, I fervently hoped, we would have secured whatever evidence Holmes wanted and would be safely on our way home.

Holmes touched my arm and indicated a large, three-story brick house behind us, built in the Georgian style. In the faint moonlight I could make out the white-trimmed outlines of its arched front doorway, and the tall bay window on the right side. The house was well set back from the road. To its left was a smaller, squared-off structure that was clearly the carriage house. In front, the moonlight illuminated a wide, curving driveway covered in silver sand.

"Mr. Worth's estate," Holmes said quietly, his lips close to my ear. "Please stay close to me at all times, Watson, and keep your revolver drawn."

He walked quickly to the front door. "Notice the tracks," he said, and indeed I could see the marks of wheels and hoof-prints, running in parallel in front, and curving in the direction of the carriage house entrance. I saw no footprints, so evidently Lestrade's man had not trespassed on the property as Holmes and I were doing. In the doorway he drew a set of picklocks from inside his coat. As I watched nervously for passersby he bent over the door handle for a few moments. Then I heard a clicking sound. The door opened and soon we stood in the vestibule, where the musty, unpleasant smell of a long-abandoned interior enveloped us. I pulled the door closed behind us and held my nose, not wanting to risk the sound of a cough or a sneeze.

Holmes seemed not to notice. He reached into his satchel and drew out a dark lantern. When he had lit it, he focused the beam on the floor of the front hall. A bleak and gray scene greeted us. The yellow light spread over empty floorboards, all coated with a thick layer of dust. As Holmes lifted the lantern slightly, so that we could see further inside, we saw a grand, curving staircase, its outlines blurred by the gray dust that clung to its wide steps and smooth banisters.

Holmes closed the lantern's panel. "It is as well not to leave our footprints for others to find. We will go outside and locate the rear entrance." In a minute we had done so. Holmes repeated his work with the picklocks.

This time the unpleasant smell was more pronounced. We were at the back of the house, looking in on what once may have been a working kitchen, but which now was a shambles of pots and pans, stacks of dishes, and various kitchen implements, all gray with dust. Even the lumps of coal in the coal bucket beside the stove were gray. Holmes shone the lantern light forward, revealing a few dust-laden steps leading down to a small root cellar or storage pantry. In its light at the foot of the stairs we could see burlap and canvas sacks that had once held flour or grain, but were now gnawed to bits by rodents. In scattered piles were what may have been the decayed remnants of their contents, mingled with droppings. The cause of the unpleasant smell was now evident.

Holmes said, "The Worth estate is still a home for vermin, Watson," and shuttered the lamp. We withdrew. I closed the door behind us, and, grateful for the fresh night air, followed Holmes to the only part of the estate that remained unexplored.

The carriage house adjoined the main house. It had no rear entry, as we soon discerned. We walked around to the front and saw the white sand of the driveway, smooth and undisturbed from where it joined the circular turnaround at the front of the house, all the way to the large doors through which a carriage might enter. To the left of these was a smaller door. For a third time Holmes busied himself with the picklocks, opened this door, and, after we entered, opened the lantern.

The carriage house was empty.

A long workbench stood to one side of the left wall. Some tools hung on the wall above it, and a hand-turned lathe was positioned in front of the side window. I caught the scents of machine oil and spirits of turpentine. The floor was smooth concrete. The lantern's beam revealed that the workbench had been swept, or wiped, more likely, by turpentine-soaked rags. I saw nothing that would provide a clue to what activity had been taking place.

Then Holmes directed the lantern's beam at the side window, away from the workbench. "There, Watson. Do you see?"

"I see a rather dirty window."

"Please turn your attention to the workbench, now that it is in darkness."

I did. From the furthest corner of the bench, directly adjacent to the intersection of the two walls, came a very faint white glow.

Holmes took a small envelope from his pocket and very carefully maneuvered the open flap into the workbench corner. Then with a delicate motion, he secured a few softly luminous granules of what appeared to be coarse white powder.

"I believe this to be white phosphorus, Watson," said Holmes.

I nodded, recalling how we had encountered that substance, known as "the Devil's element," five years ago on the moors of Devon, courtesy of our old adversary Mr. Stapleton. One of the notable properties of white phosphorous is to emit a pale yellow-green glow in the presence of air, until it has become oxidized. Another is to disrupt human neural functions, causing the rapid onset of paralysis and death.

Holmes closed the envelope. It cast a faint light onto his fingers as he slid it into his shirt pocket.

"Do you think Worth plans somehow to poison the attendees of the meeting?"

"It is a possibility, but I should like to have more facts before making a hypothesis. You know my methods."

The lantern's beam found the door briefly before Holmes extinguished it. "We are finished here," Holmes said. "Our cab should be waiting for us at the Cranford Road."

Keeping to the grassy edge of the driveway we walked quickly out to the West Common Road and headed east for the cab, which was some four blocks away. Above the trees of the Common I could see the eastern sky, barely beginning to lighten with the approaching sun. The air was quiet as we walked, Holmes at my right side and slightly ahead. Our preparations to appear as late-night revelers returning home seemed to have been pointless, as we had not seen a soul for the entire fifteen minutes' time we had spent at the Worth estate.

I felt weary and disappointed. I do not know what Holmes had expected to find—sawdust, I supposed, was the evidence that would have been most valuable—but plainly such evidence was not to be had. The house had been abandoned for at least a year, I thought. Since I knew that the unfortunate Mr. Foster had been asphyxiated by chloroform rather than poisoned by white phosphorous, I could not make any connection to his murder from the desolation we had seen at Worth's apparently abandoned estate.

Then, as we walked, I saw Holmes's top hat fly off. In the same instant I heard something strike the trunk of a large tree in front of us, and suddenly we were showered with fragments of wood and bark.

Stunned, I gazed at the tree, and saw a small white crater, about the size of an orange, that had been gouged from the bark and the wood beneath.

"Run, Watson," Holmes said quietly. "Take off your hat, and run for the cab. Stay between the trees if you can."

We ran. We ran until my lungs burned and my heart nearly burst within me. Holmes, always the faster, stayed ahead even in this instance when burdened with his satchel, every now and then looking back over his shoulder to be sure I was still behind. After what seemed an eternity I saw our hansom cab on the roadway at the bottom of the hill, and the driver with the horse, standing at the ready. My relief was even greater when we reached the cab and Holmes was beside me.

"Waterloo Station, if you please," said Holmes. "As quickly as possible!"

As we scrambled into the cab and took our seats, I turned to Holmes. "Waterloo? Why are we going there?"

There was a long silence as Holmes watched through the window. Then, apparently satisfied that we were not being pursued, he turned to me.

"Because I found what I expected to find, and I have proven what I had expected to prove."

"But Holmes!" I protested. "Other than what may be a poisonous white powder, you found nothing!"

"Nothing is what I expected to find."

The clatter of the iron-shod cab wheels seemed to grow louder. I shook my head, trying to gather my thoughts, feeling the familiar mix of chagrin and admiration that so often resulted from association with my old friend.

"I should have known you would say something like that."

"Dear old Watson. Please. Cast your recollection back to what you saw in Mr. Worth's mansion. Do you recall that there was a heavy cover of ordinary dust throughout?"

I nodded.

"And no footprints? No sign of recent activity?"

"Yes, and I am perfectly capable of deducing that therefore no one except rodents had entered the mansion from the front or from the back. But Holmes, there was no sawdust! Not in the mansion, nor in the carriage house."

"Ah, the carriage house. Please recollect what you saw there."

"It was empty. No carriage. Only a shelf and a workbench with some tools."

"And on the floor?"

I strained my memory. "The floor was concrete. That is all that I remember."

"Was there silver sand on the floor, such as would ordinarily been brought in on the wheels of a carriage?"

"The floor was bare."

"And the shelf and workbench and the tools?"

"They were clean." A realization began to dawn on me.

"They were remarkably clean, in comparison with the house. And they had been attended to recently, judging from the odor of turpentine that still lingered. The floor had been carefully swept. And outside, in front of the entrance, there were no tracks, either of footprints or carriage wheels. Do you not find that significant?"

"I had thought that the carriage house had not been used for some time."

"And that someone had flown up to its entrance, hovered there to open the door, entered, cleaned the tools, swept the floor, and then left, closing the door behind, without making footprints?"

Embarrassed, I tried to defend my position. "He might have come though the connecting door to the main house."

"Also without making footprints as he entered or left the main house?"

My fatigue and irritation were evident as I replied, "Of course when you put it that way it sounds completely absurd. But I am tired and hungry and I fear not in a frame of mind to draw logical conclusions just at this moment. Will you not tell me what you have deduced?"

"Certainly, my dear fellow. I observed that the sand of the driveway, now being smooth, had been raked all the way to the front turnaround. I deduced that someone drove to the front turn-around, got out, walked to the carriage house, cleaned the tools and whatever sawdust had been created on or near the carpenter's lathe and workbench, swept the floor, and left the building, taking with him a rake which he used to smooth the driveway sand behind him. Having reached the turnaround, he then got into the carriage with the rake and drove away."

I saw it all in my mind's eye. My fatigue vanished. Excitedly I said, "And the rake would also obliterate any signs of Mr. Foster's dragging heels as his murderers took away his body."

"You have it, Watson. Now, why should the murderers believe that it was necessary to remove the sawdust and obliterate the heel tracks, if they were taking the body some four miles away to Westminster Bridge, and preparing to drop it into the Thames?"

"They would only believe it was necessary if they knew that sawdust and silver sand had been found on Mr. Foster's body."

He nodded. "Add that information to this"—Holmes held up his top hat, displaying the holes in either side—"and we now have our evidence to prove that in the meeting room at the Diogenes Club last night, there was a traitor."

Once again, I saw. "A traitor who revealed what you said there—that we had left our rooms at Baker Street, and that we would be coming to Mr. Worth's estate to look for the silver sand and sawdust either last night or this morning." A further thought sprang to my now-awakened mind. "And I believe it was Colonel Moran whom the traitor told of our intentions."

"Why?"

"From the weapon, I think it obvious. We heard no report of an ordinary rifle, so he used a silent air gun. The hole in the tree was nearly the size of an orange, indicating that he used an exploding bullet. That is the *modus operandi* of Colonel Moran."

"Very good, Watson. And we shall learn more of the colonel in a few hours when we reach our destination."

"Are we not going home to Baker Street?" I am afraid my voice showed some of the fatigue and longing for rest that our past two days had instilled in me.

"We are going west, to the county of Devon."

"That is a four-hour journey!"

"Nevertheless we shall make it, and then we shall return for our report to the Prime Minister. I regret the strain on you, but we have, as you know, overriding obligations." His voice softened. "Watson, we must learn how Colonel Moran escaped from Dartmoor. Unless we uncover the organization that aided Moran, we cannot prevent the cataclysmic tragedy that they are most assuredly planning."

PART TWO

TREASON AND PLOT

20. A JOURNEY TO DARTMOOR

A few hours later I stared with half-unseeing gaze at the Hampshire County landscape, a pastiche of green pastures, brown hillsides, and occasional white cottages speeding by outside the window of our first-class carriage. At Waterloo Station we had placed our top hats and evening capes into a storage locker along with Holmes's satchel, from which Holmes had produced our less-conspicuous brown tweeds. Before we boarded the 7:05 that would take us to Princetown Station and Dartmoor, we had enough time to purchase copies of the morning papers and then, at the railway buffet, hot meat pies and bottled ginger beer. In our compartment I had been gratified to see Holmes methodically devour his portion. Lulled by the rhythm of the steel wheels after departure, I had dozed off, then awakened, read some of the news in the *Daily Chronicle*, and then fallen into the reverie of the railway traveler who is still many miles from his destination and is not yet ready to think about what he will do upon his arrival.

Holmes's voice startled me. "Thirty-two minutes, Watson."

He then closed his watch and produced a page of typescript from his inside coat pocket, along with a folded map of the area.

"We have thirty-two minutes until we arrive at Princetown Station. I suggest we employ the next five in studying this report from the prison officials to the Commissioner concerning the colonel's escape. It is an official report and therefore unlikely to prove conclusive, but it may be useful nonetheless. We can then look over the map and decide on how best to proceed."

Hard steel wheels clattered on hard steel rails. Holmes and I reviewed the report and studied the map. Then he lit his pipe, closed his eyes, and was silent for the remainder of our journey.

We arrived in the small village of Princetown shortly after eleven, under a cloudy sky, at a deserted railway station. Deserted, that is, but for a gray-bearded man in a drab green cloak, who sat hunched on the waiting bench puffing away at a meerschaum pipe. At Holmes's direction, we remained on the platform in order to ascertain that we were the only two passengers to alight. The old man surveyed us up and down while we waited, evidently wondering if the porter would offload some luggage of ours that would require his assistance. Of course we had no luggage and no reason to employ him. Soon the train chugged off again on its way to Plymouth. The old fellow heaved himself to his feet and, bent over, walked away toward the station entrance with that shuffling gait characteristic of the aged.

Owing to the town's proximity to the sea, the November chill had a moist, raw quality, and I was grateful that our first destination was the nearby parish church, a simple stone structure, where the Sunday service of Morning Prayer and Holy Communion was under way. There were nearly fifty worshippers present. From our pew at the rear of the church I could see only the backs of them, so it was impossible to identify the man we hoped to interview, a Mr. Dodson, the chief warden of Dartmoor. Indeed, I worried that Mr. Dodson would not be in attendance. Though his position as chief official for the major employer in the parish would naturally suggest that he set a good example for the other parishioners, he might have come to the early service, or be occupied with other matters and planning to attend later, at Evensong.

For his part, Holmes seemed entirely sanguine. We had less than four hours to spend in Princetown if we were to catch the return train to London in time to keep our appointment with the Prime Minister and his committee. Yet as the service went on, he seemed content to follow along with the other worshippers. He recited the prayers from the prayer book. He listened respectfully to the vicar's sermon, which made the point that the unknowable purposes of the Divine could cause good to come from even such a dreadful event as the 1812 wars with Napoleon and America, since the construction of this very church had been performed by French and American prisoners of that conflict. The reference to a war with America made me all the more unsettled. The explosion of the bomb at the hospital still haunted me. I worried that while we were here in Princetown, back in London Worth and Moran were now armed with more than a ton of dynamite and were plotting to turn England's hope for a stronger American alliance into an incident of divisive horror.

But Holmes remained serene. He even sang the refrains of the hymns in his strong tenor, as though he took pleasure in every word. Then, when the time came for us to go to the altar to receive the bread and wine of Communion, he got to his feet and, to my surprise, indicated I should emulate him.

We walked down the aisle, still wrapped in our tweed cloaks, not wishing to call attention to the evening attire that we, of course, still wore beneath them. We knelt at the altar rail and held out our hands, palms up in the prescribed manner, to receive the Sacrament. I was then further surprised to see, from the corner of my eye, that Holmes's open hands held a small white card on which something had been written.

The vicar was approaching, moving smoothly down the line of kneeling worshippers in his black robe and embroidered white surplice, murmuring the incantation. As he came to stand before Holmes, I saw the vicar's eyes widen momentarily at the sight of the card, but then he placed the Communion wafer in Holmes's palm and took up the card without so much as a pause in his chanted intonation of the scripture, as if to receive a message at the Communion altar might have been an everyday occurrence for him. As he moved on to stand in front of me, he pressed the white wafer into my palm with his thumb. The murmur of his chant never varied as he smoothly tucked the card into his surplice. In his eyes, however, I caught a glimmer of excitement.

21. INTERVIEW WITH A VICAR

In a few minutes' time the service concluded. We filed out with the other attendees, the vicar greeting us from his accustomed position in the church doorway. He gave us each a cordial handshake and nod of greeting indistinguishable from his greeting to the other parishioners, but followed by a barely audible request that we wait for him in the vestry office that adjoined the church. This we did. It was seventeen minutes past noon by my pocket watch when the vicar joined us. We had less than three hours before our train would leave.

He shook our hands again, this time vigorously. "What a wonderful surprise, Mr. Holmes." An energetic young man with bright blue eyes, ruddy cheeks, and curly red hair, he continued to speak as he shrugged out of his robe and surplice, hung them up in a small oaken wardrobe, and then donned the black coat typical of the Anglican clergy. His words tumbled out in a rapid stream. They were nearly as rapid as a recitation of the liturgy, but of course with more spontaneous feeling. "Even as one who deals in resurrection on a regular basis, I find myself amazed to see you! I will not ask what miracle allowed you to survive the ordeal that Dr. Watson described in *The Strand Magazine*, though I should love to hear what happened."

"Someday I may write of it," I responded politely.

"Oh, I hope so. In this part of the country we treasure all of the published accounts. But Mr. Holmes, I must say that here you are even more renowned for ending the famous curse of the Baskervilles. Sir Henry has told me something of the matter—he has now a son and heir whom I had the honor of christening last Whitsuntide—and I do hope that one day we may have the pleasure of reading of that adventure as well, Dr. Watson, if you have the time to—"

Recalling the Baskerville case, I felt a chill, for that affair had been one of the few instances in which Holmes had underestimated the murderous capacity of his opponent. I had been reluctant to share that adventure with the public, because Holmes's error had very nearly led to the death of our client. I could only hope that the vicar's words were not an omen foreshadowing a similar mistake, one that would lead to disastrous consequences.

The vicar must have seen my apprehension, for he gave me an embarrassed nod and looked down for a moment. Then his gaze turned to Holmes. "But Mr. Holmes, you cannot be here to talk about something that happened six years ago. You have come all this way because of Colonel Moran's escape."

"Quite correct," said Holmes.

"I thought so. A most malevolent individual. I have seen him on the occasions when I officiated at the mandatory chapel services. Judging from his stark and unfeeling gaze throughout, he is entirely devoid of remorse. It was unnerving to think that he escaped. And what a shameful lapse in competency by the prison officials! Warden Dodson's absence—he has been away attending to his sick mother in Liverpool these past three weeks—may be something of an explanation, but it is certainly no excuse. But, see, here again in my excitement I am talking too much. Gentlemen, please, my apologies. How can I help you?"

"We are here in an official capacity, but we would like to make our inquiries in an indirect manner. Scotland Yard is already investigating through the regular channels. We have an official report, but that is quite inconclusive. You may have heard details through conversations with your parishioners that may be helpful."

"I understand completely. I am entirely at your service."

"We are also somewhat pressed for time. Can you tell us what facts you know of the escape?"

"Ah, yes, facts. Of course. Facts. Well. There is not much news that does not get around in a country village, and when something as momentous as—but that is opinion, to be sure. Well. Facts. As I have heard from numerous sources, Colonel Moran overpowered the guard on duty in his section of the prison, a man named Trent, last Tuesday night. He beat the man senseless, then exchanged clothes with him and left him lying unconscious on his bed, locked in his cell. Moran then walked out when the night shift was replaced with the morning one."

"Did no one recognize him?"

"His physical bearing bore somewhat of a resemblance to the guard. Of course he was at least thirty years older, but he had exercised strenuously in his cell nearly every day and had the physique to show for it."

"But Moran's hair was gray," I said. My memory still held a vivid image of the colonel, and his hate-filled glare when Holmes had trapped him in the house across from our Baker Street rooms, nearly eighteen months before. "If the guard was thirty years younger, surely he was not gray-haired."

"Possibly the light was insufficient. The shifts change at six a.m. and the sun did not rise until nearly an hour later. I am an early riser myself and take notice of the celestial timetable."

"Do the guards wear uniform caps?" asked Holmes.

"Why, yes, they do. That may account for it!"

"Possibly. Do you know if Mr. Trent wore a mustache similar to Moran's?"

"Oh, my." The vicar shook his head. "Mr. Trent is one of our parishioners, and I know he is clean-shaven. A fine figure of a man, with a full head of coal-black hair. Though rather I should say, he *was* a fine figure of a man, for he remains quite infirm after his injuries, and his memory of the incident is completely gone, as I understand may be the consequence of such an attack."

I affirmed this. "Head trauma can be the cause of amnesia, which can be of short or long duration depending on the case."

"I also know poor Trent is greatly distraught over his failure—he may even lose his position, and he has a loving wife and two little girls to support—"

Holmes interrupted. "Did the morning guard not look into the cell when he made his first rounds?"

"Yes, but Trent was still in Colonel Moran's bunk, unconscious. The guard thought the colonel was still sleeping. It was only when the morning guard came to escort Colonel Moran to morning roll call that the escape was made known."

Holmes nodded, producing the typewritten report from his inside coat pocket. He consulted the page for a moment. "We are told that morning roll call was at seven and the change of shifts was at six. And that this guard, with his clean-shaven face and coal-black hair, lying on the prisoner's pallet, was believed to be the gray-haired and gray-mustached Colonel Moran when the morning guard looked in."

"He might have remained motionless under his blanket after he had been attacked. He might have still been unconscious due to his injuries," I volunteered.

"Possibly. Or he may have been drugged. Or he may have colluded with Moran, and permitted the beating and the exchange of clothes, and then hidden himself under the blanket, to provide Moran more time to make his escape."

"Oh, I protest!" said the vicar. "George Trent is a family man, a churchgoing man, and he has a fine reputation in our village. I cannot believe he would ruin his future and jeopardize the welfare of his family by doing such a thing."

"Nevertheless, it remains a possibility."

The vicar considered this, then asked to see the report. Upon reading it over quickly, he said, "This conforms to what people have been saying. Prior to evening lockup, Moran complained of a fever and stomach distress. Then when Trent was making his rounds, Moran asked to be taken to the infirmary, which was obviously the pretext to induce Trent to open the cell door. But the report omits any mention of the handcuffs."

"Indeed?"

"Yes, though it is hardly a point in Trent's favor. People have been remarking how unlikely it would be that, when handcuffed, an older man like Moran could overpower a young man in his prime such as George Trent. And yet handcuffs are required when a guard is to be alone with a prisoner as able-bodied and as intractable as Moran, or in this case, to walk with him to the infirmary. So prior to opening the cell door, Trent would have followed the procedure and required Moran to place his wrists through the aperture to receive the handcuffs."

"Have you heard whether Trent has said anything about this?"

"I have only heard that he remembers nothing of the morning's events."

Holmes stood up. "I wonder if you might be kind enough to introduce us to Mr. Trent. It would help me greatly if I might have a brief word with him."

22. AN INVALID COMES TO LIFE

The vicar graciously consented, and within five minutes we had walked the short distance to the small white cottage occupied by the Trent family. Mrs. Trent greeted us at the door, her two little girls clinging to her skirts. Her expression was worried.

"Hello, Amy," said the vicar. "These gentlemen have come from London this morning, and one of them is a doctor. Might we be permitted to have a brief visit with George?"

"He's still poorly, the dear man," she said. "You won't be upsetting him, will you?"

"We hope to help him," said Holmes. "We shall only stay a minute or two."

As we entered I saw the doorway to a small bedroom, and a reclining figure on the bed.

Then the younger of the two girls spoke up. "Is Trixie still in Heaven, Father?"

"I am sure of it," replied the vicar in a comforting tone. Then he quickly explained for our benefit, "Trixie was the name of the family kitten. She evidently had an unfortunate fall from a tree in the backyard that broke her neck, though none of us can explain why she did not utilize the ability of her species to land on her feet. In any event, we held a little funeral ceremony for her."

"When was that?" asked Holmes.

"Just this past Monday," replied Mrs. Trent. Then she went on in a hushed voice, "Too many funerals, Vicar." She glanced meaningfully toward the bedroom. "I pray we will not have a third."

The vicar nodded. We entered the bedroom, where Trent lay motionless in a white muslin nightshirt, staring blankly at the ceiling. Bruises and minor abrasions disfigured his eyes and forehead. His cheeks still bore a black stubble of beard, although a razor and shaving bowl were visible on the nightstand. Mute testimony, I thought, to his wife's unsuccessful efforts to make him presentable in the midst of his despair.

"George," said Mrs. Trent brightly, "here's the vicar, and he's brought two gentlemen with him."

"I heard," Trent said. "From London." Then he said nothing more. His gaze remained fixed on the ceiling.

Holmes bent down, whispered something briefly into Trent's left ear, then quickly stood up, his gaze fixed intently on the heretofore motionless man.

The effect of Holmes's words on George Trent was remarkable. The guard's eyes grew round as saucers. His jaw dropped open. Then he sat up. Looking at Holmes in wonderment he whispered hoarsely, "How can you possibly know that?"

"It is my business to know things," replied Holmes. He spoke quietly, and as calmly as if he had been discussing the helpful effects that a recent rainstorm would provide to the crops of the region. "Now, Mr. Trent, I beg you to take heart. I know you are blameless in this matter and I will do everything in my power to clear your name."

On Trent's features, wonderment mingled with hope. "May God bless you, sir. But what shall I do now?"

"For the moment, allow your good wife to care for you and bring you back to health as rapidly as possible. You will hear from me in a few days' time. Thereafter, I believe it will be possible for your memory to return, and for you to resume your duties. Please, though, I beg that you and your family say nothing of this visit to anyone."

"I will do just as you say, sir. And may I say again, God bless you." He looked over to his wife. "And I'm sure Amy and our girls say the same."

"Oh, George!" cried Mrs. Trent, moving forward to embrace her husband.

Holmes had already nodded his good-bye.

23. A SECOND FUNERAL

We left the house a few moments later and set out for the prison with the vicar. Both the vicar and I pressed Holmes to reveal what he had said to George Trent, but he would say only that it had been "something of a long shot, but gratifying nonetheless."

After an uneventful walk to the prison, and an equally uneventful walk to the records office, Holmes spent less than five minutes perusing Moran's file, examining the official reports and a few scraps of handwritten notepaper. Then we took our leave. The three of us were now close by the entrance to Dartmoor Prison. The gray, monolithic gateposts loomed above us, and I was glad that we would soon be away from their ominous presence. Holmes turned to the vicar.

"Your assistance has been invaluable," he said. "Might I trouble you for one more piece of information? Mrs. Trent mentioned that she hoped there would not be three funerals. I presume the service you held for the family kitten was the first. Can you tell me something of the second?"

"That would be Asher. A quiet man, and also employed at the prison as a guard. He died in an accident at Hoo Meavy, some eight miles away."

"Might he have been involved in Moran's escape?" I asked.

"There was some talk of that in the village, but I think it most unlikely. Asher worked in another section of the prison, entirely apart from the one that housed Moran."

"Were there witnesses to the accident?" asked Holmes.

"There were none. Or I suppose it would be more accurate to say that no one has as yet come forward as a witness. Asher's body was found on the road beneath a bridge, with a partially eaten sandwich and a dented flask beneath him. He was accustomed to taking long walks around that time of day, carrying his picnic lunch in a knapsack. The knapsack, containing a change of clothing, was found on the bridge, some thirty feet above the road. It seemed plain to the coroner that Asher was sitting on the bridge, eating the sandwich and drinking from the flask, when he lost his balance and fell. So no inquest was called for."

Holmes nodded. "Did Mr. Asher also have a family?"

"No, he was a single gentleman, only in town these past six months. He worked as an orderly in a London hospital prior to coming here. He kept much to himself. He did not attend church services. No one knew of a next of kin to notify, and there were only myself and the undertaker's employees at the interment service."

"And when was the service?"

"Why, Thursday noon."

"How long was that after the body was discovered?"

"Barely two days. We are a small village and do not have the facilities to preserve the dead for a long interval before burial."

"Of course." Holmes nodded in that polite but brisk manner he takes on when he has reached a conclusion and wishes to move on to something else. "Now, Vicar, it remains only for Watson and me to have a meal at the Plume of Feathers Inn prior to boarding

our train. Might we persuade you to join us? No? Well then, once
again, we are very grateful for your help. Do not, I beg you, speak
of our visit to anyone. If you learn of any further developments
that you think are significant, please send a wire to me in London,
care of the Commissioner of the Metropolitan Police."

We said our farewells to the vicar and watched his receding
form grow smaller on the pathway to the village church. A wind
had sprung up, bringing with it a cold mist from the southwest.
I consulted my watch. "It is nearly two," I said. "We shall have to
move quickly if we are to get a luncheon and catch the 3:05."

There was a moment's silence. Then Holmes replied, "Draw
your revolver, Watson."

Startled, I looked at Holmes in bewilderment. I saw that he
was taking his own pistol from beneath his cape. Then, looking
over his shoulder, I saw two burly men advancing toward us from
the prison gates. I turned, looked behind me, and saw two more.
They were blocking our retreat to the inn and to the railway station
beyond.

"Walk toward them," said Holmes, "and take care to show that
you are armed."

24. A NARROW ESCAPE

My racing heartbeat pounded in my temples. I drew my revolver and aimed it directly at the two men who were coming closer to us from the direction of the railway station. My gesture had its effect, for the two men stopped. To my surprise, I saw that one of them was the bearded old fellow we had seen on our first arrival. Now, however, he stood fully erect in his drab green cloak, and as we drew nearer I could see a mocking smile on his face.

"Walk slowly and carefully," I heard Holmes say behind me. "I am covering these other two."

About forty yards ahead of me the bearded man waited with his companion. He opened his cloak. His smile broadened.

"One of these has a shotgun, Holmes."

"Keep walking. The Prince of Wales Pub should be coming up on your right, and just beyond that is the police station. We may find shelter there."

I advanced, keeping my pistol trained steadily on the chest of the bearded man. I felt apprehension, but I was also glad that Holmes had remembered the police station from his perusal of the map.

It was clear to me what had happened. Moran had reasoned that we would try to pick up his trail by investigating in Princetown, and had positioned the bearded man as a lookout at the railway station. Then during the hours we had spent at the church and with the vicar and with Trent, three other thugs had been assembled. Two had waited at the prison, where they thought we were most likely to go. The third, with the old man, had taken a position at the railway station, where we should have to come to catch our train.

Would they try to kill us? My confidence grew as we neared the police station. Lethal intentions or no, I did not believe these men would dare to attack us there, especially in broad daylight. We were alongside the Prince of Wales Pub now, and the police station was the next building, only a few feet from where we stood.

Behind me I heard Holmes say, "I was mistaken, Watson. These two have each drawn a pistol."

Then I saw the sign on the police station's front door:
CLOSED SUNDAY.
INQUIRIES AT PRISON OFFICE.

At the same time I saw the bearded man raise his weapon to his shoulder and take aim.

"Holmes, get down!" I called. I dropped to the ground and fired my revolver, just as I saw flames burst from the muzzle of the shotgun. A rush of wind from the pellets whistled over my head. The bearded man dropped his gun and writhed on the ground, clutching his knee.

His companion picked up the shotgun. I fired again and saw the gun fall once more as the man's left arm dangled unnaturally from his shoulder.

Holmes was behind me. In the distance I heard the clatter of running boots approaching. "Make for the back of the pub," Holmes said. Then he fired twice. I ran alongside the pub, hearing no more footsteps other than those of Holmes, who was close behind. Up ahead I could see a groom standing with two waiting horses, and two travelers emerging from the pub's rear entrance.

The travelers and the groom gaped at us in astonishment as we ran toward them. Then they saw our pistols and their expressions turned to fear.

"Keep your gun out," Holmes said quietly. As we reached the three men, Holmes put away his pistol and took out his wallet. He held out a sheaf of bills.

"We are in urgent need of transportation," he said cordially. "Here is compensation for your trouble—enough to purchase a dozen horses."

So saying, he let the notes flutter to the ground in front of the amazed trio. Before the notes had been picked up, Holmes and I quickly mounted and were on our way down a small path and across a brown-gold hayfield, riding at a gallop toward the road that ran parallel to the railway line.

We reached the road, turned left, and galloped northward. About a hundred yards to my left I could see four huddled figures, one of them in a drab green cloak.

Four shots, four wounded, I thought.

We rode at full speed until the four men were no longer visible, and then continued several minutes more. Holmes slowed his horse to a walk. I did likewise, coming up beside him. We were two riders alone on a deserted road. I caught my breath. The air was growing colder, yet I was perspiring from the heat of exertion. On Holmes's grim features also, beads of perspiration mingled with the chill November mist. But there was no one else to be seen. For the moment, at least, we were safe.

Holmes's eyes flashed. "Well, Watson, that cost me one hundred pounds. Still, I thought it best not to add armed robbery and horse thievery to our last night's crime of breaking and entering." He gave a nod of satisfaction. "It is as well those four thugs were not marksmen. You saw how they waited to get close before they opened fire."

"You wounded your two, as I wounded mine."

"Against four assailants I would have been defeated if I had been alone."

"My dear friend—"

He continued before I could finish. "Our day's journey has been highly instructive. Among other things, it is plain that Moran did not miss deliberately when he shot at me in Clapham Common. He obviously wants to kill us."

"Obviously."

"We also know more about the organization that arranged Moran's escape. There is one fact in particular that I believe will prove highly useful."

One of those quick smiles flickered across his hawklike face, and I wondered just what new knowledge he had attained during our brief stay in this windswept little town. I also knew that it would be futile to press Holmes for an explanation until he himself had decided that the time was right.

Holmes looked back in the direction of the village, then forward along the empty railway track and deserted road. "We must reach Exeter in time to send a wire to the Commissioner before the train for Paddington departs at half past three. We are roughly twenty-six miles away. We shall have to ride hard."

25. MISS JAMES HAS NEWS

It was after eleven o'clock that evening when I knocked at the door of Miss James's room at the Savoy Hotel. The third-floor hallway was deserted. Miss James opened the door just enough to identify me, and to see that I was alone. Dark circles shadowed her lovely green eyes. "I got your note," she said, widening the opening and motioning for me to enter. "I saw Mr. Worth again yesterday."

Despite the late hour, her hair was still pinned up, though I noticed she now wore small pearl earrings in her delicately shaped ears, and a blue silk robe now covered her white cotton blouse and long black wool skirt. On the window seat, large parcels wrapped in brown paper were stacked in front of the heavy green velvet curtains.

She saw me looking at the parcels. "Those came this afternoon. Johnny wanted me to have some fancy things to wear. He got the dressmaker to produce them overnight and deliver on a Sunday. It's amazing what the Rockefeller name does to people. But it's still nothing serious between us. He confessed that he has a sweetheart, and he hopes he can make her jealous—or at least that's what he said he was trying to do. This is all an act, to stir up some rumors."

On the low table before me were a silver coffeepot and a half-empty cup. I was about to sit on one of the two upholstered chairs near the window, and I expected Miss James to sit on the other. But she remained standing, so I did the same. Thinking she would appreciate news that indicated we were making progress on her case, I said, "Holmes found the registration of your birth yesterday. It did not list the names of your parents but it did give a location in the county of Kent. We may be able to learn something there."

She accepted this admittedly inconclusive report without apparent interest. "Where is Mr. Holmes?"

"I do not know. We met earlier this evening with government officials. Then he said he had an important visit to make and asked me to make sure of your safety."

"Well, I'm safe enough. But I've had another doozy of a piece of news from Mr. Worth. I was called to Mr. Carte's office after the Saturday night performance, and there he was, waiting for me: top hat, white gloves, black cloak, and all. He took me to the restaurant next door. We were at the same table where I'd been with Johnny on Friday night."

"Did he know that you had seen us yesterday?"

"He asked where I'd been and I told him shopping with Johnny. He said where before that, and I said out walking, picking out the shops. He looked at me really hard, as if he didn't believe me."

"Did he threaten you?"

"He said London was a very unsafe place for a young woman to be going about on her own." She pressed her lips together, remembering. "The way he said it was ugly, but in a polite way. I felt as if he'd be disappointed to have me harmed, but that he knew he'd get over it in a minute or two. Then he said a lot of things about family and loyalty. He got all sentimental and reverent over what a great man I had for a father. He said my father is his brother, only for legal reasons his brother adopted a different name."

"Did he tell you the name?"

"He did."

She hesitated. I felt a sudden apprehension, and a moment's wish that I had not asked the question. Then she blinked rapidly and pressed her lips together again. Her eyes met mine.

"According to Mr. Worth, you are looking at the daughter of the late Professor James Moriarty."

"You poor child."

The words came out before I realized what I had said.

"Don't feel sorry for me." Lucy sat down across from where I was standing, and indicated that I should sit. "It hasn't touched my heart or anything. I know what you wrote about a criminal strain in Moriarty's blood, but I don't believe in any of that. I'm not about to go in for a life of crime, and the thought of Mr. Worth being related to me is just sickening."

"His name is listed as a witness on the birth registration." I felt I had to tell her, but she barely seemed to notice as she went on.

"He said you distorted the truth about his brother. He said my father was an organizational genius. He said one day the Professor's greatness would be recognized and his enemies would be destroyed."

26. A SURPRISE VISIT

Electric lamps formed pools of light on the deserted asphalt pavement of Waterloo Place as I paid my cabman. Grateful for the illumination, I nonetheless glanced apprehensively at the shadowy trees of Waterloo Gardens to my left and to the small stand of additional trees behind me. I could not help remembering that not twenty-four hours had elapsed since another wooded park at Clapham Common had provided cover for Moran, or some other marksman who was doubtless in the employ of Adam Worth. And even though my cabman, a trusted member of Lestrade's undercover squadron, had assured me that we had not been followed, I hurried as I approached the four concrete steps that led to the wide concrete entrance of the Diogenes Club.

Returning to Baker Street, Holmes had said, was obviously out of the question, given our circumstances, and so he had accepted Mycroft's arrangements for us to stay at the club, where attendants could keep a lookout. We each had one of the small rooms on the top floor that were maintained for the use of members. Lestrade had posted three of his most capable men at the entrances to the club. They had been instructed not to admit anyone, and, thinking of Moran and his air gun, to keep clear of windows. Holmes had sent another of Lestrade's men with a message to Mrs. Hudson to pack enough luggage for each of us to spend three nights away from home.

Lestrade's man opened the wide front door for me. "We put your things in your room, Doctor. Mr. Holmes's room is just alongside, but he's not yet arrived."

I mounted the stairs and within moments was entering my room. My battered brown leather suitcase stood upright on the carpet at the foot of my bed alongside my equally battered black medical bag.

Then I looked up and gasped in astonishment.

Hunched on the small chair beside the window, his head in his hands, sat young Henry Clevering.

Clevering looked up at me with haunted eyes. His flaxen hair, normally perfectly combed, now projected in an aura of straw-like spikes, like the stuffing spilling from a torn doll. "Where is Holmes? I must speak to him at once. It is imperative! And please, close the door behind you."

I stood my ground, refusing to take direction from this man. I felt sympathy for his obvious distress, but I was also indignant at his unannounced intrusion. "How did you get in here?"

"I never left the building. I was on my way out when the door-man handed me this note."

From the inside pocket of his coat he produced an envelope and handed it to me.

"It is my personal stationery. The handwriting is my wife's."

I read:

HENRY, MR. WORTH WAS HERE.

HE WISHES TO REMIND YOU OF YOUR POSITION.

I concealed my excitement, for the name of Worth and an evident connection with Clevering spoke volumes. I said as blandly as I could, "What of it?"

"It is a threat, Dr. Watson. He has chosen this method to remind me—"

We heard footsteps approaching from the hallway. "The door. Please," said Clevering.

I turned to close it, and saw Holmes. He was only a few steps away, still clad in the formal garb he had worn at our meeting with the Prime Minister earlier this evening. Behind him, one of the attendants in the Diogenes Club's distinctive maroon uniform and cap was carrying a suitcase into the room across the hall.

Holmes looked at me inquiringly. I also thought I saw a hint of satisfaction in his eyes. At any rate, I felt relieved that Holmes was here and safe, and able to glean firsthand whatever information Clevering might possess.

"We have a visitor," I said. "Mr. Clevering wishes to consult you on an urgent matter. Would you like to come in?"

He nodded and entered, closing the door behind him. Clevering, to my surprise, apologized for the intrusion, showed Holmes the letter, and explained once again that it had come from his wife. Holmes nodded graciously and perched on the side of my bed to face Clevering, folding his legs gracefully beneath him as if he were a Hindu Yogi.

"Mr. Worth seems to find it useful to threaten the loved ones of those he wishes to control," Holmes said. "Yours is not the first report of this method that I have run across since Friday. Let us hope that we can find Mr. Worth and bring him to justice before there is a fourth occurrence."

"Can you protect my wife and children?"

"We will come to that in due course. First, I have a few questions to put to you regarding your 'position,' as Mr. Worth refers to it."

A shrewd look came into Clevering's blue eyes. "If I tell you, will you give me your word that you will not tell the Prime Minister or the others of my involvement?"

"I will not bargain, Mr. Clevering. If you want my assistance in any form, you must tell me the whole truth. Now. How did you come to be involved with Mr. Worth?"

"I was referred to his organization by someone—at our embassy in Berlin."

"Why?"

"They had got wind of the possibility of a meeting with the Americans. They recognized that it would alter the balance of power in Europe, and so they wanted to ensure that it did not succeed. They would pay well. They needed someone to keep them informed and to supervise the payments they would make to their confederates in London."

"They wanted you to spy for them. When did this occur?"

"About five months ago, they took me aside at an embassy function and gave me an ultimatum. I had gambling debts. And there was a young woman."

"When and where had you met the woman?"

"In my Berlin hotel the previous night." Clevering hung his head. "I was manipulated."

"Of course you were. Did they try to manipulate Foster as well?"

"After he started asking questions at the Bank. But he wouldn't cooperate. That's why he had to be killed."

"When his body was found, how did you notify Worth?"

He looked startled. "How did you know about that?"

Holmes was silent. Finally Clevering spoke.

"I cannot tell you."

"Then there is nothing I can do for you."

"Mr. Holmes! Please! I am facing ruin, and the ruin of my family!"

Holmes's face was impassive.

"If the police investigate," Clevering went on, "Worth will know that I have betrayed him. His organization will kill my wife and children. That is the very message of this note!"

"I understand the threat. But if you cooperate, the police can protect your family."

"Would you take the risk, if someone you loved were involved?"

There was a long silence, and I had the impulse to shout at the man's presumptuous self-centeredness. But of course my words had to remain unsaid.

Finally Holmes spoke. "I would take the risk. Now. Tell me how I can find Worth."

Clevering closed his eyes, seeming to withdraw into himself for a moment. Then he shook his head and got to his feet. "You have boxed me, Mr. Holmes. I cannot argue with you, but neither can I find the courage to give you the information that you need. I can only hope that you find it by some other means, and rely on your mercy not to have me arrested."

Without another word, Clevering left the room. The door closed behind him.

"He thought to engage my charitable instincts toward his wife and children," said Holmes. "He still hopes to escape the consequences of his treason."

"Why did you let him go?"

"The police have been watching him at my request. If we are fortunate, he will try to contact Worth, they will observe and report, and we shall be able to follow the trail."

Holmes stood and rubbed his hands together in that brisk way he has when he anticipates a favorable outcome. "Now, Watson, let us walk down the corridor to the smoking room and you can tell me what you learned from your visit to Miss James. I believe there is a decanter of brandy on the sideboard."

I could not wait to tell him my news. "Worth has told Miss James the identity of her late father."

"And?"

"Worth says that the man was his brother."

"A family connection is not surprising, given that he witnessed the birth registration and that he serves as her trustee."

I continued, watching Holmes's face as I anticipated his reaction. "Worth says that his brother was the late Professor Moriarty."

To my astonishment, Holmes barely seemed to notice. He replied, "That is what Miss Rosario says as well. She is in the room across the hall."

"But I saw the club attendant there, with your suitcase."

"That was Miss Rosario, with her own suitcase."

I stared at him.

He continued, "I brought Miss Rosario here for her safety. You realize, of course, that she is the mother of Miss James."

27. A CONVERSATION WITH MISS ROSARIO

Holmes said nothing further about Miss Rosario that evening, other than to remind me of our most recent meeting, when she had fled from us outside the Savoy rehearsal room. Then he had me recount my conversation with Miss James and immediately thereafter announced that he was in need of a good night's rest. I retired immediately to my room, welcoming the opportunity for uninterrupted sleep.

The following morning I was taking coffee in the breakfast room of the Diogenes Club when Holmes entered, looking refreshed. "I need your assistance for the next several hours, Watson," he said. "Miss Rosario is attending an early rehearsal at the Savoy. I should like you to escort her, first stopping at her flat so that she can retrieve her violin, which she forgot to bring with her in the confusion of her travel here. I have arranged for one of Lestrade's men to drive you. You will then ensure that she reaches the Savoy Theatre in time for rehearsal. She will tell you the time that she needs to arrive. I would go myself, but the Commissioner and I have an appointment with Mr. Carte at ten. We may still be at the Savoy when you arrive, so please come by to let me know you are both safe. If you agree to make the journey, of course."

"I agree."

"And please, Watson, do not press the lady for details about her past association with Professor Moriarty. The recollection would be distressing to her, as you may well imagine."

"I quite understand—"

But before I could finish assuring him on this point, he had nodded his thanks and was already departing the room.

It was about an hour later, almost nine o'clock, when Miss Rosario and I began our carriage ride to her flat. The Strand was filled with the usual assortment of carriages, carts, cabs, and wagons one would expect for a Monday, but the driver Lestrade had assigned was a competent fellow and moved us along without undue delay. Still I felt apprehension. Something impelled me to keep looking out the window to see if we were being followed. We had about one mile to cover between the Diogenes Club and Miss Rosario's flat on Exeter Street, and then from there only a short walk to the Savoy. Her rehearsal call was for noon.

I saw nothing suspicious behind us, but I kept a lookout. Naturally I was suppressing my curiosity regarding why Holmes thought Miss Rosario might be in danger. Did she know of Adam Worth, and his connection to the late Professor Moriarty? Did Worth have reasons to silence her? He had obviously refrained from doing so up until now, but was there something connected with Rockefeller's visit and the impending meeting at the Bank of England that would change his view? I had no answers.

We had come as far as Trafalgar Square when Miss Rosario asked, "What does he think of Lucy?"

"Last night he asked to hear every detail of my conversation with Miss James. He made me go over it a second time."

"That is not what I mean. Does he realize what she could accomplish in her career?"

"I am sure he does. He admired her performance Friday night; you couldn't help seeing that." I had to lean close to make myself heard over the roar of traffic. She had a scent of jasmine. The warmth of her hopeful expectation seemed to surround me and lift me up.

"Lucy has a gift."

"Singing?"

"People. She engages easily with anyone. I have seen her at the theater. Even those who don't like her find themselves letting down their guard."

"She was with young Rockefeller Saturday, and then Worth. Though it is by her own account, she seems to have acquitted herself well with both." This statement was somewhat inaccurate, for although I was sure Lucy had completely charmed young Johnny Rockefeller, I was equally certain that her encounter with Worth had been acrimonious. Still, I wanted to keep our conversation on a pleasant footing.

"I find that I have the pride and dreams of a mother," Miss Rosario said. "Given our circumstances, perhaps that is unwise."

We rode without speaking for a time. Outside, the clatter of wheels and horses' hooves punctuated the cries of cart drivers and cabmen pursuing their morning enterprise. Then she asked, "Does Lucy know I am her mother?"

"I do not believe so."

"Does she know of James Moriarty?"

"Yes."

She turned her face away, toward the side window of the carriage. "He was one of my first students twenty-one years ago. I had only recently arrived in London from Rome with a small legacy from an uncle, and a dream of performing with the London Symphony. I had secured a position there as second violinist, but the pay was barely adequate, and the legacy was rapidly diminishing. To support myself I began giving private lessons in my rooms on Montague Street, just around the corner from the British Museum.

"Moriarty was both physically unattractive—'reptilian,' as you have described him, Dr. Watson—and also entirely lacking in ability to perform a musical composition in the spirit intended by the composer. Due to his mathematical gifts he was able to grasp the theoretical aspects of a composition instantly, that much is true. But he had no feel, no heart, to understand and project the emotion of the composer, which is, of course, the sole reason for the existence of any musical performance. His pride, however, would not let him admit that he lacked ability of any sort. He persisted in the face of my frequently expressed opinion that he should direct his energies to other matters. 'No, one more week. I am sure I can master this, just let me continue one more week,' he would say. Then, one day, I discovered that he had gone to my landlady and paid the rent on my flat for the next six months. He had learned somehow that I was in difficult financial straits. Although I should have told my landlady to return the money, I took the path of least resistance and did not. But when Moriarty insinuated that I should meet with him socially, in addition to the scheduled lessons, I told him I was no longer willing to see him at all, and he went away.

"I thought myself well rid of him and put him out of my mind, for, you see, by this time I was completely infatuated with another student, a young man studying at Cambridge, who had talent for both musical theory and violin performance. Additionally, he had such an eclectic taste, such an energetic nature, such a wonderful interest in so many things that I found myself looking forward to our weekly lessons not only for the musical experience but also for the sheer delight of encountering his exuberant personality."

She glanced at me briefly and then continued, her lovely features seeming to glow with happiness at the recollection, though her hands remained tightly clasped together.

"To my delight, the young student seemed also eager to see me, and began to ask me to spend time with him outside our weekend lessons. We walked together in Hyde Park, we strolled through the British Museum, we had tea at little shops, and we could not seem to get enough of each other's company. That was during the springtime of that year."

She stopped and drew a breath, and then her voice hardened and the words came faster. "But after the month of May he did not come for his next scheduled lesson. He sent a letter that he would be busy with his end-of-term examinations, and that during July he would be visiting a schoolmate of his for a few weeks or perhaps more during what he called 'the long vacation.' I was disappointed, but looked forward to his return. Then, on Monday the twenty-ninth of June, James Moriarty appeared at my door. When he realized that I was alone, he . . . forced himself on me. I cried out for the police but no one heard. He left me with the threat that if I told anyone what had occurred, he would have me killed."

I felt my face burn red with acute embarrassment and sympathy. She continued, "In early August I realized I was pregnant."

"How terribly, terribly unfair," I said.

"I was alone. I could not go back to Rome and my parents. They had disowned me when I defied their wishes by coming on my own to London. And they are staunch Roman Catholics, so you can imagine the reception they would have given me had I arrived on their doorstep unmarried and pregnant. So I had no one to talk to about what I ought to do. However, my landlady guessed what had happened, and one morning I made the mistake of taking her briefly into my confidence. A day later James Moriarty came to call on me again.

"His proposition was simple. First, he had a document I was to sign that released him from any liability for anything that had passed between us. Then he said he had a brother who was somewhat obsessed with family ties, and from whom he needed funds to invest in his business activities in London. He proposed to go to his brother with the news that he had fathered a child, that the woman did not wish to marry him, but had no means of support, and that he wanted to be sure the child had a proper upbringing. His brother would act as trustee for the child, who would be raised in a manner befitting the status of its father. Moriarty was convinced that his brother would reward him for having acted in that honorable, family-oriented manner. He was very open in saying that if I ever tried to contact the child or make inquiries, or tell anyone the truth of his involvement, he would have me killed, along with the child.

"That November, when my condition became too visible for me to conceal, I had to resign my position with the London Symphony. I was taken to a remote tenant farm in Kent and lived with a kind old couple, husband and wife, until the time for the child to be born. A midwife attended the birth. She took the child away immediately. I heard its first cries but I was not permitted to see it or hold it, and she would not even tell me whether it was a boy or a girl. I stayed on for a week until I recovered my strength, however, and during that time I overheard the wife say she wondered 'how the little lass would turn out.' So I believed the child was a girl. And last night Sherlock confirmed it."

"Lucy James," I said.

"Yes. I then returned to London and resumed my life. Or tried to. It was extremely difficult to overcome the sadness, just as difficult as you would imagine. I could of course no longer stay in my home at Montague Street, since I could not trust my landlady not to inform on whatever I might be doing, so I moved. Then I began imagining that the people in that building were watching me, so I moved again. Then desire to learn more of the child overcame me and I journeyed to the farm in Kent, but the old couple had gone away and the new tenants had no knowledge of their identities or whereabouts. Finally I resolved to live my life without thinking of either the child or Moriarty. Of course I did not succeed. But I did find a position with Mr. Carte's troupe and that has been a blessing."

"Did you ever meet the trustee? The brother of Moriarty?"

She nodded. "I believe so. Shortly after I returned from my fruitless journey to the Kentish farm, a tall man stopped me outside my building one evening as I was on my way to the orchestra. He said that it could be dangerous to travel in these times, because travel might lead to injury, and he was sure that it would be a disappointment to his brother if I were to be injured. He said he was certain that I knew his brother, who was a rising young mathematician and in line for an appointment as a professor. There was no doubt from his tone of voice that he was threatening me."

"Was he specific as to the possible injury?"

"He said a woman in my profession needs to protect her hands."

"Can you describe him?"

"His face haunts me still. He has a high forehead, thin nose, bushy black eyebrows, and a square jaw, with thick black side-whiskers. I remember wishing I had the courage to defy him. But he made me feel powerless. His cold blue eyes were the same as his brother's. He looked at me as though I were an insect that he might crush at any moment, on a whim."

"Adam Worth," I said.

"Sherlock told me his name. I heard his voice coming from Mr. Carte's office when you and I first met Friday night. That is why I fled. I was terrified."

She looked outside the window again. "We are almost there. My flat is in the last but one, just before the corner." Outside I could see a row of well-kept five-story buildings on the southeast side, their brick facades and concrete steps still in the morning shadows. "I have lived here nearly thirteen years," she said. "Ever since Mr. D'Oyly Carte opened the Savoy. It is very convenient to the theater."

We stopped at the curb. Lestrade's man opened the door for us. Behind him stood another policeman. "I've been on duty since nine, sir. Only residents have come in. And some of the construction chaps." He pointed to a scaffold high above, on which two workmen crouched to maneuver long boards into the building through a window.

"My new upstairs neighbor is redecorating," said Miss Rosario. "The doorman told me about it last night. He says there will be noise starting at nine every morning for the next week."

28. TWO REVELATIONS

Our two policemen positioned themselves on the stoop so that they could see the street and sidewalks in either direction. Miss Rosario used her key to open the inner door and we entered the building. "I'm afraid we have three flights of stairs," she said brightly as we started our climb. "Two more than at Baker Street."

"But a great deal closer to the Savoy."

"My thoughts exactly when I rented it. It only takes me five minutes to walk there, carrying my violin. Though I certainly did not know I would stay here thirteen years. No one could have predicted the theater and the operettas would have been such a great success for so long a time. I remember the night we opened. The electric lights were a mystery to nearly everyone back then. Mr. D'Oyly Carte stood on the stage and broke a glowing bulb, just to show the audience how safe it was."

By now we had reached her floor, and soon she was unlocking the door numbered 4A that led to her small suite of rooms. "People still think that living in a flat is somehow 'not quite nice,'" she said. "But a normal house would be impossible for someone like me to afford."

"Yesterday a man tried to make Holmes feel small because he lived in a rented flat and did not have several grand estates from which to choose."

"Sherlock never cared for that sort of thing."

We entered her sitting room. To our right there was a small fireplace, half-circled by a small couch, two comfortable chairs, and a low table upon which a substantial stack of magazines was neatly piled. At the far corners of the room, two open doors led to what were plainly a washroom and a bedroom. Both appeared to be empty. Nonetheless I drew my revolver and, motioning for Miss Rosario to keep silent, walked quietly to the washroom door and looked in. A glance showed me that no one was present. Moments later I had repeated the process of inspection in the bedroom and returned to Miss Rosario.

"We are alone," I said, pocketing my revolver.

"You are very careful."

"Holmes insisted. I have strict instructions that you are not to leave my sight until I have delivered you safely to your rehearsal."

"Thank you for your vigilance." She moved to the low table and gestured toward its contents. "Do you know what these are?"

"Of course. They are copies of *The Strand Magazine*."

"Dating back to 1887. Every one of your accounts is here. Every one, from *A Study in Scarlet* to *The Final Problem*."

"I am flattered."

"I am grateful. But at the moment you do not know just how grateful. So I would like to tell you about my other student."

We sat, and she continued, "I recall our last meeting perfectly. Late in August he had returned from his school vacation visit. He asked me to meet him for lunch. He chose the Criterion, for he was in high spirits, even higher spirits than usual for him, and said he wanted to celebrate. He said his visit had shown him the path forward for his life's purpose and career. I knew his brilliance, of course, so I understood at once what a wonderful choice he had made and how significant his role in the world would become. He was so full of plans for the studies he would pursue at Cambridge and elsewhere to prepare himself—so completely caught up in the excitement of his visions for the future."

She broke off, closed her eyes, and shook her head. "I did not have the heart to tell him of my condition. I sent him a letter afterward, saying that I had found someone new and that I was going away. I made the letter particularly abrupt, so that he would have no expectations of continuing our relationship."

She looked directly at me then, and said, "I explained all this to Sherlock last night. Of course he remembered the letter."

For a moment I was unable to breathe as the realization dawned. So many things came into focus. The tale of *The Gloria Scott* that Holmes had recounted years before as he told me of his visit to Victor Trevor, his school friend. Holmes's careful selection of the placement of our seats at the Savoy Theatre and his hasty departure from the Savoy lobby. Miss Rosario referring to Holmes as Sherlock and her knowledge that he never cared for the trappings of wealth.

"There were many years when I tormented myself with regret and doubt. Then your reports began to appear in *The Strand*. You made me see that what had occurred was for the best, at least where Sherlock was concerned. Had my relationship with him continued, Sherlock would not have had the freedom to pursue the life he was born to lead. Severing my connection with Sherlock allowed him to complete his education at Cambridge and beyond, and then go on to contribute greatly to the safety of all of us. I could understand that, each time I read one of these accounts. Dr. Watson, I have read each one of your reports again and again. I never thought I would have the opportunity to thank you in person for writing them."

It was a moment or two before I could do more than nod my acknowledgment. Then I found words. "And now you know that your daughter has grown up with a promising future."

"And I have hope that we may get to know one another." She went on lightly, "That does not seem too much to ask for, does it? Now, just let me get my violin. It is a Stradivarius like Sherlock's, so it is of some value. I keep it in a locked cabinet in my bedroom. I shall only be a minute, and then we shall get to the rehearsal on time."

I remained seated on the sofa to wait for her. Before me were the volumes of *The Strand* in their covers of yellow and black, many with Holmes's portrait inset amid the titles. Memories of our adventures contained in those pages came flooding back, each with its own wealth of characters and emotions. In my mind's eye many images flickered into life and then vanished, each to be replaced by another. I saw again the ferocious little Andaman Islander, the tall, gaunt figure of Jefferson Hope, the great Somomy stallion Silver Blaze . . .

Then I realized that Miss Rosario had shut the door to her bedroom.

I sat in silence for a few more moments, thinking that she had decided to change her clothing. Then another possibility occurred to me. My heart pounded as I got to my feet. "Miss Rosario?" I called.

There was no reply. In a moment I had reached the bedroom door and flung it open.

The room was empty. From the open window, a chill breeze dispersed what was now only a faint scent of chloroform.

Sick at heart, I ran to the window and looked down. Below me the scene was perfectly ordinary. Passersby on the sidewalk; horses, carriages, and cyclists on the street. Lestrade's two men were on the stoop, oblivious to my presence. I shouted to get their attention and then called, "Have you seen anything?" The words seemed absurd and futile even as they left my lips.

Lestrade's men looked up at me, their eyes wide and uncomprehending. Then I realized what must have happened. I twisted my body to see what was above me. There was the paint-flaked bottom of the scaffold, swinging slightly on its ropes. "Come up to the top floor," I called down to Lestrade's men. "Quick as you can!"

Without waiting for a response I ran for the stairs and up to the top floor. The stout oak door to 5B was locked. I kicked at it in frustration, then drew my revolver and fired three times at the lock. The smoke of gunfire and the reverberations of the shots filled the small confines of the hallway. I barely noticed.

Lestrade's men reached the landing, breathless from their climb, just as the smoke cleared. We could see the lock was shattered. Keeping my revolver drawn, I pushed the door open.

The rooms were deserted, empty save for some boards and dirty painters' canvas drop cloths. Cold air and traffic noise came from the open window. I ran to it and looked down.

Five stories below, the scaffold lay empty. The ropes that had supported it now were strewn in untidy coils covering either end.

My heart sank. On the sidewalk and on the street, there was no sign of the workmen, or of Miss Rosario.

29. PLANS, INTERRUPTED

"It was carefully planned," said Holmes. He and the Commissioner had come immediately from Carte's office and now stood with me in Miss Rosario's bedroom. Despite Holmes's masklike expression, I felt sure he was deeply disturbed by the consequences of my failed attempt to protect her. Nevertheless he spoke briskly as he moved about the room, reconstructing the events that had occurred.

"You see how the edges of the window sash have been coated with soap. The intruders gained entry at some time before this morning to accomplish this, possibly with the assistance of the building superintendent. Then, as you saw, they waited on the scaffold for you to arrive and come into the building. As you climbed the stairs, they lowered the scaffold and opened the window. One of them entered and closed the window so that the room would appear undisturbed. That person stood here, behind the door, as evidenced by these flecks of dried paint and the plaster dust on the floor. I have no doubt that these came from the surface of the scaffold, clung to his trousers when he knelt outside, and then fell to the floor when he pressed himself against the wall."

"I should have looked behind the door."

"Had you done so, you would have been blinded by chloroform, or your throat would have been cut."

"I let her out of my sight."

"If you had gone into the room a second time, you would have been taken from behind. The result would have been the same."

Holmes pointed to the open door of a small empty cabinet where a key was in the lock. "He waited for her to insert her key before using the chloroform to subdue her, and then took time to remove the violin. I find some cause for optimism there. No, Watson, you must not waste your energies in blaming yourself. I have no doubt that Mr. Worth or one of his associates is the 'new tenant' who rents the space above where we now stand. It is likely that he has controlled the rooms for some time. Miss Rosario having lived here more than a dozen years, he has had ample opportunity both to gain access and to injure her. The question we must ask ourselves is why he has chosen this particular time and method."

The Commissioner frowned. "The question I must ask, Mr. Holmes, with all due respect, is that in view of the threat to our nation's leaders and the momentous political import of the events that will commence tomorrow, why are you interesting yourself in the case of a kidnapped lady musician from the Savoy orchestra?"

"Because I believe the two are connected."

"Then what is the connection?"

"The connection is Mr. Worth. The lady musician has been threatened by him."

"And why would he do that?" The Commissioner broke off. "Never mind. I do not intend to be distracted from the real point at issue, which is why you believe Mr. Worth is connected to an attempt to disrupt our meeting with the Americans. I know that he is a major investor in Mr. D'Oyly Carte's enterprises, that he is of unsavory reputation, and that our men have had no success finding the location of either the town house in Westminster that he is said to rent or the yacht he rents from the West India Company that was once harbored at the Isle of Dogs. I know Carte wants to replace him. I know that at his estate in Clapham Common you and Dr. Watson were shot at by someone who very likely was the escaped Colonel Moran. But none of this is conclusive. Colonel Moran may well have been your attacker, but he may have no connection to Mr. Worth or to our meeting."

"You will recall what I said at the outset of this inquiry. To disrupt a conference of this level requires a competent criminal enterprise, with a certain level of funding and organization. I have investigated Colonel Moran's escape from Dartmoor Prison, which plainly was accomplished with the aid of an outside organization, comparable to that of the late Professor Moriarty. By the way, have you received the report from Dartmoor?"

"What report?"

"The report I requested in my telegraph message to you yesterday afternoon."

"I did not receive a wire from you yesterday afternoon. But yesterday was a Sunday, and my assistant may not have noticed the wire when he came in this morning. What was your request?"

"I need the prison records concerning a guard named Asher, who died last week."

"I'll have my assistant attend to it. But I still do not see why we are here, investigating the disappearance of a woman who wished to be protected from this Mr. Worth."

"Mr. Worth is the alias of the brother of the late Professor James Moriarty. I believe he is the same brother who wrote eulogizing letters to the press to defend the Professor's reputation."

The Commissioner gave a nod of satisfaction. "That would explain a great deal. And why do you believe Worth is a Moriarty?"

"Because that is what he said twenty-one years ago, to the lady musician who was this morning abducted from these rooms."

"Are you certain that she is a reliable witness?"

The Commissioner's tone was careful, but not without a certain skepticism. At that moment the horrid possibility occurred to me that Miss Rosario's story might not have been true, and that she might have been a willing accomplice to her abduction for purposes known only to herself and Worth. After all, I had not witnessed the abduction. The event might have been carefully staged—

But Holmes was speaking. "On balance, I do not believe the facts will support a theory that she is not reliable."

Facts! I felt relief when I heard Holmes's words, for they brought back the memory of Miss Rosario's accounts and the honest emotions she had evidenced each time she had spoken of her past. Those blushes, those halting words, those involuntary expressions in her face and eyes—those were all evidence of an honest heart. I felt ashamed for doubting her, and somewhat abashed that I had allowed my imagination to run away with me.

"I am sure there are many things you are not telling me, but we have relied on you greatly in the past," said the Commissioner, "and there is no reason not to continue. How do you intend to proceed?"

"I shall interview Mr. Perkins. And it would be most helpful if one of your men remained here to wait for the return of one of my 'Irregulars.' I had asked them to keep watch on this building. It is possible that they may have witnessed the abduction without knowing what it was."

"Consider it done. But why Perkins?"

"Perkins managed the account from which Mr. Worth invested in the Savoy. When we press Mr. Perkins with this knowledge he may reveal some useful information that will help us to locate Mr. Worth."

The Commissioner cleared his throat. "That is quite logical, but I must ask that you defer your interview."

As we stared at him, he drew a telegraph message from his pocket. "This was sent to the Prime Minister this morning."

He read aloud, "SHERLOCK HOLMES MEETS ME TODAY ON THE WHITE STAR OR I RETURN TO NEW YORK."

The signature line on the message bore but one word: "ROCKEFELLER."

30. MR. ROCKEFELLER OPINES

"Mr. Rockefeller, you are in danger," Holmes said quietly, less than an hour later. The three of us stood with young Johnny at the bow of the *White Star*, the steam-liner the American tycoon had chartered from the shipping company of the same name. A chill wind from the river stung our faces. We were in the shadows of the tall brick warehouse buildings that lined the quay, entirely out of the hearing of about a half dozen men who clustered around a temporary telegraph station that had been installed in the main cabin of the steam-liner, closer to the gangway. Holmes and Rockefeller had just shaken hands. Rockefeller's steely gray eyes widened for only a moment.

Holmes continued, "Mr. Foster is dead. He was murdered, and there is a grave threat to the meeting that you have come here to attend."

Rockefeller turned to his son. To my astonishment, he spoke with an air of satisfaction. "Didn't I tell you he'd be different?"

Unlike his shorter and more muscular son, the senior Rockefeller stood as tall as Holmes and was equally lean in body, though with closer-set features and a receding chin. Despite the warning he had just received from Holmes, there was an odd serenity about him. As he turned back to Holmes, his sparse, reddish-gray mustache only partially concealed a friendly smile.

"Mr. Holmes, you have no idea of the runaround we have been getting from your diplomatic monkeys. I told my son here that you would be straightforward and truthful. That is why I insisted they send you. Now, let us understand one another."

He drew himself up to his full height and continued, with an odd note of pride, "I am one of the most hated men in my country. I receive threats against my life on a regular basis. I spend most days surrounded by hundreds of acres of forest ringed by barbed wire and guarded by dozens of Pinkerton employees. I cannot abide anyone who would mislead me concerning my safety."

"A true understanding of the facts is the most essential requisite in any case," Holmes replied.

"Good. Now let us go inside, out of the wind. We can have lunch and talk this thing over more privately."

We were soon in the ship's first-class dining saloon, a luxurious space with a high white ceiling trimmed in gold, and white linens with gold-embroidered napkins adorning every table. The staff wore white uniforms with military-style gold embroidery on the lapels and cuffs of their jackets. "All this opulence is a waste of money," said Rockefeller, "but it would be an even bigger waste to have it removed, and then gilded up again when I'm home and done. So Cettie and I put up with it. But at least the staff's efficient," he concluded, as our waiter approached. As if to prove him right, the man took only a few moments to explain that the menu had been preselected, and to place a glass filled with ice and water before each of us.

"From a spring in Vermont," Rockefeller declared. "Far better for you than champagne, and far easier on the mental faculties when one works the long hours that I put in."

"You do not drink spirits, I believe," said Holmes.

"Cettie and I are Baptists," he replied, as if this provided a definitive answer. He continued, with an affectionate nod toward his son, "Junior here is a college man, and has been known to take an occasional glass of beer with his young friends. In moderation, of course. Now, Mr. Holmes, I want you to take a look at this."

He removed a telegraph message from his breast pocket, unfolded it, and spread it before Holmes. "It was sent Wednesday, the day after I left New York. It should have been delivered to me in Southampton Friday, but it was forwarded to my Standard Oil office in London by mistake. I didn't get it until I arrived this morning."

The message read:

NEED FURTHER INVESTIGATION AT SAVOY THEATRE. CHECKING BANK TOMORROW. FF.

"So this is the last message you had from Mr. Foster."

Rockefeller nodded. "What have you learned, Mr. Holmes?"

Briefly Holmes summarized the past events: the discovery of Foster's body, the bomb outside the hospital, the escape of Moran, the possible connection with Adam Worth, and the attempts on our lives outside Worth's estate and near Dartmoor Prison. He said nothing, however, of Clevering, or Miss Rosario, or Miss James.

Holmes concluded his summary, "The Prime Minister fears that the meeting will not take place if you, Mr. Carnegie, and Mr. Morgan believe yourselves to be in danger."

Rockefeller held his water glass as though he were proposing a toast to Holmes. "But you're telling me all this anyway."

"I am."

"And you have not been authorized to do so."

"Quite correct."

"Could get you into some trouble, I expect."

"I could be hanged for treason under the Official Secrets Act."

"I'd sooner hang whoever killed Foster. Now, here come our waiters. We can talk later and decide what's to be done."

During our meal, Rockefeller gave us a dazzling view of the international situation. He held strong opinions as to which nations would fear and oppose an increase in British and American naval power and would consequently pay to destroy the alliance he hoped would result from his visit. Russia, he said, was preoccupied with domestic concerns, though its oil resources made Russia Rockefeller's chief competitor in Europe. The South Africans were too concerned with the short-term conflict that the Boers were fomenting with Britain to invest in a long-term strategic move. That left the Germans or the French. Between these two, Rockefeller was inclined to suspect the French, for the Rothschild banking family had the capital and would love to see the British and the Americans at war, so they could then rule over the ruins and make handsome profits in the rebuilding effort. However, he admitted that his views might be biased by the Rothschilds' ownership interest in Royal Dutch Shell, the most important international petroleum distributor other than Rockefeller's Standard Oil Corporation.

These insights were fascinating, but I could see that Holmes was preoccupied. He had arranged for Lestrade to pick us up at the dock and take us to the Bank of England, where we would confront Perkins. I had high hopes that there we would learn where Worth could be found, and with that knowledge we could find and rescue Miss Rosario.

Rockefeller was saying, "Now, I'll have the police commissioner in New York City look into this. Energetic young fellow named Roosevelt. We'll see what he can dig up on your Mr. Worth. I'll have him wire me the information and I can hand it over to you tonight, Mr. Holmes, if you'll join Cettie and me here for supper."

"I regret that will not be possible. Tonight I must report my progress to the Prime Minister."

A glimmer of indignation in Rockefeller's gray eyes showed he was not accustomed to having his invitations declined. But without a pause he asked, "Dr. Watson, can you come?"

Holmes's nod told me my answer and I agreed. Rockefeller seemed mollified and returned to his half-eaten baked potato. Holmes took out his watch but Rockefeller seemed unaware of the gesture. Johnny noticed, however.

"Father, I believe these gentlemen have business to attend to."

"Oh, of course. Don't mind me," Rockefeller replied, cutting off a small portion of potato and spearing it with his fork. "Just go ahead, Mr. Holmes, and I'll have that report from New York for Dr. Watson when he returns."

Shortly afterward we had said our good-byes and met Lestrade, who waited with a hansom cab alongside the dock. The little detective greeted us with a worried countenance.

"A bad business, Mr. Holmes," he said. "We found Mr. Perkins's body in his office. His throat has been slashed."

31. MR. PERKINS'S SOUL

A macabre scene awaited us at the Bank of England. The sharp, copper-laden smell of blood hung in the air of Perkins's office. On the small table where two days before I had eaten my sandwich with Lestrade and Mycroft, the body of Llewellen Perkins now lay prostrate. A red-brown pool of blood encircled his head and shoulders like a grotesque halo. The skin of Perkins's face was gray-blue. The once-alert black eyes were now dull. The pomaded black hair and carefully waxed mustache clung stiffly to the lifeless flesh.

Between Perkins's shiny black shoes lay an empty oxblood-colored calfskin folder. Blood from the table had spilled down onto the parquet floor. The edge of the pool had stained the white border of a blue Persian rug beneath Perkins's stout mahogany desk.

Most bizarre of all was the corpse's facial expression. The lips were pressed tightly together, yet at the corners of the mouth there were the unmistakable beginnings of a smile.

Holmes had taken in all this detail at a glance and was now hovering over the desk, examining an opened appointment book. "The page for today's appointments has been torn out," he said.

"Lestrade, can one of your men find a witness? We must obtain a description of whoever entered this office or asked for Perkins at the main entry."

"We have checked. No one remembers."

"Please check again. Quickly, now!"

After Lestrade left the room, Holmes bent over and opened each of Perkins's desk drawers in turn, his long fingers rifling through stacks of papers. Then he reached farther into the center drawer. In a moment he had pressed something inside the recesses of the desk, pulled the drawer completely away from its slot, and held it up. A cascade of bills, papers, pencils, and erasers and a small bottle of mucilage fell noisily from the drawer onto the desktop.

"Watson, if you will kindly step over here and witness what I am about to do?" There was urgency in his tone, and I was at his side in an instant as he laid the drawer down on the desktop and pressed both corners of a boxlike structure built into the inside back of the drawer. There was a wooden click.

The two halves of the box top snapped up to stand at either end of the drawer, revealing a cavity roughly two inches in depth and width, and two feet in length.

The cavity was filled with gold sovereigns.

"A thief, Watson!" His tone was bitter and disappointed. "Perkins was a thief, but not a blackmailer. Unless . . ."

He tilted the drawer upright, and the gold coins spilled with a metallic clatter over the already-littered desktop.

Holmes's long fingers sorted rapidly through the pile. After a few moments he uttered a grunt of satisfaction. From amid the heap of gold coins his fingertips extracted a small brass key.

He held the key up to examine it. "A double bit, with a three-ring bow and a barrel stem. Manufactured by the Eastlake Company."

His eyes glittered as he carefully scanned the room. There were none of the customary potted plants, nor chairs other than the one behind the desk and the four around the table upon which the body lay. The austere beige wallpaper on each of the four walls was barren of pictures or other decoration.

Holmes grasped the corners of the heavy desk. "Quickly, Watson! A safe may lie beneath the rug!"

As the two of us bent over the desk, however, Lestrade reentered the office. At first he stared with astonishment at the glittering chaos on the formerly tidy desktop, but after a few words of explanation from Holmes he came forward to help. Soon the three of us had pushed and lifted the desk clear of the rug, which we pulled aside to the edge of the room.

The squares of the parquet floor shone smooth and undisturbed, with nothing to indicate the presence of a floor safe.

"Watson, I have grown slow-witted!" Holmes dropped to his knees. I fully expected him to manipulate the parquet squares, but instead he turned to face the mahogany desk, pressing his palms flat against the vertical boards of its front panel. Holmes pressed in and then sideways toward the outer edges of the desk. The thin boards parted. Each slid to the outside, revealing beneath a polished steel door with a recessed handle below a keyhole. Holmes inserted the key and turned it. The door emitted the sound of a sharp and most satisfying metallic click, and then it opened.

Standing on its edge in the shallow metal recess was an ordinary schoolboy's black notebook.

Within moments Holmes was on his feet and had the book spread open on the desktop. The volume appeared new, with writing only on its first page. There we saw, written in blue ink, in a small, neat hand, columns of letters and numbers. Some of the numbers appeared to represent dates and amounts paid on those dates, but the letters seemed to me an entirely incomprehensible jumble.

10/10	jahqhudyf guxz mrudje kxyit	10000
11/10	sx jahqhudyf jlte	9000
25/10	jahqhudyf guxz mrudje kxyit	40000
26/10	sx jahqhudyf jlte	35000
31/10	jahqhudyf guxz mrudje kxyit	300000
01/11	sx jahqhudyf jlte	295000
04/11	jahqhudyf guxz mrudje kxyit	1000000
04/11	jahqhudyf sx klybhu2 jlte	995000

klybhu2 990000 rwxy trjjhtt sx
ehyun critxy ulnzxyt
198 wdjjltdaan

"It appears to be in code," said Lestrade.

"A record of receipts and disbursements," said Holmes. "Made as recently as today. There are four progressively larger sums, each followed by a smaller. Possibly this indicates the deduction of a fee. The final three notations are something different."

I had a sudden thought. "Mr. Perkins died protecting this book," I said. "Perhaps he was successful in withholding the information that his murderer wished to obtain. Perhaps that accounts for the look of grim satisfaction on his face."

"Let us hope so. Now, Lestrade, we have no time to lose. Did you find anyone who can enlighten us regarding who came to see Mr. Perkins today?"

"No one remembers anyone asking for Mr. Perkins."

Holmes considered. "Possibly Perkins met his visitor at the entrance to the bank, as he did when we arrived Saturday. The visitor evidently had an appointment, since today's page was removed from Perkins's appointment book."

"If Perkins escorted the visitor to his office, the person's identity would be less memorable to other bank employees," said Lestrade. "But where does that leave us?"

Holmes handed the notebook to Lestrade. "You must deliver this to Mycroft immediately. Tell him to drop whatever he is doing and decipher its contents. When he has done so, he is to telephone me at once. Watson and I will be at the Savoy Theatre. We can be reached through the office of Mr. D'Oyly Carte."

On our way out of the bank we again passed the room where the clerks stood in a row, all cranking gold sovereigns through their tall, black weighing boxes. I wondered how the soul of Llewellen Perkins was faring as it was being weighed on the scales of his Maker.

32. A BACKSTAGE DISCOVERY

We could hear the smooth voice of D'Oyly Carte as we opened the door to the center aisle of the Savoy Theatre auditorium. The dapper producer stood at the front row, entreating the cast, crew, and orchestra assembled in the seats before him to rise to the heights of greatness that company tradition would demand. "The circumstances will be unusual—I might even say unique. You will perform before a particularly august audience whose identities we must keep secret, at an uncertain location, on a yacht of American origin."

I turned to Holmes. "Morgan's yacht."

He nodded, but held a fingertip to his lips.

I scanned the audience members, hoping against all reason to find Miss Rosario among them, but of course she was not there. However, I felt a surge of relief when I saw Lucy James seated with Jesse Bond about four rows from the front, in an aisle seat to my right, paying polite attention to Carte's remarks as he continued.

"Carriages are waiting to transport you to the West India Docks, about an hour's journey from here. We have arranged for a yacht to be provided there for rehearsal purposes, and while the layout may not be precisely as you will encounter tomorrow night, it will be of great assistance, I am sure. On both nights there will be awnings to protect us from the elements, and electric lights strung throughout. The generator will be positioned far enough away so that the noise of its engine will be barely audible. We shall rehearse the performance in its entirety tonight. Tomorrow night I have no doubt that despite the somewhat unusual conditions, each of you will acquit yourselves with honor and, if I may be so bold, with glory."

There was a smattering of polite applause, and a "Hear, hear!" from one of the male actors.

"Will the carriages wait for us during the rehearsal?" asked Miss Bond.

"They will. And when we have concluded our work, a light supper will be provided."

More applause greeted this announcement.

"Now, if there are no further questions . . ." Carte hesitated then, for he recognized the two of us standing at the back of the auditorium. He went on smoothly, projecting his voice to address Holmes, "May we proceed?"

Holmes nodded graciously.

Carte nodded in return. "Five minutes, then!" he told his audience. They began to stand up. I saw Lucy glance in our direction, and then an expression of delight appeared on her lovely features as she recognized us.

Holmes saw her as well. He made a warning gesture. "She must not approach us, Watson. For her own safety." I was about to make a similar gesture, but Miss James recognized Holmes's cautionary signal and looked away.

Carte was coming up the aisle. To my relief, he spoke quietly, not using our names. "Gentlemen!" he said. "How may I be of service? As you can see we are somewhat at sixes and sevens, but I will be pleased to take as much time with you as you wish."

"We will be brief. We have a question to ask of you, and one favor."

"Certainly."

"Were any of your current staff hired because of a recommendation from Mr. Worth?"

Carte's manicured fingers lightly stroked his neatly trimmed goatee as he reflected. "Now that you mention it, Mr. Blake was recommended by Mr. Worth. He joined us after one of the ushers was injured. An accident with a lorry, I believe."

"Anyone else?"

"Why, yes: Cleo, our makeup girl and seamstress. We needed someone after Mrs. Brennan had to leave to attend her mother, who had unfortunately fallen down the stairs of a railway station. I believe it was Waterloo Station. Or possibly—"

"Many thanks, Mr. Carte," Holmes said briskly. "Now, if you please, we do have a favor to ask. We need to search throughout the theater. May we have a set of keys?"

"Of course. There is a set in the upper right-hand drawer of my office desk. You know the way. Please feel free to go anywhere you like. Your timing is excellent, for we shall all be away at rehearsal. Just please lock up after you are done. Oh, and if our first violinist arrives while you are here, would you please tell her where we have gone and put her in a cab?" He pulled a ten-pound note from his pocket. "West India Docks, the *Shamrock*. This should cover the fare. I must confess I am worried. She has been with us for nearly twenty years and has not once been late."

After the little impresario bade us farewell and hurried out, we reached his office without being observed. Holmes quickly retrieved a ring of keys from the desk where Carte had told us they would be. "What are we looking for, Holmes?" I asked.

"One moment." He cranked up the telephone on the wall behind Carte's desk and gave a number to the operator. In a few moments I could hear a ringing through the receiver, then a man's voice answering.

"Do you recognize my voice?" said Holmes. "Good. The line is not safe. Please do not call me here. Remain where you are. I shall call upon you presently.

"Now, Watson," he said after hanging up the receiver, "Mycroft will wait for us at the Diogenes Club while we conduct our search."

"Do you think Miss Rosario may be hidden somewhere in the theater?"

"That is a possibility, but unlikely, given the number of people who would notice her being brought in. No, we are looking for whatever caused Mr. Foster to become suspicious enough to send that telegraph message to Mr. Rockefeller. We can only hope that he did not reveal the cause of his suspicions to his murderer."

Backstage, we groped our way for a few steps until Holmes struck a match and we located the box of switches that controlled the electric lighting. We were standing behind the tall panels of framed canvas that formed the facade of Ko-Ko's garden, the setting for the second act. Holmes stood on tiptoe beneath each one, gazing up to the top of each wooden frame. Then he moved to where four wooden steps of about five feet in width led up to a sturdy platform of flooring planks, worn smooth by many years of service.

"I see nothing suspicious here, Holmes."

"Sawdust, Watson. Look for sawdust." He dropped to his knees and then lay prone beneath the platform. A moment later came the sound of a match being struck and the shimmering glow of a flame. Then the glow vanished. Holmes extricated himself and got to his feet. "Nothing. Now, Watson, we must take a different tack and put ourselves in Mr. Foster's place. Someone circled the name of Lucy James on a theater program and delivered it to the Savoy Hotel in an obvious invitation for young Mr. Rockefeller. Mr. Foster told young Mr. Rockefeller that he would investigate."

"Then surely he would not be looking beneath a platform on the stage."

"On the contrary." He bent to rap the top step with his knuckles and listened. "He would want to know that the theater was a safe place for young Mr. Rockefeller to attend." He stood once again. "He might have looked anywhere and everywhere. He might have hoped to attract attention, and in turn, to provoke a reaction. He may also have gone to the theater office and inquired directly about Miss James."

To my astonishment, I heard Lucy's voice coming from the wing to my left. "Miss James is"—we turned and she emerged from behind the curtain—"here!" As we stared, she continued. "Forgive me. I could not resist the theatricality of the moment. I was hiding, hoping to catch up with you after the others were gone. Why have you come? Has something happened?"

Holmes reached out and gently touched her shoulder. "Something indeed has happened. There are two things I must tell you. To begin, last night I met with your mother."

In a few words he explained how knowing the date and place of Lucy's birth, and Adam Worth's identity as a witness, had led to Miss Rosario's full acknowledgment of her motherhood when Holmes had subsequently visited her in her flat. "Your identity has been hidden from her all these years. She is most anxious to meet you."

"How did you know to do that?"

"I had known her during my university days, before you were born. Friday evening after your performance at the Savoy she approached Dr. Watson and told him she was afraid of both the late Professor Moriarty and Adam Worth."

"She confirmed Moriarty was my father?"

"She said he forced himself upon her. I regret to say that."

Lucy grimaced. Then she continued, "I felt a curious connection with Miss Rosario—and I noticed she was looking at me during rehearsals. But if she is truly anxious to meet me, why did she not come to rehearsal today?"

"That is the other thing I must tell you," said Holmes. Quickly he explained how Miss Rosario had been taken from her flat and that he believed Adam Worth's organization to be responsible. "The police are searching his estate in Clapham Common. I also hope to hear from the Irregulars, who were instructed to watch her building."

"They took her," Miss James responded, "so they may have reason to keep her alive."

"That is my hope, yes."

She considered this. Then she said, "I need to tell you about Blake."

"You believe he is connected to Worth?"

"He brought Worth to Carte's office, didn't he? But that's not what I was getting at. I heard his voice a few minutes ago when I was hiding. I couldn't see him, but I'm sure it was Blake! And I thought it must be important and I'd better tell you, because he said, 'Holmes was with Carte just now,' in a worried way, as though your being here made him, well, worried, and then the other person answered—and I knew right away who she was. It was Cleo, who's in charge of makeup and costumes. Cleo said, 'No, we'd be missed. Besides, I've already locked up.' And then they both left. Together."

"Do you know where Blake was going when Cleo stopped him?"

"I can figure it out. Let me show you."

She took us to the edge of the curtain at the very back of the stage. "I was here, behind this curtain, facing directly downstage. Blake would have been coming from off stage right. So Cleo would have been coming from off stage left, which leads to the wardrobe area and the construction workshop."

Holmes elected to begin with the construction workshop, on the theory that Blake would be more likely to go there than to the wardrobe area. One of Carte's keys fit the lock to the very tall double doors, large and wide enough to admit oversized portions of a theater set. We were soon inside a spacious room with a high ceiling, illuminated by a row of large barred windows along the far wall. Workbenches occupied most of the room's perimeter. Most of them were bare, stained and flecked with varnish and paint from a decade's use.

"Over there," said Holmes, striding swiftly to one workbench that had not been properly swept. Miss James and I followed him. He was looking at an untidy heap of wood shavings, sawdust, snippets of copper wire, and some bits of coarse cotton fabric. In a row beside this little pile of scraps were three small, white ceramic cones.

They were identical to the ceramic insulating connectors the Commissioner had shown us after the explosion at the hospital.

33. A JOURNAL DECODED

Rain had begun to fall about one half hour later as the three of us alighted from our cab and took shelter under the wide front portico of the Diogenes Club. One of Lestrade's men stood guard at the main entry. His eyes widened when he saw Miss James, who at Holmes's insistence had covered her usual attire with a policeman's uniform we had appropriated from the Savoy Theatre wardrobe room. The disguise was adequate for its temporary purpose, for her long hair, pinned up as usual, was completely covered by the round bobby's helmet and the odd bulges in the trousers created by the folds of her skirt were not noticeable at a distance. But up close the deception was impossible to maintain. Her lovely face and wide green eyes beneath the rain-soaked and dripping helmet brim caused Lestrade's man to break out into a smile. "What's all this, Mr. Holmes?"

"She is an important witness under my protection," Holmes replied smoothly. "Though she must get to her rehearsal with the D'Oyly Carte Troupe before she is missed."

"I do not go on until midway through the first act," said Lucy.

Holmes ignored her. "Has Inspector Lestrade arrived?"

"He is with your brother, sir. They said you'd telephoned. They're waiting for you in the library."

Miss James caught my eye and her lips silently formed the word *Mycroft* with the same excitement as she had shown when Holmes had mentioned the Irregulars in our rooms two days before. As we mounted the stairs, she took off her helmet and turned to Holmes. "Will you introduce me to Mycroft as Moriarty's daughter?"

"It would only complicate matters," Holmes replied without hesitation, and we continued up the stairs.

We entered the library to find Mycroft and Lestrade bent over some papers on a table, along with the ledger book of the unfortunate Mr. Perkins. Naturally, each of them looked up in surprise at the sight of Miss James.

"Gentlemen," said Holmes, "I rely on your absolute discretion." As they nodded, Holmes adopted a more formal tone. Turning to Miss James, he continued, "Miss Lucy James, this is my brother, Mycroft, and you have already met Detective Inspector George Lestrade of the Metropolitan Police. Gentlemen, this is Lucy James. This morning her mother, a violinist with the Savoy Orchestra named Zoe Rosario, was abducted from her flat on Exeter Street. As Lestrade knows, I believe the man calling himself Adam Worth is responsible. You gentlemen should also know that for the past twenty-one years Mr. Worth has been the trustee responsible for the upbringing and education of Miss James in America, although she has not known his identity until very recently."

Holmes paused to let the implications of this revelation sink in.

"So, Lucy," said Mycroft. "Worth is a Moriarty, and his brother's first name is your surname. Lucy James; James Moriarty."

"He seems to have an obsession with family." There was worry and urgency in her voice as she continued, "But none of that matters at the moment! What is important is to find my mother."

"Quite right," said Mycroft. I saw respect in both his gaze and Holmes's as he leaned over the table and indicated the notebook, a similar set of words and figures arranged in neat columns on a single sheet of Diogenes Club stationery, and two strips of paper. "Let us get to the matter of this coded ledger, for I believe it has a bearing on the matter of Miss Rosario."

The two strips of paper each contained the letters of the English alphabet, but the second strip contained an additional *a*.

abcdefghijklmnopqrstuvwxyz
abcdefghijklmnopqrstuvwxyza

"This is the encoding and decoding key for the telegraph code, as published by my friend the Reverend Charles Dodgson and used by those who wish to conceal their messages from telegraphy personnel. It requires both sender and recipient to know which letter of the alphabet has been used as the key letter, which of course Mr. Perkins's ledger does not tell us. However, after several unsuccessful attempts I remembered that Perkins's first name was Llewellen and tried the letter *L*. Here is the result."

He held out the page, where we read:

10/10	Clevering from Zurich bonds	10000
11/10	to Clevering cash	9000
25/10	Clevering from Zurich bonds	40000
26/10	to Clevering cash	35000
31/10	Clevering from Zurich bonds	300000

01/11	to Clevering cash	295000
04/11	Clevering from Zurich bonds	1000000
04/11	Clevering to banker2 cash	995000

banker2 990000 upon success to
Henry Judson Raymond
198 Piccadilly

"Perkins was converting bonds to cash. After deducting his fee, he gave the remaining cash to Clevering," said Mycroft. "See how the cash payments grow larger, presumably in proportion to the importance of the task performed. See the second payment, occurring October 26, just at the time of Moran's escape. And the third, more substantial payment occurring November first, the day the hospital was bombed."

"Possibly a reward for a successful demonstration," Holmes said.

"And today, he receives a million pounds, takes his fee, and provides the remainder to Clevering to deliver to a second banker, with delivery instructions to be carried out 'upon success.' I do not like to contemplate the malignity of the task that the instigator of this wickedness values at one million pounds."

Lucy asked, "Why do you think this has bearing on my mother's kidnapping?"

"Clevering has been making payments on Worth's direction," Mycroft replied. "I believe the name of Henry Judson Raymond may be Worth's alias, and that Worth may be found at the address indicated here: 198 Piccadilly."

"Lestrade?" Holmes looked meaningfully at the little inspector.

"Not without a warrant. And this paper doesn't have the word *Worth* on it."

Holmes nodded. "Then perhaps Watson and I will pay Mr. Raymond a visit."

I was nodding my concurrence when the library door burst open and the small, ragged figure of Flynn ran to us, followed by one of Lestrade's men, equally breathless.

"It's all right, officer," said Holmes. "This boy's name is Flynn. He and his associates have been on a mission for me concerning our mutual interest. Flynn, as soon as you have recovered from your exertions will you please give us your report."

The boy nodded and took a deep breath. "We lost 'em, Mr. 'Olmes, and sorry I am to say it. We 'ung about Exeter Street this morning and a few minutes after Dr. Watson and a lady went in, the painters came barrelin' down the side of the building on their scaffold with a big canvas bundle. It was heavy-like, cos it took both of 'em to lug it into their van, which didn't 'ave no sign or nuffing on it, and then the one of 'em got in—smaller than the other, 'e was, and walked with a limp—and the other climbed up to drive. 'E whipped up the horse and off they went, with Brooks and me runnin' after. Well, we stayed with 'em to Covent Garden and then Leicester Square, but then traffic thinned out and we couldn't keep up." His shoulders sagged dejectedly. "So we lost 'em."

Holmes spoke kindly. "You did your best, I am sure. Where did you see them last?"

Flynn hung his head. "We lost 'em on Piccadilly Circus."

34. BREAKING AND ENTERING

Within fifteen minutes Lucy, Lestrade, Holmes, and I stood across the street from 198 Piccadilly, waiting impatiently for one of Lestrade's men to return with a warrant to search the premises. Number 198 was located in an imposing three-story row of white granite structures built along classical lines. A luggage shop was on the ground floor, one of a number of elegant stores similarly situated throughout the block. The exclusivity of the residences in the two floors above the shops was evidenced by a well-maintained sculptured facade decorated by serene classical figures amid various filigrees and tall windows in a pleasing variety of proportions. Balconies, each with a graceful wrought iron railing, were provided for the first-floor residences above the shops, enabling the fortunate occupants to overlook the passersby below.

Lestrade looked nervous. "Swells," he said, glancing up at the majestic building. "I don't much—Mr. Holmes! Where are you going?"

Holmes was striding rapidly across the wide street. In a moment we saw him enter a florist's shop several doors down from Number 198. Shortly after, he emerged bearing a large basket of roses. He then entered the luggage shop, and popped out a few moments later, still bearing the flowers, and entered the building again through an imposing, unmarked black door several shops to the left.

Several minutes passed as we watched the black door. Then Holmes's voice came from behind me.

"Henry Judson Raymond resides on the top floor." We turned in astonishment as he continued. "I left the flowers in his hallway. There is a service entrance coming from an alley behind the building. It leads to St. James Churchyard. Come, Watson. We have a delivery to make."

"I'm coming with you," said Miss James.

"Watson and I are accustomed to working together."

"Not the way Watson tells it. You never let him know anything until the end."

"Nevertheless—"

"Let us be reasonable. Whoever answers Mr. Raymond's door will be far more relaxed at the sight of a young woman bearing the flowers than that of a hawk-faced gentleman in a frock coat."

"I cannot allow you to expose yourself to danger."

She pulled Holmes and me away, out of Lestrade's hearing. "When I was eighteen I was attacked by a man in the riding stables of my school. He did not survive the encounter."

I stared at her, amazed.

"Fortunately I had recently read Dr. Watson's account of the racehorse named Silver Blaze. So I reconstructed the scene to indicate that the man had attacked the horses, and that the horses had successfully defended themselves."

On the busy street before us, the horses drawing their cabs, carts, and carriages seemed to take on a new and sinister demeanor as they moved past.

Miss James looked at them, then at us. "Growing up as an orphan teaches one self-reliance. Now, are we going to make this a contest of wills, or are we going to find my mother?"

A brief smile from Holmes immediately defused the conflict. "You must understand, Lucy. I really do not want to tell your mother I have lost you."

Regrettably, the remainder of our visit to Piccadilly bore us no fruit. We crossed the street and entered quietly through the tradesman's door in the rear. We climbed the stairs. Holmes and I drew our revolvers and stood in the shadows as Lucy knocked. No answer was forthcoming, so Holmes picked the lock. We entered to find the flat beautifully furnished, but empty. There were no clothes in the dressers or closets. No food in the kitchen pantry. No serving dishes on the sideboard. No sheets or blankets on the beds. No sign that anyone was living there.

"And yet Perkins told us that when in London, Mr. Worth spends most of his time in his flat in Westminster, which we know to be the one in which we are now standing." said Holmes.

"So he has another flat," said Lucy.

"Or Perkins was lying," said Holmes.

35. PHILOSOPHY WITH MR. ROCKEFELLER

Rockefeller Sr. greeted Holmes and me on the deck of the *White Star*. Holmes had changed his mind about attending dinner, since the report on Worth that Rockefeller had promised had become of far greater importance now that Perkins was dead. We had still wanted to keep our relationship with Lucy unknown to the Rockefellers, so Lucy had made arrangements with Johnny to have him escort her directly from her rehearsal on the *Shamrock*, which was docked barely fifty yards away.

A mischievous twinkle shone in Rockefeller's keen gray eyes. "I'm glad you could join us after all, Mr. Holmes. Mr. Roosevelt has sent us some interesting information about your Mr. Worth. But first, shall we have our supper? As you saw at luncheon, I generally allow one hour for the sake of efficiency in digestion. Will that suit your schedule? It is now six o'clock."

"Perfectly," Holmes replied, to my relief, for I was very much anticipating a splendid supper from America's wealthiest man, after what I thought had been a rather abstemious midday meal. Also, the arrangement would allow us to be on time for the PM's committee. They met at nine o'clock, so after dining with Rockefeller we would have two hours to make the six-mile journey to the Diogenes Club. In the carriage Holmes could peruse Roosevelt's report while also considering the implications of some new material that Lestrade had provided concerning Clevering's recent activity.

"Fine, then." Rockefeller indicated the stairs leading to the dining saloon. "Cettie is looking forward to meeting you. She is below, with my son and his young acquaintance from Connecticut."

A few moments later we were once again in the spacious and well-lit dining area. Rockefeller introduced us to his wife. From a small settee Mrs. Rockefeller rose to greet us, graciously inclining her head toward Holmes and me but not extending her hand.

"Mr. Holmes, Dr. Watson, I am Laura Celestia Rockefeller. Usually they call me Cettie. Welcome to our supper table." She was primly dressed in an embroidered white blouse and dark blue jacket and skirt, her dark hair severely parted precisely in the middle. She was smaller than her husband, but seeing them side by side I could not help thinking that somehow they had grown to look alike. Each had the same bright eyes and suppressed intensity, and a tight-lipped way of making those around them feel under close scrutiny.

Mrs. Rockefeller continued with her introductions. "You've met my son, Johnny, at lunch, I believe." She went on, with a slight tinge of apprehension, "This is his friend from school in America, Miss Lucy James."

Johnny and Lucy were already standing. The younger Rockefeller gave a polite nod and smile of acknowledgment. Lucy's smile was more direct, though not revealing any connection with us. I noticed that she wore no jewelry, and that beneath her black wool jacket were the same style of white blouse and long black skirt that she had worn at the theater. I wondered if she had seen pictures of Mrs. Rockefeller in the papers, and had deliberately not worn any of the new outfits Johnny had purchased for her so that she would not outshine the plainness of Mrs. Rockefeller's attire.

"I've heard of you, Mr. Holmes. Johnny tells me you're a famous English detective. Well, now, before you make any detective deductions about Johnny and me, I need to tell you I'm just here as an actress, more or less. That's what I do at the Savoy Theatre, and then by day I'm playing another role on Johnny's behalf."

I saw Mrs. Rockefeller's eyes widen momentarily, and then relief showed on her face as Lucy continued.

"He has a sweetheart back home, you see. But right now the lucky girl is traveling in Italy or Paris or some such place and not writing or paying him much attention at all. So he hit on this idea of starting a rumor that he had captured the heart of a London actress, which I've been lucky enough to become, at least for the past few days. Of course we don't know whether this little strategy is working, but I have high hopes that it will make Johnny's sweetheart just as jealous as she deserves to be."

Johnny was blushing furiously by this time. His mother, however, seemed delighted. "You never told me about a sweetheart!" she exclaimed with a happy smile. "Is she the senator's daughter?"

Johnny nodded.

Mrs. Rockefeller beamed. "Though I'm not sure about starting a rumor about a London actress." She turned to us. "We're Baptists, you see, Mr. Holmes. Neither John nor I ever set foot in a theater."

"The play that Miss James is in is perfectly proper, Mother," said Johnny. "Everyone's dressed in long Japanese robes, and the music is by the same man who wrote 'Onward, Christian Soldiers.'"

Rockefeller added, though without enthusiasm, "Johnny tells me we're to see it tomorrow night, Cettie. As a business matter—it's to show friendship with the English. They're very proud of their plays, you know. But the actors will perform right here in the harbor, on the deck of Morgan's yacht."

So Rockefeller knew the performance was to be on the *Corsair*. I wondered if Foster also had known, and if that was what really had prompted his investigation of the Savoy Theatre.

Rockefeller was continuing, "—and it's just a short walk. Mr. Holmes is in charge of making sure everything is safe for us."

I knew that such a responsibility was the last thing Holmes wanted, and I shuddered inwardly to think of the consequences if another dynamite bomb, with far greater explosive force than the one at St. Thomas Hospital, were to somehow be detonated on the *Corsair*. Yet Holmes was too polite to contradict his host, and too considerate to draw Mrs. Rockefeller's attention to the danger we were facing. He merely nodded.

"I hope I shall feel well enough to go with you," Mrs. Rockefeller replied.

Then the attendants appeared with the serving dishes, and with a bright "Shall we?" she bade us all to the supper table.

To my disappointment, the fare provided for our supper meal was identical to that of our luncheon. We were given lettuce, peas, green beans, baked potato, and broiled fish, with iced barley water. Yet to my surprise, the abstemiousness of the meal occasioned a remarkable congeniality between Rockefeller and Holmes. Holmes paid compliments on the freshness of the vegetables, which it turned out had been brought, on ice, from one of Rockefeller's gardens in America. Holmes noted that barley and potato had been the main staple of his extremely simple diet during the two years he had recently spent in Tibet, where the lamas in the monastery at Lhasa took their tea in small and very infrequent sips in order to facilitate digestion, precisely in the way that Rockefeller imbibed his barley water. And when Holmes observed that the longevity of the lamas sometimes reached more than a century, Rockefeller exhibited the keenest of interest.

"I knew I was on the right track!" He turned to his wife, and I had the distinct impression that the two had had numerous debates on the subject. "You see, Cettie? This is the way to live to be a hundred!"

"But, John, it's not just what they eat. Those people in a monastery don't have the business cares that you do."

"I'd expect their leaders have their share of headaches all the same. Human nature is the same wherever you are, I've been told, and it takes a lot of effort to manage people. Wouldn't you say that's true, Mr. Holmes?"

"Very likely," Holmes replied. "I have always preferred to work more or less alone. Still, I can tell you that the head lama did not mention dietary rules when he told me the secret to his longevity."

He paused, and we all leaned forward expectantly, myself included, for Holmes had never before spoken of his experience in Tibet, much less talked about the philosophy of Tibetan religious leaders. To my surprise, Holmes turned to look directly at Lucy. He seemed to be speaking only to her as he continued, "The secret is to have a quiet heart, and to celebrate each moment of life so as to have no fear of death."

Lucy's beautiful green eyes widened. She held her napkin to her mouth, as if to conceal her emotion. I do not know whether it was because of the message imparted in the words, or simply the heartfelt tone in which Holmes was addressing her, or the fact that she might be receiving guidance of this sort from a man of Holmes's experience and stature for the first time in her life. Whatever the cause, it seemed to me that she was suddenly overcome with feeling. She did not speak.

All three of the Rockefellers had listened to Holmes's words with polite attention.

"Makes sense," said Rockefeller Sr. "But of course it's easier said than done."

"I believe the Gospels say something similar," said Mrs. Rockefeller. "Now, John, I know you have some papers from New York that you wanted to discuss with these gentlemen. Lucy, would you like to come up on deck for a breath of air?"

36. COMMISSIONER ROOSEVELT'S REPORT

When the ladies had departed, Rockefeller Sr. took a two-page telegraph message from the inside pocket of his waistcoat and handed it over to Holmes. To my surprise, Holmes did not unfold the message. Instead he looked up at Rockefeller.

"Watson and I are most grateful for your help, and for your hospitality," Holmes began. "I wonder if I might presume upon your kindness a bit further?"

"What did you have in mind?"

"It concerns Miss James. I believe her to be in danger from Mr. Worth's organization. I do not wish to alarm her, but Watson and I must soon leave to make our report to the Prime Minister and I have reason to believe that if she returns to the Savoy Hotel this evening she will not be safe. I wonder if you could give her shelter here for the night."

"Nothing easier. We have the entire ship. She can have her pick of thirty cabins." He paused. "And our Pinkertons are top-quality men. She'll be safe. I'll just have a word with Cettie. It's all right with you, Johnny? Then consider it done."

"I am most grateful," Holmes replied.

"Now, have a look at that message," said Rockefeller. "Some interesting history about Mr. Worth, and it gave me an idea."

Holmes opened the telegram and held it so that we both could read its contents. Worth, the report said, was the false name of Adam Moriarty, one of two sons of an immigrant tailor in the poorer section of Boston. He had taken the identity of Adam Worth from a dead American soldier after the battle of Bull Run and used the name to enlist in both Union and Confederate armies several times, each time collecting the enlistment payment and then deserting to another regiment.

Four years after the war, using the name of William A. Judson, he had rented a store adjacent to the Boylston National Bank of Boston, and sold bottles of patent medicine to an unsuspecting public while his brother and other associates dug a tunnel from the basement of the store to the steel wall of the bank vault. The gang then used augers to drill into the steel again and again, making a series of holes in a large circular pattern, until they had isolated and removed a large disc, creating an opening large enough for a man to climb through.

Before dawn one Sunday Worth and his brother entered the vault and emptied it of nearly a million dollars in cash and bonds, as well as all the safe-deposit boxes, which were then loaded into boxes labeled as nerve tonic and shipped by rail to New York City. By Monday morning when the robbery was discovered, Worth and his brother had boarded the USS *Indiana* at the port of Philadelphia and were sailing for Liverpool with their ill-gotten gains, Worth traveling under the name of Henry Judson Raymond.

The report concluded:

BIGGEST ROBBERY IN US HISTORY BUT STATUTE OF LIMITATIONS APPLIED IN 1889. MORIARTY/WORTH/ RAYMOND SUSPECTED IN OTHER CRIMES IN EUROPE, WHERE WE HAVE NO JURISDICTION. ROOSEVELT.

"I had thought of holding our meeting at the Bank of England," Rockefeller said. "But this Worth seems to know his way around banks. I think we ought to stay clear of Threadneedle Street, or at least be sure there hasn't been any tunneling going on over there."

"I agree you should stay away from the Bank," said Holmes. "And this report, coming as it does from the Commissioner of Police, will be excellent evidence to present to the PM. I will try once again to have the conference postponed, or relocated somewhere far away from London."

"Unless you have stronger evidence, no one will agree, and everyone will think you are admitting failure."

"If I am not successful, failure is precisely what I will have to admit."

"You British and your word games. What you need to admit, Mr. Holmes, is that you can't just tell two nations to stand aside and wait. You must do your job now, Mr. Holmes, and you must succeed."

37. A TRAITOR IS UNMASKED

Promptly at nine that evening Holmes and I were called with Lestrade into the library of the Diogenes Club. Seated around the polished mahogany table were the men whose expectant and authoritative faces had by now grown familiar to me. Tonight, however, there was an additional intensity in the atmosphere. Unspoken was the threat that a horrific disaster might befall us within twenty-four hours, when the all-important meeting with the powerful American industrialists would begin with the performance of *The Mikado* on Mr. Morgan's yacht.

Tonight I also noticed a marked difference in Clevering's demeanor. At our other meetings he had leaned forward aggressively over the table as though eager to do battle. Now, he sat rigidly upright, lips pursed, staring fixedly ahead. He had the look of one who was steeling himself for a moment he dreaded.

"Well, Mr. Holmes?" asked the Prime Minister.

On the table before him, Holmes carefully placed the ledger notebook from the unfortunate Perkins's office and the telegraph message from New York City Police Commissioner Roosevelt. "Gentlemen, my investigations have led me to the conclusion that

Colonel Sebastian Moran is intimately involved in a well-funded and organized conspiracy to murder those who plan to meet with Mr. Rockefeller. I will begin by explaining to you the means by which the colonel escaped from Dartmoor Prison. My explanation will be brief, and it will also clear the name of an innocent man."

Around the room the PM's committee members nodded their heads; all, that is, except Clevering. He remained rigid, eyes fixedly staring forward, his monocle dangling unnoticed from its gold chain and collar pin.

"I shall begin with the day of Moran's escape," said Holmes. "That morning, the guard assigned to Moran's wing of the prison was a trustworthy veteran named Trent, a man of similar size and build to Moran. In another wing of the prison was a guard named Asher, who had been at his job for only six months. Using some pretext, the guard Asher entered Moran's wing of the prison. He struck Trent from behind, knocking him unconscious. He used Trent's key to unlock Moran's cell. Asher and Moran beat Trent around the face and drugged him so that he would remain motionless under the blanket of Moran's cot. Then Moran donned a black wig—supplied by Asher, through a confederate. He exchanged clothes with Trent, covering the wig with the guard's uniform hat. Asher returned to his post. At the end of the shift, he and Moran left the prison.

"In Trent's uniform, Moran walked toward Trent's house so as not to be noticed to have departed from the usual routine. But instead of stopping there, he went to Asher's rooms and donned civilian clothes that had been left for him, either by Asher or another accomplice. He hung Trent's uniform in Asher's closet, where, to a casual observer, it would appear to be one of Asher's. He walked to the bridge at Hoo Meavy, some eight miles south, where an accomplice had hidden yet another change of clothing and some money. When Asher arrived as instructed to receive payment, Moran doubtless told him to count the money or diverted his attention in some other manner. He crushed Asher's skull and threw him over the bridge onto the road below. He placed his first set of clothing in Asher's knapsack. Partially devouring Asher's sandwich and drinking from his flask, Moran threw them both from the bridge to make it appear that Asher had fallen to his death while having his lunch. Moran remained in the area only long enough to place the remnants of the meal beneath Asher's body. He then took the train to London, where, this past Friday morning, he set off the bomb that we all experienced at St. Thomas Hospital."

The Commissioner spoke. "I have obtained evidence that supports the story Mr. Holmes has just recounted. And the guard Trent will be cleared of all suspicion. However, Mr. Holmes, it would no doubt be welcome to all of us if you will explain the relevance of what we have just heard."

"Thank you. I was coming to that. The relevance relates to the death of Mr. Trent's family kitten."

A few murmurs of impatience came from the committee members, but Holmes continued unperturbed. "The animal was found beneath a small tree with a broken neck the afternoon before Moran's escape. That evening Trent received a note, instructing him to forget whatever would happen at the prison on the morrow, or he would find that his three-year-old daughter would suffer the same injury as the kitten. Mr. Trent verified this to me personally this past Sunday afternoon. When I told him I knew he had received the note, the statement brought Mr. Trent out of his despair-induced torpor. The threat is relevant to our present circumstances because the same vulnerability to threats against an innocent family member was exploited by the gang in order to manipulate the behavior of one of us here at this table."

Amid the immediate gasps of surprise from the committee members, Holmes continued, "Is that not correct, Mr. Clevering?"

Clevering continued to stare fixedly ahead, saying nothing.

A hush fell over the room. Holmes picked up Perkins's ledger notebook and explained the system: how the bearer bonds were sent by diplomatic courier from Zurich to an embassy in London, where they were picked up by Clevering, converted to cash by Perkins at the Bank of England, and then returned to Clevering, minus Perkins's fee, so that Clevering could deliver payment for services rendered to someone in the Moriarty gang. As Holmes read the dated entries from Mycroft's decoded transcript, murmurs, first of shock and then of repugnance, seemed to pass through the room each time he said *Clevering*.

Clevering did not respond. Holmes went on, "Mr. Clevering, this last entry indicates you delivered a million pounds in bearer bonds to Mr. Perkins this morning. Will you confirm that you obtained the bonds from the German embassy?"

A murmur of shock went round the room, but Clevering remained silent.

"The German government has an obvious motive to fund the disruption of this meeting, does it not? A network of naval ports and the conversion of the British fleet to oil would enable, in turn, the construction and operation of battleships far larger and more powerful than those possessed by any nation today. And a long-term alliance between our country and America would profoundly strengthen our military powers for generations."

A smile flickered across Holmes's features. "So the stakes we are discussing are enormous. The situation is one that the German government would find intolerable, one they would pay huge sums to prevent."

The Prime Minister nodded in acknowledgment. "Theoretically, Mr. Holmes, your supposition is quite possible." He looked around the table, measuring his words as he met the gaze of each man in turn. "But we must take great care, gentlemen. These are deep waters, and we have no way of knowing who sent the funds—only from whose embassy they were sent."

"Quite right, Prime Minister," said Goschen. "The British public would be unlikely to honor that distinction, if a tragedy at the meeting were to take place and the source of the funding became known. There would be an outcry calling for war with Germany."

"And other nations might want such a war to take place," the PM replied.

Goschen continued, "The French, the Italians, the Turks—any of them would be pleased to see our two nations annihilating one another, hoping they could then preside supreme over the ruins. The Fenians too, consider any enemy of England to be a friend of Ireland. They would also be delighted to see us at war."

"Or the Boers," said the PM. "This might be their doing, for we know they have tried to obtain German military support for their present quarrel with us in the Transvaal."

"And they would have ready access to the German embassy—"

"Let us not get ahead of ourselves, gentlemen," said Holmes. He turned to Clevering, and his voice now held a distinctly threatening note. "Would it surprise you, Mr. Clevering, to learn that you were being watched this morning by Lestrade's men? And that you were seen entering and leaving the German embassy and going directly from there to the Bank of England?"

I saw the shrewd, calculating glint in Clevering's eyes that I had observed the previous night. Still, Clevering did not speak.

"I will be candid," said Holmes. "You were seen entering the Bank of England, but Inspector Lestrade's men unfortunately did not see you leave, and so we do not know where or to whom you delivered the cash you obtained from the unfortunate Mr. Perkins this morning."

Clevering spoke at last. "So you want a name."

"With a name, we can have the man arrested. The papers will trumpet the name and his role as paymaster in a conspiracy to interfere with an upcoming diplomatic conference, the precise nature of which we need not disclose. When he sees the newspapers, Mr.

Worth will realize that his plot has been discovered and that he has no prospect of being paid, at which time he will have no motive to carry out the assassination."

"Come, Clevering," said the Prime Minister. "You must see that Mr. Holmes's plan gives you the opportunity to prevent great harm to your country."

Clevering hid his face in shame for a long moment. Then he turned to the Prime Minister, his voice coming almost in a whisper. "I want full amnesty."

"Impossible," said the Prime Minister.

"However," said Holmes, "public knowledge of your treason might be minimized. You might plead guilty, and your family might be spared the shame of a sensationalized public trial. Your wife and children might thus escape a stigma that will otherwise make their lives—"

Suddenly, Clevering's voice hardened in petulant resentment. "My wife and children? What do you know of a wife and children, Mr. Holmes? You, with no family save for that fat brother of yours—"

"Enough of that, Clevering," said the Commissioner. "Will you cooperate? Or shall I order Lestrade's men to take you to jail?"

"I must see that my family is safe. Worth has threatened their lives. They must be protected."

"They will be," said the Commissioner. "Now. The name of the bank official and his bank."

Clevering shook his head. "Not until I see that my family is under protection. Also, I want a decent opportunity to say my farewell. After that I shall tell you everything you want to know."

The Commissioner gave a reluctant nod, at which Lestrade stood up and left the room. We waited uncomfortably for several minutes. Then Lestrade's men appeared at the library doorway to indicate that the police wagon was ready to transport Clevering, guarded by two police officers, to what would be his last visit to his home.

As Clevering turned to leave, he looked long and hard at Holmes. "You had me followed. Hardly the behavior of a gentleman, after I came to you in confidence Sunday night."

"It was on Saturday morning that we began to have you followed," replied Holmes.

Lestrade's men then shackled Clevering by the wrists and marched him out of the room. Holmes moved quickly to the front window and looked down. Below us in the glare of the electric lamps we saw the wide entry steps to the club, the police wagon waiting on the pavement, and the driver, who stood at attention with another guard before the opened side door of the wagon.

The Commissioner came to watch with us at the window. "Once again, we owe you our gratitude, Mr. Holmes."

"Not yet" was Holmes's reply.

Clevering and his police escorts then appeared directly below us. The three men walked forward and down the wide steps. Clevering bowed his head and took his place inside the wagon. One of the policemen closed and locked the door behind him. The other turned to walk around the rear of the wagon to enter from the far side.

In the next instant a strange flickering yellow glow appeared behind the wagon. Then the glow was coming from within it, and we could see yellow flames through the small rear window.

"No!" cried Holmes. "Get him out!"

But it was too late. With a sharp thunderclap, a dazzling flash of light momentarily consumed the wagon and then dissipated, leaving behind a smoking ruin.

Though stunned, I was nonetheless aware of the shadowy figure of a tall man moving directly away from us and from the smoke of the explosion. He had an odd, crouching way of walking that seemed familiar to me, but I could not place it at the time.

When my addled eyes finally focused, he had very nearly crossed the wide pavement of Waterloo Place. Moments later he had vanished into the darkness of the trees on the far side.

I turned and saw Holmes running from the room. The Commissioner and I followed him down the wide stairway to the entrance of the club.

From atop the entry steps I tried to take in the scene. The door of the police coach hung at a crazed angle on one of its hinges. Embedded in the blackened surface of what, moments earlier, had been its interior finish, innumerable shards of glass sparkled coldly in the electric light amid a hideously glistening sheen of shadowed crimson. Mercifully, the explosion had spared the two police officers and the police coach driver. They were struggling to their feet as we descended the wide granite steps.

I strained to see within the shadows of the trees across the plaza pavement where the killer had fled and where, I was certain, Holmes had run in pursuit, though putting his own life in danger.

I was about to follow and offer what assistance I could, when I heard a moan from within the coach. I clambered inside and saw Clevering. The injuries he had suffered were as catastrophic as any I had seen on the battlefield in Afghanistan, and it was with a sense of hopelessness that I took off my belt, instructed the Commissioner to do the same, and improvised tourniquets, applying them as best I could manage.

Clevering was of course in shock, the detached state that a merciful Nature creates to obscure overwhelming pain. As I tightened the tourniquets, however, his gaze began to clear, and I thought he recognized me. I saw my opportunity. "The banker, Clevering. Can you say the name of the banker?"

He nodded, with a tight-lipped smile. He drew a deep breath. I leaned forward to hear the all-important name.

Then his eyes widened. His manacled hand grasped my wrist. As his grip tightened, he emitted a long, shallow, fluttering breath, and died.

For a long moment I felt overcome by sadness and frustration, on the brink of the same dark abyss that had confronted me in Miss Rosario's flat when I had first seen the open window that evidenced my failure to protect her. I had been so close to the name we needed! The name of the banker could have signaled to our adversary that even if he succeeded in his lethal plan, he would receive no payment. But now Clevering was gone.

PART THREE

I SEE NO REASON

38. A SMALL GLASS VIAL

I washed Clevering's blood from my hands and changed into a fresh set of clothes, hoping to expunge the memory of what I had just witnessed. I needed to clear my mind if I was to be of assistance to Holmes. But as I entered the library of the Diogenes Club a few minutes later, I still seemed to feel the pressure of Clevering's spasmodic final grip upon my wrist.

I found Holmes in a leather wing chair, in the glow of the fireplace. Lucy James stood behind him, holding a sheet of notepaper at an angle so that each of them could read it. In the strong electric light the circles under Holmes's eyes were plainly visible. The worried, urgent set of his eyebrows told me that his concern over Miss Rosario's whereabouts was still very much with him. The look on Miss James's features showed me that her anxiety was equal to his.

The two noticed my entry and looked up. Holmes spoke. "The Commissioner will join us soon. When he returns, we shall make plans. Meanwhile, Miss James has news."

Lucy's green eyes flashed. "The *Corsair* has arrived twelve hours earlier than scheduled. I saw it docking, close by Mr. Rockefeller's ship."

"We ought to warn Mr. Morgan," I said. I thought this was a perfectly sound observation; however, Holmes held up his hand.

"There is more," Holmes said, nodding to Miss James to continue.

"Also, I saw Blake and Cleo leaving the *Shamrock* after the rehearsal this afternoon. I ran to the *White Star* and persuaded one of Mr. Rockefeller's Pinkerton men to follow them. I received the report about an hour ago on the *White Star* and came straight here. Both Blake and Cleo were seen entering 198 Piccadilly. I believe that is where we will find my mother."

I shook my head in bewilderment. "We were at 198 Piccadilly this morning. We found nothing."

"But if there is really nothing there, why should Blake and Cleo go inside?"

"I still do not follow."

Holmes's voice was kind. "Lucy is deducing that there is a portal, Watson. A connection between Number 198 and one of the other flats."

Lucy said, "There could have been a false wall. Or a hidden staircase."

I understood. "You think the building is where Miss Rosario is imprisoned."

"Exactly," Holmes said. "We will arrange for a police coach to take us there as soon as we can speak to the Commissioner." I knew he was saying this last as much for Miss James's benefit as for mine, for plainly she was anxious to take action. In my fatigued and worried state, I also felt a troubled uncertainty about the effect Miss James's determined presence would have on Holmes. He was accustomed to directing all aspects of his investigations, and now, on the eve of the critical meeting with the Americans, he had to contend with the inner tumult he must have felt at Miss Rosario's peril, intensified by the voice and emotional urgency of Miss James. She was, after all, not just another client, whose pleadings could be more or less objectified; she was Miss Rosario's daughter. And clearly he intended to take her with us in the police coach. But how well would he be able to function with her at his side, knowing that she was also in danger?

I tried to shake off these doubts as Holmes took the paper from Miss James and thrust it into my hand.

"Meanwhile," he said, "examine this. It is the police account of Clevering's movements from Saturday morning until tonight when he arrived here at the Diogenes Club."

The typewritten account showed that Saturday Clevering had gone from his home to the German embassy, to the Bank of England, to Lord Lansdowne's estate, and then to our meeting here at the Diogenes Club before returning home. Yesterday he had traveled only from his home to Lord Lansdowne's and then here, and then home again. Today he had repeated his Saturday pattern of movements, though of course he had never reached his home.

"Does anything in this account strike you as noteworthy?"

"He did not attend church on Sunday."

"And yet he did travel to Lord Lansdowne's estate that day, and each of the other two days that he was being observed. A visit to Lord Lansdowne would be a considerable inconvenience, since, as you are likely aware, the Lansdowne family has for more than a century been seated at Bowood House near the town of Derry Hill, a two and one-half hours' journey from London by train."

"It was Clevering's duty to report to Lord Lansdowne, whatever the inconvenience."

"He could have reported by telephone."

"If indeed the lines have reached so far from London."

"They have," said Holmes. "While you were changing clothes, the Commissioner telephoned Bowood House to report the need for a successor to Mr. Clevering. Lord Lansdowne is still unwell, so the Commissioner spoke to Lady Lansdowne."

I failed to see the significance of Clevering's making the journey rather than using the telephone. I said, "Clevering might simply have been trying to impress his superior with his zeal, or to show his concern for Lord Lansdowne's health."

Holmes looked thoughtful. "Or his visits—"

"—may have been the cause of Lord Lansdowne's illness," Lucy finished.

"Quite possibly," said Holmes, and the flicker of excitement in his gaze told me that, far from being annoyed at Lucy's interruption, he shared her opinion.

I was struggling to understand what Holmes and Lucy were getting at, when the Commissioner entered the room. Upon seeing Miss James, he looked startled, for it was unusual for a woman to be present in the club, particularly at a late hour.

Holmes spoke in a matter-of-fact manner. "Commissioner Bradford, this is Miss Lucy James, of the D'Oyly Carte Troupe. She has been staying on the Rockefeller yacht and is a friend of young Mr. Rockefeller, who has told her of the upcoming conference. She is also the daughter of Miss Rosario, and she has come here tonight with important information concerning Miss Rosario's whereabouts. As you know, we believe Miss Rosario has been abducted by Mr. Worth, and finding her may lead us to him."

"Which could end the threat to our meeting."

"Unless Colonel Moran is arranging that side of the affair, and is operating with no further communication required from his . . . employer."

"We must follow the trail nonetheless. You shall have a police coach to accompany you."

Holmes nodded his thanks. "We must go to 198 Piccadilly as soon as we have dealt with matters arising from the explosion here. Now, have your men discovered anything new from further examination of the police coach?"

Fatigue showed on the Commissioner's face. "The explosive device appears to have been a bottle bomb. A pint glass bottle, packed with gunpowder and nails, an oakum fuse soaked in kerosene, probably lit with a cigar. Easily concealed."

"Unlike the bomb from Friday morning, which employed dynamite, detonated electrically with a timing device of some sort, and was intended as a demonstration of capabilities. Tonight there was a different purpose."

"He wanted to kill Clevering."

"But he could have done that with a pistol at close range. He could have shot Clevering and got away just as quickly, and with less risk. The fuse of the bomb might have taken longer to burn than he had foreseen. The officer might have seen the flame, opened the door, and pulled Clevering to safety. If our killer had used a pistol, such a risk would not have presented itself."

"And yet he used the bottle bomb."

"Indeed." Holmes pressed his fingertips together, musing. He continued, "Assuming there is a method at work here, there is also a message. And the message is either deliberate or unintentional. Either way we would benefit from knowing it, and as yet I cannot say I understand." He shook his head. "But let us set that puzzle aside for the present. Has Mrs. Clevering been told of her husband's death?"

"Lord Salisbury delivered the news personally by telephone."

"And what did the Prime Minister tell her?"

"That her husband had died at the hand of an unknown bomb thrower as he was leaving after tonight's meeting."

"Nothing was mentioned about Clevering's involvement with Worth?"

"We thought it best not to do so. He is being judged by a higher power than ours, and having newspapers trumpeting the story of a cabinet minister's chief assistant engaged in a treasonous plot . . .

Well, that would prove disastrous for our meeting. It might even bring down the government."

"Where is Mrs. Clevering now?"

"She is staying with the children. Two servants of the family are coming to arrange for transport of the body."

Holmes nodded. "I trust the manacles have been removed from Mr. Clevering's wrists." Then, at the Commissioner's startled look, he continued, "Let us go downstairs to confirm that. Something else has just occurred to me."

Once outside the club, we found a ring of policemen protecting the entrance and the nearest part of Waterloo Place. They had no difficulty keeping back the few curious onlookers who had been attracted by the noise of the explosion. Behind the damaged police coach, a police ambulance had been drawn up, and inside it Clevering's body lay on a gurney, covered by a khaki wool blanket of the same variety that had covered Mr. Foster's remains less than four days earlier.

Holmes drew back the blanket, and we saw the manacles, blackened and stained, on Clevering's wrists. Fortunately the locks were still working despite being exposed to the heat of the explosion, and Holmes, after getting a key from one of the attending police guards, was able to remove them without difficulty. I noticed with admiration that Miss James did not flinch from the sight.

Handing the manacles to the guard, Holmes asked, "Have you removed the contents of the victim's pockets?"

"Yes, sir." The guard nodded toward a metal box beneath the gurney.

Holmes lifted the lid of the box and bent down to inspect its contents. "Billfold, pocket watch, coins, half-empty cigarette case, contents all slightly scorched, as one would expect. And . . . this."

He showed the guard a small object. "Can you tell me which pocket this was taken from?"

"It was in his waistcoat pocket, along with his pocket watch."

"Thank you." He handed the object to the Commissioner, and in the light of the streetlamp I could see it was a small glass vial with a cork stopper. "Commissioner, I can assure you that it will be best if we retain this. It will have no value to the Clevering family, and it may have some bearing on this investigation."

"What is it?" asked the Commissioner.

Holmes looked at Miss James for a moment. "I believe it is the reason why Mr. Clevering's killer employed a bomb rather than a revolver." Holmes turned to the guard. "I must request that you say nothing of this to those who will soon arrive to claim the body." The guard having nodded respectfully, Holmes turned to the Commissioner. "Sir Edward, may we now proceed with a police coach?"

39. A WALK IN THE FOG

The young sergeant who was to be our driver gave Holmes a quizzical glance when he heard that our destination was 198 Piccadilly, barely a quarter mile away. But Holmes explained that we were going there in search of a woman who might very well be in need of medical assistance, and that the police coach might have to function as an ambulance on short notice. At this the young man drew himself up to attention. "I'm your man, sir. We have a first aid kit on board."

"We shall walk," Holmes said. "Please remain behind us and when we arrive, watch the entrance. The mist is turning to fog so you must keep a sharp lookout. If you see someone leaving in haste, stop him. Or her. Are you armed?"

"I have my revolver on board, sir. Fully loaded."

"Watson?"

I felt the reassuring weight of my own weapon in my coat pocket and nodded. "Mine is here, and I have a spare in my room upstairs. Would you like me to—"

"One will be sufficient. We shall have the element of surprise on our side."

The chill dampness in the November air seemed to cut through my coat as the three of us set out on Regent Street. I was grateful that the distance was short and that we would soon be at our destination, for better or worse. The mist, as Holmes had observed, was coming in from the Thames behind us. Holmes kept a brisk pace, and it was with some apprehension that I saw Miss James fall in beside me, her black woolen shawl drawn tight beneath her chin, her lovely young features set in a determined frown. Was it wise, I wondered, to allow her to come with us, and subject her to the peril that could lie ahead? But I dismissed the thought. Holmes had made that decision once before, at Miss James's insistence, when we had entered the flat at 198 Piccadilly less than twenty-four hours earlier. No doubt he had once again weighed all the considerations.

After a time I noticed Holmes was farther ahead of us than when we had begun, and called out for him to slow down lest the sergeant following in the coach lose us in the thickening fog.

Holmes stopped immediately. "Quite right, Watson. Your warning is most sensible."

"You think Colonel Moran is waiting for us?" asked Miss James.

"Quite possibly. Although the fog may hamper the use of his customary air gun."

As we reached Jermyn Street, the fog enveloped the light from the streetlamps. By the time we turned left on Piccadilly our view of the doors to the shops and other buildings was all but obscured. The streets were deserted, for this was a section of London in which the fashionable shops had long since closed their doors, after the Whitehall workforce had gone home for their evening's rest. We kept close to the facade, in order to see the street numbers, but this of course increased our distance from the street and the following police coach. I worried that the sergeant would have lost sight of us, until I heard the steady clip clop of his horse's steel-shod hooves on the hard pavement. As we passed the dark recess of the St. James Church courtyard my fretful mind turned to the possibility that our search, even if we found Miss Rosario, would not lead us to Mr. Worth and his accomplices. Then Holmes would be accused of placing a personal relationship above matters of national importance. I recalled an ironic poem by Mr. Kipling, the gist of which was that we ordinary people frequently take an attitude of superiority to soldiers, until the shooting starts and we need them to protect us. The critics of Holmes, I thought, would not hesitate to turn on him if he failed in his mission.

My fatigued brain continued to swirl with these pessimistic and most unprofitable thoughts, when I saw a plaque with the number 198 above a doorway just ahead. I realized, with a shock, that the door was ajar, and my heart began to pound as I saw the door open wider.

Holmes saw it, too, for he held up his hand, motioning Miss James to step back. She did so instantly, and I drew my revolver.

In the next moment a burly figure emerged. Standing well back, out of the man's line of vision, Holmes let him step out onto the pavement. The man then turned, bending to lock the door behind him.

Holmes said, "Mr. James Blake, is it not?"

The man looked up and with a snarl of rage flung a ring of keys at Holmes. Then he leaped at me, hands outstretched for my revolver. In the fraction of a second that followed, I swung my revolver as hard as I could and hit him in the face. Blake shook off the blow and lunged forward, crashing into me, his hands trying to wrest the revolver from my grip. I struggled with him, trying to keep my feet beneath me and not be shoved off balance by his powerful frame.

Then I saw Holmes before me, pressing his revolver against Blake's temple. "Release him, Mr. Blake. Do not move, or the next impact to your head will be that of a bullet."

I covered Blake with my revolver while Holmes bent to search Blake's pockets. In a few moments Holmes had withdrawn and put away a revolver and a wickedly curved knife. "Most interesting," Holmes said as he tucked the knife into his coat. "I wonder if someone on Threadneedle Street will remember you as a visitor to Mr. Perkins at the Bank of England this morning."

By now the sergeant had dismounted from the police coach and was at Holmes's side, holding a pair of handcuffs. "Shall I do the honors, sir?"

"If you please. And take special care with this one, Sergeant. A nasty piece of business."

Blake twisted for a moment but I gestured with my pistol and he stood erect, glaring, his lips beginning to swell. I heard a metallic sound as the sergeant applied the cuffs and clicked the locking rod into place.

"I do thank you for providing us with these," said Holmes as he picked up Blake's key ring. "Sergeant, you may take him to the coach. Please guard him carefully."

"I'll keep him safe." The sergeant handed me a police whistle. "Just use this if you need me."

"But before you leave us, Blake," said Holmes, "where is Mr. Worth?"

Blake said nothing, but I saw his eyes flicker upward for a moment before he set his jaw and stared defiantly back at Holmes.

"Others will question you," said Holmes, "and they will have fewer scruples than I, particularly when interrogating traitors to our country. You should think about your alternatives as you wait for us."

Blake remained silent. The sergeant led him to the police coach and pushed him, none too gently, inside.

"Holmes, Worth is upstairs," I whispered.

Miss James added, "I saw Blake look up."

Holmes tried the door. Blake evidently had not finished locking it, for it opened noiselessly. Holding a finger to his lips, Holmes motioned us to come inside.

40. THE MORIARTY FAMILY

An electric sconce illuminated the stairway at each of the building's three levels. We quickly mounted the steps to the doorway of the flat we had entered some twelve hours earlier. Holmes produced the key ring. In the shadowy electric light of the hallway he was about to select a key to open the adjacent door when Miss James placed her hand on his wrist. "Look for a matched pair," she said quietly. "If there is a connection between the flats, the keys to each will likely have been made by the same manufacturer."

Holmes smiled appreciatively. "Quite right. And if there is a connecting flat, Mr. Blake would have possessed a key to it."

But Holmes probed the locks of the other two flats on that floor with all the keys on the ring, to no avail. We then walked up the remaining flight of stairs. Holmes paused before the doorway positioned directly above the one we had entered. "This is a Chubb lock, and so is the lock on the door directly below us." He gestured at the bottom of the door and the small dark gap above the threshold. "Someone is inside," he said, his voice barely audible.

"I see nothing."

"That is how I know someone is there."

I nearly expressed my exasperation, but Lucy put her hand on my arm, held a finger to her lips, and whispered, "We saw a light in the window when we were on the sidewalk. Someone must have switched it off."

On Holmes's second attempt the key turned noiselessly in the lock. Holmes eased the door open a crack. I saw only darkness inside.

I drew my revolver and looked to Holmes for guidance. In answer, he nodded at my revolver and eased the door open another inch or two.

At that moment, the lights of the room flashed on, the door was jerked open, and before us stood Adam Worth, training a double-barreled shotgun on Holmes's midsection.

He spoke in that same harshly intrusive voice we had heard in D'Oyly Carte's office.

"No one moves, or Holmes dies."

We froze. Then a woman stepped from behind the door. She, too, had a shotgun, which she leveled at Miss James's face.

"Now, Dr. Watson," Worth said. "Kindly set your revolver down on the floor and kick it very gently toward me. Very gently."

I caught a warning glance from Holmes, nodded slightly, and did as instructed, whereupon Worth motioned the three of us to step inside. We did, and I recognized the woman as the costumer and makeup artist we had seen earlier that afternoon at the Savoy Theatre. After taking the ring of keys from Holmes she locked the door behind us. Then, still brandishing the shotgun, she moved to stand on the other side of Holmes, yet at such an angle that would enable her to shoot either Holmes or Miss James without endangering Worth.

"Mr. Holmes. Allow me to introduce my daughter, Cleo James. You have already met my son, James Blake, and my niece, Miss James, whom you have brought with you this evening for a purpose that I shall soon discover. You may already have deduced that Cleo, James, and Lucy are all three named in honor of my late brother, James Moriarty."

"*Honor* is hardly an appropriate term to associate with that name," replied Holmes.

"We shall not debate, Mr. Holmes, though I am sure you would like to distract and delay me with your quibbling. And even you will concede the futility of changing my opinion of my late brother. Certainly you, Dr. Watson, must understand the strength of my feelings, for you mentioned my letters defending my brother's honor in your abominably distorted account of his passing in Switzerland."

"Where is Miss Rosario?" said Holmes.

"She is in the next room, securely bound and gagged. As you and Dr. Watson soon will be. If you do not cooperate, the four of you will die." Worth's tone of voice was as matter-of-fact as if he were discussing tomorrow's weather.

"What is it you want?"

"My son Blake, of course."

"You were watching."

"The fog obscured your identities. I could have shot you from the balcony, but that would have called attention to this flat, which I did not realize you knew about until you entered. How did you learn of it, by the way? Clevering could not have told you, for he did not know of its existence."

"The banker Perkins kept a hidden diary. Whoever cut his throat failed to discover it."

At this remark I saw Worth dart an angry glance at Cleo. When she gave an apologetic shrug in return, the identity of Perkins's murderer was confirmed. Holmes saw it, too, for he said, "Ah, Miss Cleo. I see that you share your family's lethal propensities. You also were involved in the untimely end of the unfortunate Mr. Foster. You kept Mr. Foster's attention focused on your fascinating features and conversation, enabling your brother to take him from behind. Your costume must have been so alluring that he did not even notice the odor of chloroform."

"We heard all about your fanciful theories from Mr. Clevering," said Cleo smugly.

Holmes continued, speaking amiably, and the movement of his right hand toward his coat pocket was barely perceptible. "So when you learned Mr. Foster had seen what you were constructing at the Savoy, you lured him to your carriage house in Clapham Common."

Cleo smiled more broadly and looked positively triumphant. "Another theory, and it only proves you know nothing about Mr. Foster."

"Here, now, that's enough chatter." Worth gestured menacingly with the shotgun. He held it left-handed, favoring, I supposed, his good shoulder, and I wondered momentarily if we could somehow turn that infirmity to our advantage. "And keep your hands steady, Mr. Holmes, there's a good fellow. Cleo, search Mr. Holmes's pockets."

Cleo soon had extracted Blake's revolver and knife, along with the policeman's whistle the sergeant had given us. Worth smiled as Cleo laid the weapons on the couch. "You are so unlike my brother, Mr. Holmes. He was a master of delegating the various tasks that our organization required. You, however, insist on doing everything yourself. My brother never found it necessary to carry weapons."

"And like him, you employ others to murder for you," replied Holmes.

"Mr. Holmes, I begin to lose patience with you. I take it that this whistle is to be used to signal your policeman friend?"

"Your identities are known," Holmes replied. "You and Colonel Moran will not live to spend the payment Perkins received via the German embassy. You will be hunted down and brought to justice on the gallows."

"I have taken other identities before. A million pounds sterling buys a great deal of influence and anonymity. You will be remembered as a spectacular failure. My brother will look down on your humiliation and smile."

"Your brother is in Hell, where you will soon join him."

Worth shrugged. "Until then I shall be enjoying myself in San Francisco or Johannesburg under another name. Now, Cleo and I must go to free my son, and I would prefer not to alarm the policeman guarding him with the noise of our shotguns. Of course if you choose not to cooperate, you can die here, and possibly be remembered as a martyr. But I think you will choose life, because you do not wish to watch Dr. Watson and Miss Rosario in the agonies of a painful death. Also I am sure you are vain enough to think that you may be able to escape and somehow prevent Colonel Moran from carrying out my orders."

"You allow me to live now, and yet you engaged men to kill me and Dr. Watson at Dartmoor."

Worth gave a small, self-satisfied smile. "I have recently changed my plans."

"What about Miss James?"

"As my niece, she is welcome to join me when we leave the country. Provided, of course, that she can give me a satisfactory explanation for her presence here." Worth's voice turned silken, which made it even more menacing. "Lucy, how do you happen to be in the company of Mr. Holmes and Dr. Watson this evening?"

Lucy's eyelids fluttered. Then her jaw slackened, her knees buckled, and with a shudder, she sank to the floor, apparently unconscious.

Involuntarily I took a step forward to assist her, but Worth's voice stopped me.

"No, Dr. Watson. Or Cleo shoots Mr. Holmes. You and he will kneel." He pocketed the police whistle that Cleo had placed on the table. Then he trained his gun on me. "I said *kneel*, Dr. Watson."

"Do as he says, Watson."

I knelt. Holmes did likewise.

"Cleo, use the cords from these drapes and tie the three of them together."

She cut the cords with the curved knife. As she tied us, she showed her teeth in a twisted smile of mockery. Triumph glittered in her coal-black eyes.

Worth stood directly before us, his shotgun still at the ready. "Now, gentlemen. As I said, the fog obscured your identities, so I did not see which of you struck my son. Each of you will therefore pay the penalty."

Whereupon he grasped the shotgun by the barrel and swung it like a club. The wooden stock smashed into the side of Holmes's face. Holmes took the blow in stoic silence. Before I could move, Worth turned to me and, smiling broadly, delivered a similar blow. In a blinding flash of pain I felt myself toppling onto my side. I heard Worth's voice.

"Now, Cleo, fetch three hand towels and gag them. Mr. Holmes, these relatively gentle measures will delay you long enough for me to continue with my plans. I look forward to our next meeting. At that time you will feel pain considerably greater than what you have just experienced."

41. A CALL FOR ASSISTANCE

About five minutes after Worth and Cleo had departed, the three of us were struggling with our bonds. My jaw throbbed, but the pain had none of the sharpness or intensity that would have indicated broken bones. I hoped Holmes had fared similarly well.

Lucy was the first to free her hands. She quickly removed the towel that had gagged her. "I saw him hit you both," she said, her fingers now busy undoing the towel from Holmes's face. "Are you all right?"

Holmes nodded. "Thank you, Lucy."

"Worth is a coward." She undid the cords from Holmes's wrists. "I didn't know how to answer him, so I pretended to faint. I guess I was convincing enough."

Soon Holmes and I were both free. Holmes went to the balcony window. "The police coach is gone," he said. "They have taken the young sergeant."

"Why has he allowed us to escape?" I asked.

"He is toying with us, Watson," Holmes replied.

"Letting us go, the way a cat plays with a mouse," said Lucy grimly.

We found Miss Rosario in the adjoining room. She lay on a single bed, blinking her eyes and twisting as Lucy turned on the electric light. In a moment, Holmes removed the hand towel that had gagged her and set to work loosening the cords that bound her wrists and ankles. She asked for water. Lucy went to the kitchen to fill a glass. Shortly after, we were relieved to see Miss Rosario sit up, take a few sips and then a long drink. She appeared alert, but confused.

"I have no recollection of how I came to be here," she said. "But I am grateful that you came to rescue me. I heard voices—are you all unhurt?"

Holmes nodded. "Do you think you can stand up?"

"I think so." She looked at me somewhat dazedly. "One minute I was with you, and about to fetch my violin from its cabinet, and the next . . . I was here." She shrugged. "I have been awake for some time, but I have no recollection. A mystery."

"But not insoluble," said Holmes. "Can you recall anything at all from when you were in your flat? Something in the air, perhaps?"

Her beautiful dark eyes widened in recognition. "There was a strange odor. Dust or smoke. Then something wet, clapped over my mouth and nostrils."

"There is still dust on your forehead," said Holmes. He took from his waistcoat pocket the small vial we had obtained from Clevering's possessions, drew out the cork, and held the open vial up to where Miss Rosario could catch the scent.

"That is the odor I recall from this morning," she said. "What is it?"

"A South American herb known as Devil's breath, or hyoscine. It induces a temporary amnesia. Native tribes use it in their religious rituals." He turned to me. "I believe Mr. Clevering was employing it to keep his superior minister in a state of incompetence, so that he could act as his replacement and attend certain high-level government meetings."

"So that is why he traveled to Bowood each day," I said, as the realization set in. "And Clevering's murderer knew that he carried the vial with him. He used a bomb rather than a gun in hopes of destroying that vial and preventing the police from learning how Lord Lansdowne had been manipulated."

"The effects are quite temporary." Holmes looked reassuringly at Miss Rosario. "You were also injected with a sedative, or forced to drink one. But since that has clearly worn off and you are awake, you should be able to come with us."

"But why were you taken in the first place?" asked Lucy. "Can you remember anything they said?"

"Perhaps later I will be able to recall something useful."

Holmes's voice took on a note of urgency. "We need a police coach to take us to a place of safety. Also, we must have a warrant issued for the arrest of Worth, Blake, and Cleo on charges of kidnapping and murder. Watson, can you please determine if there is a telephone here? If there is, please call Scotland Yard and arrange for them to send a police coach as quickly as possible. We cannot stay here long, and I do not want the four of us to be walking unarmed in the fog." He gave a glance at the doorway and continued, "Colonel Moran may be nearby, in the flat connected to this one. While you make the arrangements, I shall remain here with Miss Rosario and Miss James."

I found the telephone in a cramped little alcove built for the purpose into a small room that was lined with shelves and leather-bound books and contained a desk and two small chairs. There were no papers on the desk, only an inkwell and an ink-stained blotter. I was sorely tempted to go through the desk drawers, for I believed the room was Worth's office and I thought it possible Worth might have left some clue as to his operations. But time was short. We needed to alert the police to the events that had occurred.

I rang the Diogenes Club, hoping that the Commissioner was still there. There was no response. Then it took me several minutes to reach the duty officer at Scotland Yard, and several more until I was able to convince them to send help.

Shortly afterward we waited together for the police coach to arrive. Miss Rosario sat beside Lucy. I was grateful to see that she appeared stronger and more alert, although she leaned against Lucy for support.

Miss Rosario said, "I have remembered something. I was just awakening in the room where you found me, not long before you arrived. Mr. Worth was talking to a man he called Blake. They were discussing how they would send a message to you—a note, giving the location where I was being held and demanding that you go there if you wanted to see me alive."

"Was the location here?"

"They said something about a carriage house."

"They wanted you to go back to Clapham Common," I said, "where they could kill you as they did Foster."

"More likely they wanted to hold me prisoner there."

"And then savor your humiliation, after they had completed their mission. You heard Worth say he wanted you to be remembered as a spectacular failure."

"He also said he had recently changed his mind," said Lucy. "So the plan to humiliate you was not part of his original scheme."

Holmes nodded. "I am not so vain as to suppose my humiliation would have a value of one million pounds sterling. Yet Worth has added this personal touch, which demonstrates his strong desire to avenge his brother. Let us hope that we can somehow use his emotional attachment to our advantage." Then he turned to Miss Rosario. "They were watching when I visited you Sunday night. They saw me take you away. They followed us to the Diogenes Club. They knew you would return to your flat for your violin. Seeing us together, they deduced that you were . . . important to me."

"So was I to be the bait for a trap?" she asked.

Whatever response Holmes would have made to this observation was lost, for at that moment came the sound of a police whistle. Looking down from the balcony we saw the fog had begun to clear. A police coach was coming to a stop outside.

42. A MATTER OF HONOR

After a brief ride in the police coach we stopped and Holmes asked me to get out. I did so, immediately feeling a strong wind from the north. The fog had vanished. I realized that we had stopped on Pall Mall just opposite the Diogenes Club. Before us were several tall residential buildings, their white limestone facades gleaming cold and austere in the light of a nearly full moon.

Holmes climbed down to stand beside me and drew a key from his pocket. "This is Mycroft's building. His rooms are on the second floor. We had best not bring the ladies to the Diogenes Club, since we know Moran has already struck there. It would likewise be foolish to risk the half hour's drive through the dangerous side streets of the Docklands in order to take them to Mr. Rockefeller's yacht. But we must find a safe haven where Miss Rosario and Miss James can rest and recover."

He handed me the key and continued, "Please open Mycroft's outer door as soon as you see the ladies step out of the coach. We can then all mount the stairs and explain the situation to Mycroft. He will understand the need for his immediate hospitality."

So it was that I approached the heavy black-painted door to Mycroft's building, my memory going back to the predawn incursion Mycroft had made on our Baker Street rooms less than three days before, and thinking that now we were about to return the favor. Then I heard a familiar, youthful voice call, "Dr. Watson!" I turned and saw young Mr. Rockefeller running at full speed toward me across Pall Mall.

He drew up beside me, his breath coming in frosty clouds after his exertion. "Have you seen Lucy? She said she was coming to the Diogenes Club but she is not there. Mother is quite worried."

Then Holmes was beside us. "We need to be mindful of the dangers of moonlight, Mr. Rockefeller. We can escort the ladies as soon as Dr. Watson has opened this door."

Soon the five of us had mounted the wide, carpeted stairs of a luxuriously appointed entry hall, and I was knocking at the dark-stained heavy oaken door to the second-floor flat.

There was no response. "Mycroft," said Holmes. "Are you there?"

From within came Mycroft's cheery voice. "Where else would I be at this hour?"

The door opened, and Mycroft stood before us, a red silk smoking jacket wrapped over the wide expanse of his evening shirt and white tie. We were quickly ushered into his spacious sitting room. Electric lights on the wall and ceiling revealed comfortable leather furniture as inviting as any of the chairs at the Diogenes Club. Glancing around the room I saw dark green walls hung with landscapes and other memorabilia, and five chessboards lined up on a long side table, each evidencing different stages of play. Beside each lay an opened letter neatly clipped to a mailing envelope. I also caught the scent of a rather sweet cigar, which was puzzling, since no one in the room was smoking and I did not recall Mycroft ever having indulged in the habit.

Mycroft greeted Miss James and young Mr. Rockefeller by name and nodded respectfully to Miss Rosario. "Well done, Sherlock," he said. "I take it this is Miss Rosario? Madam, you are most welcome here. Would you ladies please be seated on the sofa? I perceive you are in need of sustenance, Miss Rosario." He turned to a young and extremely competent-looking man who had appeared behind him. "This is Stamford, my valet. He will bring scones and tea with plenty of cream."

A very short while later we had all been served and Miss Rosario, looking far more comfortable, thanked Mycroft for his hospitality. Mycroft continued, "I have another unexpected guest this evening." Raising his voice slightly, he continued, "Richard, will you please join us? I believe you know all these people."

Whereupon we saw gliding in from the adjacent library, holding a lit cigar and wearing his customary evening wear, Richard D'Oyly Carte.

Carte looked quite as self-possessed and assured as he had in his office Friday night. "Mr. Holmes and Dr. Watson! And Miss James and Miss Rosario. And the name of this young gentleman is . . ."

"John Rockefeller Jr., at your service."

"Of course, and what a coincidence!" Carte shook young Rockefeller's proffered hand. "Young man, I came here because your father telephoned me! He was concerned about the security at our performance tomorrow evening, and he worried that Miss James had gone missing." Carte turned to Holmes with a smile. "But she is clearly safe, thanks no doubt to you, Mr. Holmes. Perhaps you can reassure me that Mr. Rockefeller—Senior—has no cause for concern?"

"To the contrary. He and all who attend the meeting are in danger. As are you and your troupe."

Carte took several rapid puffs on his cigar. "Mr. Holmes, I thank you for your candor. However, before we continue, I cannot help but observe that two of my most important performers are here with us at a late hour and in what must be a state of fatigue. If there is a telephone here, I should like to summon a carriage from the Savoy to take both these ladies to wherever they choose to rest for the night. Each of you is welcome to stay at the Savoy as my personal guest."

"I should not advise staying at the Savoy," Holmes said. "Mr. Worth has managed to place two of his associates in the Savoy organization."

"Who?" Carte asked.

Holmes went on. "James Blake and Cleo James. This evening, Mr. Worth introduced them as his son and daughter. They are both murderers."

At this, Carte's dark eyes widened. "And they both know about the performance tomorrow night."

"They do."

"But not where it will take place. Even I do not know that."

"You will be told soon, however, and the set and costumes that now are located on the *Shamrock* will have to be moved to the new location. When that move takes place it will be observed by whomever Worth has assigned to the task."

Carte put his hand on the settee to support himself. "I am appalled. I feel responsible." He shook his head. "This is what comes of being overextended and therefore too willing to accept investment capital. But who would have thought—never mind, it is no good making excuses. I *am* responsible, and I cannot allow my company to be used in a way that could endanger my performers, let alone our national leaders! Tomorrow's performance will not take place. We will find an excuse. The influenza, perhaps—"

Lucy spoke up. "I have another idea, Mr. Carte. You gave me the leading role at the direction of Mr. Worth, did you not? I believe his family pride was his motive for elevating me, and it might really get his dander up if he were to read how much I loathe his brother. Could we get that into the newspapers? If he saw it, he might make a mistake."

Holmes held up his hand. "Thank you, Lucy. You are very brave, but I cannot deliberately expose you to danger."

The room fell silent. We all looked to Holmes as he continued. "Mr. Rockefeller, Mr. Morgan, and Mr. Carnegie must be invited to join the Prime Minister's committee. At our meeting tomorrow morning we must tell them the truth."

"Others may disagree with you, Sherlock," said Mycroft.

"Let them," Holmes replied. "Making our allies aware of the perils that confront us is the only way for our nation to retain its honor. But now the hour grows intolerably late and we must find shelter for Miss Rosario and Miss James. Mycroft, I propose that you leave your two bedrooms to them and that the rest of us spend the hours that remain until tomorrow morning at the Diogenes Club."

43. ON THE FIFTH OF NOVEMBER

At nine o'clock the next morning we reached Rockefeller's *White Star* liner. Once outside our coach, we were immediately buffeted by a powerful western wind that chilled my very bones and exacerbated my sense of foreboding. What would Holmes say to our nation's leaders, and what would be the consequences, both to our nation and to him? These and similar worries filled my thoughts as Holmes, Mycroft, and I came on board accompanied by a Pinkerton guard, who escorted us down to a lower deck to stand before the PM's committee.

The five members were seated at the round captain's table in the magnificent high-ceilinged first-class dining saloon, with Lord Lansdowne in the place formerly occupied by Clevering, his assistant. Carnegie, we had been told, had been delayed, but Rockefeller Sr. and J. P. Morgan sat somberly on either side of the Prime Minister, directly facing us. There were three vacant spaces on our side of the table, without chairs. Lord Salisbury gave no indication that we were to join the group at the table. He sat at the center, ashen-faced, and I noticed he fingered the curls of his flowing beard as he spoke.

"Mr. Holmes, you are here at the invitation of Mr. Rockefeller and Mr. Morgan. They both telephoned me very early this morning to request that all of us meet here to discuss security arrangements for the conference that has brought them to London. They are aware of certain events that occurred last night, involving a bomb at the Diogenes Club. They refuse to divulge the source of their information."

Baron Halsbury, the Lord Chancellor, held up his hand. "If I may, Prime Minister." He was seated closest to us on Morgan's side of the table, and as he continued, his pug-like features were set even more firmly in the dour frown he had exhibited at our first meeting with the committee at St. Thomas Hospital. "The position of Mr. Rockefeller and Mr. Morgan notwithstanding, however, it is my duty to inform you, Mr. Holmes, that the Official Secrets Act governs anything you may have said to either of these gentlemen, and that the penalties—"

"Oh, to hell with your penalties, Stanley," Morgan interrupted. His florid, choleric features glowed with indignation and his lightning-eyed gaze seemed to overpower the room with the sheer forcefulness of his personality. He turned to Lord Salisbury. "Robert, if you want John D. and me to stay, you had better let us get down to the business at hand, namely whether all our lives are truly at stake here, and what can be done about it."

There was an awkward silence, and then Lord Lansdowne leaned forward. His high, dome-like forehead bore a waxy pallor, but there was a determined earnestness in his wide, brown eyes, as if he were prepared to do the right thing at any personal cost. "Gentlemen," he said, "the responsibility for any risk to our lives is mine, since my late assistant created the danger with his treachery. I am most grateful to Mr. Holmes for discovering the cause of the incapacity that allowed Mr. Clevering to attend meetings of this committee in my place. The knowledge has been a great relief to me and to my wife. I for one should be greatly distressed were Mr.

Holmes to receive anything but praise from this committee for the energy and acumen he has employed thus far on our behalf."

Goschen and the Commissioner nodded their assent. The PM was about to speak, but Mr. Rockefeller cut him off. "Mr. Holmes," he said blandly, with no indication that Holmes and he had ever met, "I understand you are in charge of security."

"I have been asked to advise—"

"Do you have a plan, sir?"

"I have a course of action to recommend."

"I expected no less. What do you recommend?"

"I recommend that 'sources in the government' announce to the press that Mr. Rockefeller and Mr. Morgan and Mr. Carnegie have come to London for a conference, but in light of certain pressing matters in America they must return home at once."

"Call off the conference?" Goschen said, his voice rising.

"No, sir. *Announce* that you have called off the conference."

"What precisely will that achieve?"

"Mr. Worth will believe that he has attained his objective. He will go to the banker who has the bearer bonds—"

Chancellor Halsbury interrupted, "Mr. Holmes, I must protest. You are disclosing confidential—"

"Balderdash," said the Prime Minister. "Go on, Mr. Holmes."

"He will go to the banker from whom he expects payment. We can place watchmen at as many of the banks as could possibly be involved, and, if we are fortunate, we will apprehend both Worth and his paymaster. From this we may confirm whether or not the Germans are behind this affair."

"What makes you think we will succeed?"

"We may or may not capture Worth, but we will succeed in preserving your lives. The meeting that is no longer secret due to the traitorous disclosure of the late Mr. Clevering can vanish. Your next meeting can be secret, indeed. You can meet at another place. All that is needed is for the *White Star* and the *Corsair* to depart

London Harbor, giving the impression that their masters are on board."

"I like it," said Morgan. "When Carnegie arrives, we can all sail on the *Corsair*. I'll wager we'll have an agreement before we reach Southampton. But I want Mr. Carte's troupe to perform on the *Corsair* tonight. All the arrangements have been made."

"Does Mr. Carte know the location?"

"I told Carte I thought a performance on shipboard might be an amusing novelty. But I did not say where."

"He has rehearsed his troupe on the *Shamrock*, the smaller vessel docked between this one and yours."

"Well, that shows foresight."

Holmes refused to be distracted. "Two of Mr. Worth's associates were part of the D'Oyly Carte Troupe until last evening. They witnessed the rehearsal on the *Shamrock*. Worth will have others watching the docks. If the performance is to be on the *Corsair*, they will know, and you will not be safe. You *must* postpone your evening's entertainment."

"Oh, come now, Mr. Holmes," said Chancellor Halsbury. "Are we to turn our tails and run at the threat of a few criminals, when we have an army and a navy at our disposal?"

"I believe these criminals have in their possession more than a ton of stolen dynamite."

"And your evidence for this belief is what, precisely?"

Holmes was silent.

"Gentlemen, I propose a compromise," said Lansdowne. "We shall carry on as previously arranged, but the conference will be under the guard of the Pinkertons and a thousand men from the various branches of the British military—under my command. Does that satisfy you?"

Rockefeller and Morgan nodded, as if being the object of such grandiose arrangements was for them an everyday occurrence.

Holmes remained silent.

44. RETURN TO THE *SHAMROCK*

Shortly thereafter Holmes and I climbed the staircase from the dining saloon to the boat deck in silence. As we reached the daylight at the top, Holmes spoke.

"They are willfully blind, Watson. None of them can bear to look weak in front of the others."

I took in the bracing chill of the November wind, the scents of the tobacco, grain, fish, and other cargo that daily passed through the great harbor, and the sheer scale of the vista surrounding the wide, glittering gray waters of the Thames. I tried to buck up Holmes's spirits.

"At least there will be additional security forces."

"Our leaders and the Americans imagine that there is safety in numbers. That reaction is entirely foreseeable, and therefore Mr. Worth has foreseen it."

The pale November sun had just begun to rise above the gigantic brick warehouse structures that faced us from across the quay. I had the lonely sensation that Holmes and I were indeed on our own.

The *Corsair* had docked immediately beside the *White Star* on our right. The ship had been in the shadows when we had first arrived just before sunrise, but now it was plainly visible. Though smaller than the *White Star*, it had a more dashing look, a proud air of command. Beneath its steeply raked black smokestack, which gleamed as though freshly painted, its brass rails and polished wood deck and trim seemed to exude a superiority that defied the elements and, by implication, any man foolish enough to challenge the House of Morgan.

Holmes noted my fascination. "Yes, Watson. A most imposing vessel, and we shall board her soon enough. But at present we must turn our attentions to the *Shamrock*."

From our elevated position on the boat deck of the *White Star*, I looked past the *Corsair* to where the *Shamrock* lay docked, some fifty yards up the quay. Before her bow, several carriages and cabs had lined up and were discharging their passengers. Beside one of the cabs we saw Miss Rosario and Miss James, with young Mr. Rockefeller, who had escorted them to their morning rehearsal as Holmes had requested.

We strode purposefully toward them along the quay, but before we had reached the halfway point the two ladies turned away from young Mr. Rockefeller and walked up the gangplank to board the *Shamrock*. Young Mr. Rockefeller turned his back on them and, hands in pockets, shoulders hunched, walked in our direction with downcast eyes. As we drew closer I could see that his face was deeply flushed.

"Good morning," said Holmes as we came within a few paces.

He looked up, startled. "Mr. Holmes. Dr. Watson. Forgive my inattention. I have brought the ladies from your brother's flat to their rehearsal. If you will tell me how I can be useful to you, I will be very grateful."

"We are about to organize a search of the *Shamrock*," said Holmes.

"Then I'll join you there soon. I just want to reassure my mother that everyone is safe." And with a polite nod, he turned and continued his walk toward the *White Star*. On the wide quay, with the massive brick warehouses rising up darkly on his right and the two imposing steamships towering above him on his left, Johnny appeared quite solitary and vulnerable.

"Holmes, did young Mr. Rockefeller seem upset to you?"

"Youth can be a difficult advantage to bear," said Holmes.

45. LUCY MAKES AN OFFER

"Well, he practically proposed to me!" said Lucy. "After all that folderol about wanting to make that senator's daughter jealous, he just up and changes his mind—"

She broke off, shaking her lovely head in frustration. We were with Zoe on the boat deck of the *Shamrock*, the four of us huddled at the stern, looking out over the wide, dark waters of the Thames and the many small craft that plied their trade amid the larger vessels, like small fish following greater ones. Behind us members of the chorus and orchestra waited while Carte's crew arranged chairs for the orchestra and, behind them, the props and stage backdrops that had been put away overnight. Holmes, I knew, was eager to begin the inspection, but his gaze never wavered from Lucy's face as he asked, "What did he say to you? Try to recollect his words as precisely as you can."

"He said I was a really good sport for going along with his idea to stir up the rumors. He said that he had never felt so alive as when we were together. He said he wanted us to be together after this was all over. He said he could find some way to arrange that."

"What did you say to him?"

"The truth. That he is still a college boy. That it's way too soon to think about such things. Then I laid it on a little bit. I said his destiny was to carry on what his father had begun, and . . . well, that I needed to have my own destiny." She gave an ironic smile. "I was being polite, actually. What I wanted to do was say, 'So you think I'll be overjoyed by your fickle flip-flopping, just because you're a Rockefeller?' But I didn't want to hurt him. He looked pretty done up, though, all the same, so I suppose I did."

Miss Rosario stood at Lucy's side. "Loving someone and not wanting to cause hurt are very different things," she said kindly. "And even a young millionaire cannot expect to go through life without experiencing pain. Young Mr. Rockefeller will get over you soon enough, if you are willing to let him."

Holmes's gaze shifted from Lucy to Zoe, and then back. "Johnny may want to convince you," Holmes said, "as long as the two of you are in London. Even if he is fickle, he also has his pride."

"I'll just stay away from him. I have plenty else to do. Speaking of which, Mother, rehearsal is about to start."

She turned and was about to go when Zoe pressed a letter into Holmes's hand. "This was delivered a few moments ago. The stage manager gave it to me as we were coming on board."

Holmes opened the letter. I had a glimpse of Zoe's name written in crudely printed block letters in black ink. Holmes read aloud, "'If you wish to recover your Stradivarius, come alone to your flat.'"

"I don't want to go."

"This is an obvious trap, or, more likely, a distraction. We shall ignore this message. Better yet, we can send police to your flat."

Zoe nodded. "But Sherlock, you defeated this man's brother, and it nearly cost you your life. Now Worth has had years to plan his revenge, and he has told you as much. I hope you will not underestimate him."

Holmes smiled briefly. "That would be unreasonable."

"I could shoot him," said Lucy. As the wind lifted her wide-brimmed hat, she secured it and held it firmly, all in one easy, graceful movement. "I could leave a message for him at the Savoy, ask him to meet me at the restaurant—" She broke off. "But there isn't time, is there? And he's not going to show himself now."

I could see that Lucy's youthful bravado was causing discomfort to Holmes as well as to Miss Rosario. Each of them looked ready to reply sharply, but at that moment came the stage manager's call for the actors and musicians to take their places on the set.

46. A FRUITLESS SEARCH

Shortly afterward, Lestrade strode up the gangplank with a bright-eyed naval officer on either side of him. After he introduced us, Lestrade explained that each officer had a dozen able seamen under his command, and that they would arrive in a few minutes to inspect all decks of the *Shamrock*.

"We will also need two skiffs," said Holmes.

"Skiffs, sir?"

"Each with a long-poled gaff, to be scraped along the hull of the *Shamrock*. The entire length, mind you. We want no hidden lines dangling in the water, ready to pull up some submerged weapon or ammunition."

The Navy men regarded Holmes with new respect, and the older of the two said, "I'll see to it, sir."

"Also, throughout the interior of the ship, pay particular regard to any new wood construction. Sawdust was found in two areas frequented by those who are suspected of this planned attack. Pay particular attention to elements of the stage set that are to be moved to the *Corsair*. Any areas where a bomb or a weapon or a man could be concealed should be gone over thoroughly. Also, the

coal from the ship's hold should be moved to ensure that no dynamite has been buried beneath it. Any wires or electrical apparatus
should be traced to the source and their functions determined to
be innocent."

The Navy men set off to make their arrangements. Holmes
showed Lestrade the crudely printed note. Lestrade agreed to send
two policemen to Zoe's flat. Then Holmes said, "Now, Inspector, I
have a favor to ask."

Lestrade's ferret-like features took on even more of a guarded
look.

"I need to know as much as I can about an unfortunate
prison guard named Asher, who died near Dartmoor last week.
I telegraphed the Commissioner Sunday asking him to make the
request of the prison, knowing the prison would respond far more
rapidly if the request was made in an official capacity. The report
may already have come to the Commissioner's office and been
buried among all his other messages. But I need that report. It may
lead to an arrest of extreme importance."

"You want me to find a report?"

"Or communicate directly with Dartmoor if needed. Get me
that information, Inspector. It could be a matter of life and death."

"I'll see to it, then."

Lestrade departed. Within the hour the two skiffs arrived, and
each circumnavigated the *Shamrock* twice, finding no ropes or
lines of any sort other than those securing the vessel to the dock.
Examination of the stage set revealed that the platform for the garden scene in the second act had, at its base, three large steps, and
this elevation provided enough space beneath the platform to conceal several men. Moreover, a hinged panel facing the center of the
stage had been newly constructed and installed. Holmes spoke to
Carte, and we learned the hinged panel served no useful purpose
in the performance. Holmes ordered the panel to be nailed shut,
which was done immediately.

At about one o'clock the Commissioner arrived. The troupe, with Lucy and Zoe, had just repaired to the *Shamrock* dining saloon for a buffet luncheon provided by Carte. Holmes informed the Commissioner of our progress. Sir Edward frowned. "Do you think this crawl space you discovered beneath the garden platform was a threat?"

Holmes shook his head. "Almost certainly not. It is too obvious. And impractical—they would have to bring an assassin on board, with his weapons."

I saw a danger. "The actors are in costume, with makeup. Many of them wear robes, where a weapon might be concealed."

"Thank you, Watson. We must make certain that Carte is present to identify every actor who comes on board. All the costumes must be also inspected."

The Commissioner looked thoughtful. "Of course we must do that, and every other precaution we can think of. Yet the more our inspection uncovers, and the more precautions we implement, the more secure the committee will feel, and the more likely they will want to go on with tonight's performance as planned."

The strain of the past few days was evident on Holmes's features as he lit his pipe. "So we must look to the *Corsair*."

47. MR. MORGAN'S DEMAND

Morgan received us in his private study, a spacious dark-paneled chamber at the stern of the *Corsair* that took up the entire width of the vessel, with portholes on all three walls. Dismissing the attendant who had brought us to the door, he ushered us in, nodding at a grouping of comfortable chairs and a sofa upholstered in brass-studded leather. "We'll sit over here," he said casually. "Now, you should know I want an agreement to build and operate three naval seaports and I want it by tomorrow noon. So I need you to guarantee our safety for"—he made a show of consulting his watch in the light of an ornate brass electric floor lamp styled as a Grecian column—"less than twenty-three hours. Can you accomplish that?"

The three of us sat down. "If the *Corsair* remains where she is presently docked," Holmes replied affably, "I must say that I cannot. But if you will sail for Southampton—"

"We can set sail after Carnegie arrives and Carte's troupe finishes their performance."

"I fail to grasp why Carte's troupe is essential to the success of a negotiation regarding naval ports."

Morgan leaned forward. "Because we are all accustomed to overzealous security men—not to say that you're of their number, Mr. Holmes, but you must realize that if we changed our plans every time somebody threatened us, none of us would accomplish a damn thing. Every day we all evaluate our own risks and make our own decisions." His tone softened, and he shrugged. "I know you mean well, Mr. Holmes. I know there's a lot to indicate that this Worth fellow is mixed up in this and that his brother nearly killed you. But there's no evidence that he can defeat the British Army and Navy in their own backyard. Bring us some new evidence, though, and we may change our minds. We're not stupid."

"I understand," said Holmes. "Now, I had understood arrangements had been made for you to meet at the Bank of England."

"Rockefeller was looking into that. But only as an alternative. From the time this conference was first conceived six months ago, the understanding has been that we would meet on the *Corsair*."

"Did the Prime Minister know this?"

"Of course. So did Lansdowne and Goschen. I've had very successful experience getting powerful men to settle their disputes here on the *Corsair*," Morgan said, as though remembering past triumphs. Then he frowned. "Hang it all, Holmes, what difference does it make?"

Holmes seemed lost in thought for a long moment. Then he blinked rapidly and nodded. "We cannot afford to overlook anything. I shall need complete access to the *Corsair*."

"You have it."

"Including every one of the staterooms."

"Fine. I have no other guests on board. But I will not have the police mucking over my own stateroom, and there is one adjoining it—"

"I shall inspect those personally," said Holmes with a deferential nod.

"Good. Then we go forward as planned?"

"You and the committee will all be told of any dangers uncovered by the inspection, and then a decision can be made to proceed or not proceed."

Morgan nodded, and I had the impression that the interview was about to be concluded. But then he frowned. "This Clevering, who was killed last night. How did he get mixed up in this business?"

"We are in the realm of supposition here," said Holmes cautiously. "But Clevering made frequent visits to the German embassy and to Germany as assistant to Lord Lansdowne's predecessor, who I believe was born in Munich. Clevering is a family man, but he had gambling debts and had been seduced by a German courtesan. Once Lansdowne was appointed as the new Secretary of War, and after he chose to keep Clevering in his position of assistant, the situation would have been known to the Germans as an opportunity to be exploited."

Morgan's gaze hardened. "So Wilhelm is behind this."

"We have no proof of that. Our only evidence is that Perkins, the late and traitorous banker, was seen entering and leaving the German embassy yesterday morning."

Morgan continued as if he had not heard. "The arrogance of that little swine! Holmes, I do not want to slink off to Southampton like a coward. I want these villains stopped, and crushed, and publicly executed, and I want the word of their complete humiliation to get back to Wilhelm."

48. THE REPORT FROM DARTMOOR

"We have the telegraph message from Dartmoor," said Lestrade. He stood with Holmes and me on the upper deck of the *Corsair*, at the upper edge of the gangway, where a network of velvet ropes and brass columns had been set up to funnel new arrivals and ensure the close inspection of all who came on board. It was nearly two o'clock. The afternoon shadows were lengthening and Holmes's patience was growing strained. The final rehearsal for *The Mikado* had concluded on board the *Shamrock*. The set and costumes had all been thoroughly examined and were safely on board the *Corsair*, which had received a full inspection. On the quay, a large dogcart approached us, piled high with orchestral instruments in their cases. One of the ushers from Carte's company drove while two walked alongside the horse. I also recognized young Flynn and two of his ragged associates, trailing behind the dogcart.

Holmes gestured to Flynn, and then to the men guarding the gangway, indicating that they were to let Flynn pass.

"I will read you the report," Lestrade was saying. He squinted at a telegraph message that he pulled from his jacket pocket. 'Asher, Harold Stuart. Date of employment: 14 May, 1895. Termination

date: 28 October, 1895. Reason for termination: death by accident. Former employer: London Bridge Hospital, London.
Recommended for employment by: Warden Dodson.'"

Lestrade looked at Holmes expectantly. "Is this what you
wanted?"

"It is precisely what I wanted," said Holmes. "Now. I take it
your men have seen no further activity at Mr. Worth's Clapham
Common estate? Good. Please have them continue observation
there. Now I have something else you must do right away."

He took Lestrade and Flynn aside and walked a few paces
from me as he spoke. Holmes's voice was too low for me to hear,
but I saw Lestrade's eyes widen in surprise and his hand move to
cover his mouth. Then he nodded. "I'll attend to it."

"Take the fastest police launch you can find. You must use
extreme caution. Flynn, you and the Irregulars are to be guided by
the inspector and stay out of danger. His men may need to shoot
to kill."

"Holmes, what will they need to shoot?" I asked, after Lestrade
had departed.

"I hope nothing at all."

49. OUT OF TUNE

A few minutes later we saw Lucy and Zoe queued up with the others of the company within the velvet rope network. As they waited to be identified and vouched for by D'Oyly Carte, Lucy saw us and waved, then pointed at us and then to herself and Miss Rosario, indicating that they had some news. A few minutes after that the two joined us and we retreated to a place along the rail where we could talk privately.

"I noticed something odd during rehearsal," said Zoe. "The percussionist could not seem to get his tympani tuned properly. It has never happened before, so I thought I ought to mention it."

As she spoke, I immediately saw in my memory the drawing the Commissioner had shown us at the Diogenes Club four days previously, and heard his voice once again, saying a*bout the size of a loaf of bread.*

"Holmes," I said, "one of the tympani would provide space for Moran to conceal a dynamite bomb."

"And the presence of a foreign object within the drum would shrink the volume and change the sound harmonics, making it difficult to tune," added Lucy.

Holmes looked across the deck to where the seats for the orchestra were being arranged. Beside them five Navy men, under the supervision of two uniformed officers—one from the Navy and the other from the Metropolitan Police—were unpacking and inspecting the instruments. "We had better look into this right away," he said. "Thank you very much for your vigilance, both of you. Now could you please go below to the dining saloon? Watson and I will come to you with a full report as soon as possible, but meanwhile I should greatly appreciate having a deck of solid steel between whatever may be hidden in that kettledrum and the two of you."

As Lucy and Zoe retreated, Holmes and I made our way to the orchestra section, and not long afterward the Navy men lifted each of the kettles from its stand and carried it down the gangplank and out to the edge of the quay. Holmes and I followed. Two other policemen were assigned to keep the area clear as Holmes bent over the first of the two drums. We did not know which of the drums was the one that had been difficult to tune, and, since Holmes did not want to take time to locate the percussionist or alarm the other musicians, he simply opened up the one nearest him. He carefully loosened each of the tuning bolts, removed the circular brass head protector, and then gently peeled back the goatskin membrane.

The drum looked empty. In the reddish late-afternoon sunlight the copper-colored bottom of the instrument appeared smooth and undisturbed. Quickly Holmes turned his attention to the second drum. But when opened, that one also appeared to contain nothing but air.

"Hope he knows how to put it back together," whispered one of the seamen to his companion. But Holmes did not appear to take notice. He bent lower into the drum and reached his hand inside, running his fingers around the inner surface of first one drum and then the other.

"Watson. There is a false bottom in each of these instruments. Your pocketknife, if you would be so kind."

I handed him the knife and moments later he had pried back a thin metal disc that had been cleverly glued to the inside perimeter. Underneath, fastened to the true bottom of the drum with what appeared to be a medical sticking plaster of the sort I had often employed in Afghanistan, were two sticks of dynamite. They lay alongside a mechanical apparatus of the same type as the one drawn on the sketch the Commissioner had shown us.

As Holmes pried up the metal disc from the second drum to reveal a second dynamite bomb, the Commissioner joined us. At a glance he recognized the contents of the two drums, and his tired face lit up in a weary smile. "Mr. Holmes," he said, "I congratulate you."

"Not yet," Holmes replied, looking at a police launch that was steaming rapidly toward us.

50. LESTRADE AND FLYNN REPORT

The police launch docked moments later. We saw Lestrade and young Flynn clamber out. Then they were hurrying up to where we stood on the quay, in front of the *Corsair*. Both their faces were flushed with excitement and exertion.

"We found it, Mr. 'Olmes!" cried Flynn. "In the 'ospital carriage 'ouse!"

Holmes nodded. "Good work, Flynn. There will be five shillings for you and each of your lads, along with a crown as a bonus, if you will please call upon me at Baker Street tomorrow afternoon."

Lestrade added, "There was no one in the carriage house, so we did not even have to use our weapons. The men have taken it to the Yard for safety. Flynn and I came back in the launch."

"Thank you, Lestrade."

"But how did you know it would be there?"

"London Bridge Hospital is only a short distance from Threadneedle Street. I knew that Mr. Foster had been killed immediately after his investigations took him to the Bank of England. And before Mr. Worth arranged for him to be employed at Dartmoor, the unfortunate Mr. Asher had worked at London Bridge Hospital."

I could not contain my curiosity. "What are you talking about, Holmes?"

"I am talking about a direct attack on the Bank of England, averted less than one hour ago by Inspector Lestrade, young Mr. Flynn, and their associates."

"In the hospital carriage house we found a large ambulance wagon," Lestrade said. "Packed up to its roof with dynamite."

"The Ardeer dynamite missing from the railway shipment to Newcastle," said Holmes.

"Well, that is good news all around," said the Commissioner. "Mr. Holmes, would you kindly elaborate?"

Holmes nodded. "Friday morning we witnessed the detonation of a dynamite bomb outside St. Thomas Hospital. I believe that was a demonstration to prove to the Germans the capability of the detonation device. Clevering would have reported the successful deployment. The actual attack would have taken place near the Prince Street corner, closest to where the gold reserves of the Bank are stored. Perkins might have provided the architectural plans. The extent of the damage would have been enormous, an impact great enough to justify the enormous sum Worth demanded from his employers in Germany."

"Mr. Holmes, this relieves my mind considerably," said the Commissioner. "I shall take this news to the committee. They have convened on the *White Star* and are waiting to decide whether or not to proceed. I may at last congratulate you."

"I must repeat, not yet. Not until Worth and Moran are in our custody."

"But the stolen dynamite has been found and recovered. The *Corsair* and the *White Star* will be ringed with soldiers and sailors. The Pinkertons are on each vessel, and I have stationed patrolmen at the entrances to all the warehouses." He pointed to a naval vessel now docking in the slip to the immediate starboard of the *Corsair*. "This is the *HMS Daring*, a torpedo boat destroyer. Her men will provide additional security for the entire area. Surely there is no reason to change the plan."

Holmes said, "That is what troubles me."

51. LIGHT BECOMES DARKNESS

Holmes and I now stood together in the twilight shadows. Sunset had come and passed in a red haze over the darkened buildings to our west, and we were side by side at the boat deck rail of the *Corsair*, very nearly at the prow on the starboard side. All around us a swarm of activity was taking place in preparation for the performance of *The Mikado* that would occur if the PM's committee, against Holmes's repeated wishes, elected to proceed with the conference.

Before and below us to our right on the edges of the quay, electric streetlamps were being unloaded from Navy wagons and set up on tall wooden poles roughly twelve feet high, inserted into heavy metal stands to provide stability. As soon as one of the lamps was standing, a wire at its base was immediately connected to a long cable that ran along the dockside to the *HMS Daring*. There was obviously an electric generator on board the *Daring*, for the moment the connection was accomplished, the lamp atop the pole immediately flashed on, casting a pool of harsh white light over the quay in a radius of nearly thirty feet.

Holmes indicated one of the Navy wagons passing along the quay to our left. "They will extend the reach of the lamps past the *White Star*," he said. "No one will be able to cross the quay during the performance without being seen, challenged, and shot. You see, Watson, the Army riflemen emerging from that omnibus in front of the *Daring*, and there are four more omnibuses queuing up behind it, waiting to discharge their occupants."

As we watched, the men marched to the side of the quay and formed up in single file, all looking very smart in their khaki uniforms, blue spiked helmets, and shouldered rifles. They marched with a certain excitement, as if they knew a distinguished audience would soon review their parade in the white glare of the electric lamps.

"Ready to be inspected by the Prime Minister himself," Holmes remarked. "Let us hope that is the most difficult challenge these young men will have to face this evening."

From behind us came the sound of the wind flapping the fabric of the canvas roof that nearly a dozen Navy men had hoisted over the green-striped canvas partition walls. The enclosure towered above us, nearly twenty feet in height, sheltering nearly all of the boat deck, from just behind where we were standing all the way to the stern rail. Once inside, the performers of *The Mikado* and their exclusive audience would be protected from the elements. This was a matter of necessity tonight, for although rain was unlikely, the cold wind would make it impossible for anyone, let alone high government officials, American millionaires, and their spouses, to enjoy an outdoor theater performance. Even in my warm wool ulster I felt the chill as I cast a somewhat longing glance at the canvas entryway that seemed to beckon, like a circus tent, indicating pleasures and warmth to be found within.

As if a benevolent providence had somehow divined my thoughts, the tent flap at the entry opened and toward us came Lucy James and Zoe Rosario, each carrying a small tray with some scones and a steaming mug of tea. "We thought you'd appreciate something warm," Lucy said. "We have a few minutes before we need to be in costume—though no one's said for certain that we're really going to perform tonight."

"We wondered if you could tell us anything about that," said Zoe.

Ignoring the tea, Holmes nodded toward the lights and soldiers below us. "We have heard nothing official. But to begin such a flurry of military activity and expense and then send everyone home—I cannot imagine the committee doing that unless there was new evidence that indicated imminent danger."

Zoe pulled her black woolen shawl tight around her. "The police and the Navy men have looked everywhere. One of them even inspected the inside of the violin Mr. Carte borrowed for me. He held it over an electric torch and peered inside—he twisted his head around until I thought he would injure his neck. But nothing."

Lucy said to Holmes, "You don't look happy, though."

"Something is not right. We are forgetting something."

"Then take some tea," said Zoe. "It may help you to remember."

"Anyway, we have news of another kind," Lucy said. "Mr. Carte has invited us to join a touring company in Rome. We would leave this coming Saturday."

"Did you have something to do with that, Sherlock?" asked Zoe.

"I should be relieved to know both of you were safely out of London."

"And Rome? Which gives me the opportunity to introduce Lucy to my parents? You didn't suggest that to Mr. Carte?"

"I've never seen Rome," Lucy said brightly. As Holmes remained silent, she went on, "I know I can't stay on as a lead at the Savoy. The role really belongs to Miss Perry. She's already well enough to sing—in fact she'll be in the chorus tonight."

Lucy stopped, looking past Holmes. "Oh, my. There's Johnny!"

Young Rockefeller was standing at the roped-off entryway, in animated conversation with one of three Navy guardsmen. Holmes took a few steps in their direction and caught the attention of the guards. Soon young Rockefeller was with us.

"I came over to tell you that the performance is on for tonight," he said. "I just had the official word from Mother, who had it from Father. Oh, and all the men on the Prime Minister's committee are still waiting for Mr. and Mrs. Carnegie at the *White Star*. Father has assigned each one of them a stateroom to use as a dressing room and they're having their evening clothes sent over. Their wives are being brought here in separate carriages, each with two Army officers as escorts."

"What did you see of the meeting?" asked Holmes.

"I came in with Father, but then he thought it best if I made my exit. Some old fossil started yammering some nonsense about an Official Secrets Act."

"That would have been the Chancellor," I explained. "The chief legal officer, in charge of all British courts. He has always been a hidebound reactionary on the bench, and now he seeks to impose his views even though he is but one member of a committee."

"What an idiot," said young Rockefeller. "What do you suppose ails the fellow?"

"The old tiger cannot change his stripes," I said, offhandedly.

Holmes stared at me as if my words contained a dreadful hidden meaning. Then he was at my side, his voice hushed so that only I could hear him. "Moran is watching us."

As I struggled to understand, Holmes turned to young Rockefeller, gripping his forearm with an urgency that made the young man wince.

"Mr. Rockefeller. Would you please return to the *White Star* and tell your father that he and the committee should not board the *Corsair* unless they have heard directly from me that it is safe to do so."

Rockefeller looked puzzled, but nodded assent as Holmes turned to Miss Rosario. "Zoe, would you tell Mr. Carte that the troupe is to remain below until he has received my personal assurance of safety." Then he drew closer to her, his lips nearly touching her ear, and spoke too quietly for me to understand.

The effect of his words on Miss Rosario was immediate. She folded her arms as if to protect herself. A deep blush suffused her cheeks. She looked downward, then at Lucy, and finally at Holmes. I barely heard her say, "As you wish."

Holmes turned to me, and I saw in his glittering eyes both determination and despair. "Watson, we must go immediately."

As we strode away from the astonished trio, Holmes gestured toward the quay, and upward, and beyond, to the row of darkened warehouses that loomed above us, shadowed against the night sky.

"Moran has set up his huntsman's blind once again. The old tiger hunter is watching us from one of these warehouses, Watson, just as he did last year, from the empty house on Baker Street."

"But the warehouses are under police guard."

"I tell you the old *shikari* is looking down upon us even now, and all these shining new streetlamps have perfectly illuminated his target."

PART FOUR

NEVER FORGOT

52. TAKEN

A few faint yellow gas lamps guided us through the squalid darkness of Dockland Way. The street was deserted, for this part of London was not a place to remain after the ground-floor shops had closed. On our right, one block distant and through an alley between two large warehouses, a faint white glow came from the newly installed streetlamps on the quay that separated these buildings from the *Corsair*, the *Shamrock*, and the *White Star*.

Walking rapidly beside Holmes, I felt uncertain and apprehensive, for I did not know our destination or what we were looking for. I must also admit that my feelings were heightened by simple fear, since neither of us could see exactly what dangers might surround us in the shadows.

Holmes seemed to sense my apprehension. "Bear with me, Watson," he said, slowing his pace only slightly. "Moran is in one of these buildings. We must look for clues to his whereabouts."

"But why are we alone? Why did you not ask for policemen to accompany us?"

"There are police guards posted at each of the entrances to each of these buildings. When we find our quarry, we shall enlist their aid."

I looked up at the looming bulk of the huge warehouses, trying to see within the Gothic curves of the huge glass windows. "Are we looking for a glimmer of light?"

"We are looking for a police carriage."

"But there are police carriages at every corner."

"We are looking for the one Worth stole last night in Piccadilly. When we find it, you must go straight to the Commissioner and bring as many of his men as he can spare. You will stay close to the buildings along the quay, in order to—"

He froze. We had come to a second alleyway, dividing one of the warehouses from the next. I could see the shadowy outline of a carriage waiting at the far end, silhouetted against the streetlamps, but I could not see a driver. The light being against us, it was impossible to say whether the vehicle was a brougham, a hansom, or a police carriage.

"His means of entry and escape," said Holmes. "Quietly, now."

We advanced as silently as we could, crossing the narrow road and entering the alleyway. I could hear the wind from the dock as it swirled between the high brick walls. I heard the rustle and clink of leather and brass as the horse shifted its weight in its harness. As we came closer, I could see small clouds of steam emanating from the horse's nostrils, shimmering like luminescent fog before the streetlamps.

Finally, I could see the rear of the carriage, which was taken up nearly entirely by a large, partially opened door. "I cannot see anyone, Holmes," I whispered.

"Stay here," he replied. "If there is a driver I shall distract him. When you see movement, run to the opposite side of the vehicle, get to the quay, and tell the Commissioner to send help."

I held my breath, watching as Holmes walked silently to the carriage. His revolver at the ready, he opened the rear door.

I saw only darkness within the rear compartment. Holmes turned to look at me. His eyes widened with alarm.

Then at the back of my neck I felt a hard and metallic pressure.

"He has a shotgun, Watson," said Holmes.

Behind me, a man spoke. "We saw you come across the quay as soon as you left the *Corsair*," he said. "You were quite visible in all this lamplight, but you did not see me behind you."

The words were indistinct, as if the man had difficulty forming them. "This gun has two barrels. How appropriate. Drop your gun, Mr. Holmes, if you want your friend's head to remain on his shoulders."

It was the voice of James Blake.

53. THE OLD *SHIKARI*

Blake marched us at gunpoint to the entrance at the front of the building. The entrance was unguarded. Inside the doorway we passed the crumpled body of a policeman, leaned against the stairway wall. Step by step, Blake marched us up the six flights of stairs at the front of the warehouse. The staircase had windows, and in the light from the new streetlamps outside I could see Blake was keeping his shotgun trained on Holmes. Each time we reached a landing and our path turned upward, I visualized myself turning around and making a dive at Blake. But each time I held back, knowing my attempt to stop him would endanger Holmes, for I could see that Blake always remained at a distance far enough away to dodge me, yet close enough that his first shot could not fail to hit its target. His swollen and bruised lips twisted into a grim smile each time our eyes met, as if he was anticipating the moment when he would pay me back for the injury I had given him.

At the top of the staircase, we passed through a doorway and found ourselves at the edge of a dark, cavernous expanse, illuminated on our left by the pale white glow from a long row of tall windows. About sixty feet away, dark rows of wooden crates had been stacked nearly twenty feet high, blocking our view of the far end of the warehouse.

The window light revealed the crouching figure of a man seated on a plain wooden chair. Between the man and the nearest window, several opened crates of ammunition lay beside a tripod-mounted Maxim gun. I drew in my breath, for I knew that the weapon before me was capable of delivering 500 rounds of lethal ammunition and killing hundreds of men, all in less than one minute.

The man spoke. "Yes, Mr. Holmes. We are at the front of the warehouse, almost directly across the quay from the *Corsair*. I have not forgotten our last meeting."

He sat up and turned to face us. Light from the window shone on his lined, gaunt features and high, bald forehead. It was unmistakably Colonel Sebastian Moran, the murderer we had captured in a deserted house seventeen months previously, just after his air gun bullet had smashed through our front window at Baker Street. On that occasion the bullet had exploded harmlessly within a wax sculpture of Holmes's head, and we had triumphed. I feared that now the tables had been turned.

Holmes said, "Your complexion is more pallid than before you went to prison, and I see you are attempting to grow back your mustache."

"Much has changed, Holmes," Moran replied. "But now you are the one in the trap."

"Where is Worth?"

"He departed shortly after you left the *Corsair*. He saw something on the quay."

"What?"

"Something that interested him. He will return soon enough, and your curiosity will be fully satisfied at that time, I can assure you."

"Dr. Watson and I appreciate your courtesy. And yours also, Mr. Blake. Though I am sure each of you would prefer a different course of action if left to your own devices. I take it Mr. Worth has instructed both of you that we are not to be harmed until he returns?"

Neither man spoke. Blake had moved to stand before the window at our right, so that his shotgun would not endanger Worth if he fired in our direction.

Holmes went on, "And you are compelled to obey, since Worth knows how to retrieve the fortune in bearer bonds that you hope to earn for your night's work here. But I wonder how you intend to ensure that you collect what has been agreed upon between you and Worth. Of course, if Worth disappears with his son and daughter when he has the funds in hand, you, Colonel, will not find it easy to locate him. Will he reward your loyalty? I notice that he did not reward your loyalty for traveling with the Professor to Reichenbach and then pursuing me for three years. He allowed you to languish in Dartmoor. And I suspect he arranged for your escape rather more because he had a use for you than because he wanted to reward you. Or do you see it differently?"

"Don't listen to him," said Blake. "He's just trying to stir you up."

"I also wonder," Holmes went on, "how you will explain away the brown stains on your fingertips when you attempt to play cards at any of the fashionable clubs which you formerly frequented. You developed the stains, of course, by picking oakum ropes for so very many long and tedious hours in Dartmoor. But now those stains mark you as a convict. People in polite society are inclined to look askance at stained hands, at least if they are attached to someone trying to pass himself off as a gentleman."

"You persist in goading me, Mr. Holmes."

"I merely hope to satisfy my curiosity on a few more points. For instance, I wonder how Mr. Worth came to walk in that slightly twisted manner of his. I know he claims it is the result of a wound from the American Civil War, but a report I received from the American authorities makes no mention of this. I fancy there was a wound, however, for I know that a shattered shoulder blade, improperly healed, produces that same twisted effect in a man's posture. So I wonder, Colonel, just who shot him in the back. Likely it was someone he allowed to get close to him, which would mean a betrayal of his trust. And the betrayal was one of which he was ashamed, since he took pains to conceal it by fabricating an alternative explanation. Given his fixation on perpetuating the Moriarty family line, a betrayal by a family member would bring on a sense of failure and shame. So my question: was it Professor James Moriarty who shot him?"

"I have nothing to say."

"You do not have to say anything. I wonder if he shot his brother shortly after they came to England with the fortune obtained from the Boylston Bank robbery. Perhaps there was a dispute over the shares? Or perhaps the brother who would become a professor wished to use the funds to invest in a new criminal network in London, and the other brother was not willing to take such a risk?"

"Are you trying to distract me, Mr. Holmes? It will not work."

"Ah, well. Perhaps Mr. Blake has taken an interest in his family's history."

Holmes was about to continue, but a noise of machinery came from behind us, from the opening to the motorized platform lift beside the stairway door. Moran turned to look as the lift rose to our level and revealed a shadowy group of figures standing behind the protective metal grid. I hoped momentarily that we were about to be rescued. But Blake seemed to be perfectly sanguine about the new arrivals. As he had done throughout Holmes's narrative, he continued to stare dispassionately at us while cradling his shotgun.

The lift stopped, the metal grille slid open, and the white glow from the windows now silhouetted five people coming toward us. I recognized Adam Worth, unmistakable in his twisted posture, and another man who wore a policeman's uniform. Each of them carried a shotgun.

The three others held their hands in the air and shuffled slowly toward us, faces rigidly forward, as though wary of making any sudden movement. My heart sank as I recognized Johnny Rockefeller, Zoe Rosario, and Lucy James.

54. A REVELATION

I could see the dismay on the faces of Lucy and Johnny when they realized that Holmes and I were also prisoners. Then their dismay turned to alarm as they saw the Maxim gun and the huge piles of ammunition alongside it. I dared not look at Holmes.

Johnny Rockefeller made a brave attempt to knock the gun from its tripod, possibly hoping to damage the firing or feed-through mechanisms. As he passed Moran, he turned sideways and launched himself at the apparatus. But he fell short, landing on the hard concrete floor with a sharp impact, just before a kick from Moran's boot connected with his shoulder. Young Rockefeller lay still for a moment and then sat up, glaring at Moran, who stood over him as though prepared to repeat the attack.

"Show some sense, Worth," snapped Holmes. "This particular prisoner is a valuable hostage, and you may need him to bargain with."

"My apologies, Mr. Rockefeller," Worth replied. He gave Moran a sharp look, which caused the man to retreat to his chair and sit down, the Maxim gun within easy reach. Then Worth beckoned to Lucy and Zoe, indicating they should sit beside young

Rockefeller on the concrete. In the light from the window, Worth's face appeared to glow with triumph.

"I will not sit," said Zoe.

"Nor I," said Lucy.

But the young policeman stepped behind them and kicked each woman hard in the back of the knees. Each fell. Instinctively I took a step forward. Blake and Worth reacted simultaneously, brandishing their shotguns, and I saw that, for the moment at least, resistance was unavailing. Worth spoke gruffly.

"Thank you, Cleo."

The policeman removed the helmet, shook loose an array of shining black hair, and the smiling visage of Worth's daughter was before us.

"The young sergeant's uniform required a few alterations," she said. "But it fooled the guard at the front of the building."

"You killed them both," said Holmes.

"Never mind that, Mr. Holmes," Worth said. "You and Dr. Watson. You will sit."

I followed Holmes's example and sat cross-legged on the cold concrete, my knee joints and the muscles of my inner thighs protesting from the unfamiliar position as Worth, Blake, and Cleo trained their guns on us. I wondered why Worth had not ordered us restrained in some manner. Then I realized how quickly we could all be shot.

Lucy looked at Holmes and seemed about to speak, but Holmes gestured for her to remain silent. "Come now, Worth." Holmes's tone was exasperatingly calm and reasonable. "What were you thinking when you set up this weaponry? Were you planning to rain down death and destruction on the *Corsair*, knowing that your niece and her mother would be killed?"

Worth consulted his pocket watch. "We have nearly twenty minutes until the performance begins at six o'clock. So there is ample time for you to understand that I am neither a poor planner nor a heartless uncle. Even now, a young street urchin waits in the crowd outside the military barriers. He holds typewritten notes addressed to each of these two ladies, instructing them to come at once if they value their lives. He awaits my signal, but of course that will not be necessary. So Lucy can continue the brilliant career that I have helped put into motion. She will need to sing under a different name, of course, for I am also not such a bungler as to think that after the tragic events that are about to ensue, people might not have cause to question why she and Miss Rosario were not present among the victims. Besides, I shall want to be able to see them both from time to time, and you will naturally understand that it may not be possible for me to remain in London."

Then, to my astonishment, Holmes said, "Miss James is not your niece. There is no blood connection between her and that reptilian brother of yours." Holmes turned to Miss Rosario. "Zoe, I would be most grateful if you would confirm this."

As I stared in wonder, Zoe replied, her voice perfectly composed, "Professor James Moriarty was not Lucy's father."

"Then you lied to me," said Worth.

"Your brother lied to you. He wanted to control me. Since I had rejected his attempt to possess me in one manner, he said he would find pleasure by possessing me in another. Had I told you the truth, he would have had me killed and Lucy would have been left an orphan. I had no choice. He told me he also would gain favor with you if you thought he was continuing the Moriarty bloodline. He said you were obsessed with family. He said you were the oldest, and that your parents took to drink and abandoned you both when you were ten years old. He said he needed access to the funds that you controlled in order to build what he called an 'organization.'"

She paused and looked at Worth. "You still appear to doubt me. Do you think I could have obtained that information from some other source than your brother?"

Worth stood motionless, his face a mask. Holmes said, "I can supply further corroboration. Your brother spoke to me on the subject when we were together at Reichenbach, though I did not realize his meaning until later. I now see that even twenty-one years ago he had wanted to cause me emotional pain."

"You were a nobody then, Holmes. Why should my brother have cared about your feelings twenty-one years ago?"

"He was jealous," said Zoe. "After I rejected him, he had seen me with Sherlock on a number of occasions. He said a trust would be established for the care of my child, but only if I never spoke to Sherlock again. If I failed to obey, both my child and I would be—to use his word—'discarded.'"

Recognition began to appear on Worth's cruel features. "Just what did my brother say to you, Mr. Holmes?"

"We were at the Reichenbach Falls. He had just told me that Colonel Moran would kill me if I happened to survive the struggle that we both knew was about to occur."

"Do not waste my time, Holmes."

"His exact words are still fresh in my memory. He said, 'I broke your heart, Holmes, and you never knew who it was that had caused you such pain. Over the years I have savored that knowledge, and I will take that joy with me to the grave.'"

Holmes paused reflectively. "At that time, of course, I was not sure of his meaning, and it has been a vexing puzzle ever since. But Miss Rosario understands the truth of the matter. She has told you how Professor Moriarty forced her to end her relationship with me. She can now confirm that Lucy James is my daughter."

55. MR. WORTH REACTS

For a long moment there was silence. The shadows around us, the cold light from the windows, the looming presence of the tall dark rows of crates on our right—even the air itself in that cavernous enclosure—seemed to be alive and to press heavily in upon me. I stared at Holmes, then at Zoe, then at Lucy. My heart pounded as I waited for Zoe to reply.

"She is Sherlock's daughter," Zoe said firmly. "A few minutes ago on the *Corsair* he told me that he had deduced the truth. Lucy, he made me promise to tell you—if he did not return."

Questions whirled through my mind. How long had Holmes known? How had he deduced the truth? How must he feel, knowing he was Lucy's father? I recalled when we were in Worth's Piccadilly flat, Holmes had said that we might use Worth's emotions to our advantage. Was this a last, desperate attempt to infuriate Worth, though at the cost of the only motive Worth had for allowing Lucy to remain alive? Then I realized that we all might die here and that those questions and a thousand others would forever remain unanswered.

Lucy's eyes were shining, locked on Holmes. Johnny was staring at Lucy in amazement.

It may have been my imagination, but it seemed to me that
both Holmes and Lucy were gathering their strength, waiting to
spring at Blake or Cleo if either shotgun were to waver. It occurred
to me that since I was closest to Worth, I should be following the
same plan. It seemed certain that the news of Lucy's real father—
which meant Worth had been supporting the daughter of his mortal enemy for more than two decades—must take its emotional
toll. I felt certain that Worth was bound to react soon, and that
when he did I must be ready to move. I waited.

"I apologize for misleading you, Lucy," said Zoe. "After keeping
the truth from Sherlock for twenty-one years, I was too ashamed
to tell him what had really happened. So I took the path of least
resistance and continued with the lie. Sherlock, I am sorry."

"You need not apologize," Holmes said. "I am glad you had
no physical contact with James Moriarty. To be anywhere near the
man was most unpleasant. Even when I was pulling him over the
precipice at Reichenbach and sending him to his death, I felt a very
strong repugnance."

Worth was staring at Holmes, blinking rapidly at what I was
sure was Holmes's deliberate provocation. I gathered my inner
forces, hoping my middle-aged sinews would not betray me and
that I would be able to get to my feet in time.

Then, to my astonishment, Worth turned to me. His face shone
with a triumphant smile.

"Dr. Watson," he said. "Now that I know the true circumstances of Lucy's birth and the relationship Miss Rosario had with
Holmes, I know that both these women are dear to him and, therefore, to yourself. So you will act as I demand, or in the remaining
time that we shall spend together here you and Holmes will watch
both Lucy and her mother suffer most horribly."

The shotgun trained on me remained steady. "In just a few minutes the colonel must commence work with his specialized weaponry. So let us begin."

56. AN IMPOSSIBLE DEMAND

Worth advanced toward me, cradling the shotgun. Then he allowed it to point downward for a moment, holding it under one arm while he reached into his coat pocket with his other hand. As he moved, I felt this was my opportunity to somehow wrest control of the weapon from him. But he was coming closer, and the light was clear enough for me to discern that his finger still grasped the shotgun trigger. Horrible possibilities swept through my imagination: the gun firing both barrels into the concrete; the gun swinging up and the blast connecting with Holmes, or Zoe, or Lucy . . .

I did not act. Still, I thought, if not now, when? Hardly any time remained; Worth had said so himself. I vowed I would stay focused on every moment and not shrink or hesitate if my chance arose.

Worth pulled a rectangular object from his pocket and in one motion tossed it in my direction. It slid across the concrete and landed at my feet. "Please pick it up, Dr. Watson," Worth said pleasantly. "And please remain seated. You also, Mr. Holmes."

I picked up the object. It was a leather-bound notebook, of exactly the type that I used to prepare my narratives of the cases that Holmes and I had worked on.

Worth gave no explanation for the notebook. He stepped back from me a few paces toward the window so as to encompass the others in his remarks, puffing out his chest and widening his stance as if he were an orator on a stage or a professor in an auditorium. "To celebrate this Guy Fawkes Night," he said, "there will soon be a large explosion at the Bank of England."

"There will be no explosion," Holmes interrupted. "We found the dynamite your minions stole from the Ardeer factory train. It was in the carriage house of the London Bridge Hospital. It is now at Scotland Yard."

Worth blinked rapidly for a moment. "You are so clever, Mr. Holmes. But I am the one holding the gun."

I realized yet another attempt of Holmes's to distract him had failed.

Worth continued, "Here, as you see, there is no way for the Queen's Army, Navy, or police forces, or the Pinkertons, to stop us. We hold the higher ground, the militarily superior position. Not one of them will be standing after a few thousand rounds have been fired from our artillery."

He gestured at the Maxim gun, from which a belt of ammunition cartridges descended, folding upon itself into a pile that filled a large wooden crate to overflowing. A second crate lay beside the first, also overflowing with a cartridge belt. "We also have something special planned for the ships," he said with a cruel smile. "This second box contains a new form of ammunition supplied by Herr von Herder, whose innovations in weaponry have served Colonel Moran so admirably in the past. These are incendiary bullets, tipped with phosphorus, which as you know is highly combustible. We possess here the modern-day equivalent of the flaming arrows that our ancestors employed to soar over the high walls of a medieval castle and send the occupants running terrified and helpless in the ensuing blaze. Our parallel here is not quite exact, since the fortresses in question are steel ships, and we are shooting down upon them with many thousands of metallic missiles. Also the havoc that results should be greater."

I drew in my breath as the horrific consequences of this lethal attack flashed through my imagination. Even though the fire might not penetrate the boat deck, the fumes from the conflagration that would consume the upper portion of the ship would poison the air supplied to those below. Rockefeller, Morgan, D'Oyly Carte and his troupe, and many more—they would all die in agony.

"You stored the ammunition on the workbench in your Clapham Common carriage house," Holmes said.

"Oh, did you find residue?" He glanced at Blake, then shrugged. "That would be an oversight on Blake's part."

"He also left Mr. Foster's identification papers on his body. Was that another oversight?"

At Worth's shrug, Holmes continued, "I thought not. You killed Foster because he was investigating at the Bank of England. But you wanted to divert attention from the Bank to prevent discovery of your dynamite plot. So you allowed Foster to be identified, and ordered Blake to tell the police that he was investigating at the Savoy Theatre. Blake also left three white ceramic connectors for us to find in the Savoy workshop, and he left an inert dynamite bomb in one of the troupe's kettledrums—two more of your diversions."

"You continue your attempts to divert *me*, Mr. Holmes. But we have very little time remaining here. I have promised myself this moment, and I shall have it. And then hundreds will die in a hail of bullets, and hundreds more will perish in the fires that will come down upon them like brimstone on the judgment day. Blood will have blood."

"You are mad, indeed," Holmes said.

Worth ignored the insult and once more he assumed the pose of an orator. "On Saturday I visited the offices of *The Strand Magazine*, for the idea came to me that I might go beyond my charter, so to speak. In addition to hoodwinking you, succeeding in my mission, and being rewarded in a handsome enough fashion to ensure that my family could build a dynasty forever, I might also rectify the harm that you and Dr. Watson here have done to my brother's reputation and to our family honor. I might add, the idea sprang to my mind, fully formed."

Worth looked at me. "So now to business, Dr. Watson. Saturday, a clerk at the *Strand* offices was perfectly willing to show me your notebooks in exchange for a mere five pounds in ready cash. The notebook you hold, as I am sure you are aware, is identical to those you have employed to present your fictionalized concoctions to your editors at the *Strand*. Since publishing your abominably libelous tale of my brother and Holmes, they have not told your readers that Holmes has returned. Your readers would gladly pay for news of their lost hero. Your editors would gladly pocket the revenues. So you will write a new account of Mr. Holmes's latest adventure. The *Strand* will eagerly publish, knowing it is unassailably authenticated by your own handwriting in one of your own notebooks."

My heart sank as I recognized the truth of this statement. I shuddered inwardly at the anticipation of what he would say next.

"Your millions of followers will soon read how Sherlock Holmes has confessed his participation in a long-standing criminal venture for his own profit. They will also read how he lied about my brother, intending to deflect blame by casting the innocent Professor James Moriarty in the role of the Napoleon of crime, the role that was in reality played by himself. The final stroke will be his confession of complicity and profit in the plot to assassinate the highest officials of the British government as they assemble here, on Guy Fawkes Night, and his boasts of how he succeeded two hundred and ninety years after the original plan was foiled. Holmes will confess—that is, you will write—that following this last climactic event of his criminal career, he intends to vanish from public view and assume another identity, using his well-known powers of acting and disguise."

Holmes interrupted. "You let us escape from your Piccadilly flat so that you could recapture us here?"

"No, Mr. Holmes, I am not so driven by my emotions that I would put our main enterprise at risk in order to avenge my brother. The discovery of your bodies might have created a sensation, and caused Mr. Rockefeller and Mr. Morgan to go elsewhere to conduct their business with the British government. If that contingency had arisen, I would have lost a very substantial fee. One million pounds." Worth bared his teeth in a brief smile. "But your humiliation is a most gratifying bonus for me, nonetheless."

"How did you know I would deduce your location and come to the warehouse?"

"I did not *know*. But given your knowledge of Colonel Moran's previous methods of assassination, it was a reasonable assumption that you would. But the point is no longer relevant. For you *are* here. And, Dr. Watson, you will now write as I direct you to."

My heart pounded in my chest and I could barely speak, so stunned was I at the enormity of the outrage I was being commanded to perpetrate. "Never" was what I managed to say.

"In that case, Mr. Blake, will you please carefully deliver a blast from one barrel of your shotgun directly at Miss James where she now sits before us, so that you shoot off her right arm."

I could not help looking at Lucy as Worth spoke his terrifying command. Her eyes rolled back in their sockets and she slumped sideways, collapsing on the concrete floor.

I heard Holmes's voice behind me. "Do as he says, Watson."

"I knew you would be reasonable," Worth replied. "Mr. Blake, you will train your shotgun on Mr. Holmes, and shoot him dead if he moves. Doctor, you will find a reservoir pen fastened in its leather loop inside the cover of the notebook. I shall dictate. You shall write. Begin."

His hideous distortions and lies came thick and fast. My pen flew across the notebook pages.

After an eternity that was actually not more than five minutes, Worth paused. "There," he said, coming closer. "Now, let us see how well you have kept up with me. Hold the first page up to the light so that I can read it."

I did, and Worth saw the seven words I had written, on each page, over and over and over again:

ADAM WORTH IS A DANGEROUS, RAVING LUNATIC.

57. ACTION AND REACTION

I did not know what would result from my refusal to obey Worth's order. I really had no expectations at all. Holmes doubtless would have anticipated the various forms Worth's reaction might take, and the consequent advantages or disadvantages that would attach to any subsequent counter move on my part. I, on the other hand, was merely acting from the heart, or perhaps from a stubborn streak in my Scottish makeup that urged defiance against any man like Worth, regardless of risk or peril.

I did not plan my next action, either, nor did I consciously register my surroundings or Worth's reaction. Holmes would doubtless chide me for my lapse in attentiveness—I can hear him now: "You see, Watson, but you do not observe." Nonetheless, the events that followed are etched into my recollection as clearly as I see my journal and pen before me at this moment.

Crouched over me, Worth gave a cry of outrage. At the same instant I thrust the point of the reservoir pen upward toward his face. I wanted to blind him, but he shrank back reflexively and the point of the pen lodged in his throat.

With a roar he flung the notebook aside. His free hand yanked out the pen, as with his other hand he brought up the shotgun to fire at me, point-blank. Still seated and off balance from my lunge, I could see the opening at the end of each barrel coming to bear on my chest. I struggled to get to my feet. My muscles cramped. With an awful sense of inevitability I realized I would be too late.

Then two things happened almost simultaneously. On my left, Holmes dove past me, colliding with Worth, hitting him below the knees. And from behind me a shotgun roared, scorching the left side of my arm. I now know that Blake had fired both barrels to stop Holmes from reaching Worth, and that Holmes's dive had taken Blake by surprise before he was able to adjust his aim downward. What I saw in that moment was a great red stain in Worth's white shirt fabric, in the area of his left shoulder. Then Worth and Holmes were on the concrete, each struggling for control of Worth's shotgun.

I moved forward and was reaching to pull Worth's hands away from the gun when I heard Lucy's sharp cry. "Behind you!"

Turning, I saw James Blake, kneeling, snapping closed the breech of his reloaded shotgun and raising it to his shoulder. I gathered myself to spring forward when from behind me came two gunshots, each with the whiplike crack of a smaller weapon. Blake looked surprised as a small dark spot materialized in the center of his forehead. Then his expression went slack and he toppled onto his right side.

"Get his gun!" called Lucy.

The shotgun came easily from Blake's lifeless fingers. Turning back, I saw Holmes was on one knee and getting to his feet. He held Worth's gun.

But Worth had vanished, although dark stains on the concrete led my gaze to an aisle between two of the dark rows of crates that towered over us. Urgent questions filled my mind as I struggled to understand what to do: Ought I to follow the trail? How badly had Worth been wounded? Was he armed? Was he capable of shooting? I felt the same hollow uncertainty that had gripped me a few minutes before, when Holmes and I had walked the darkened streets in the shadows of this warehouse and the others. What danger lay waiting here and now, in these interior shadows?

I could see young Johnny Rockefeller beyond Holmes, locked in struggle with Moran, clinging grimly to him from behind like a Greek wrestler while Moran struggled to reach the Maxim gun. And a few yards to their left, Zoe and Lucy grappled with Cleo, Zoe trying to wrest control of the shotgun from her while Lucy hit at Cleo's face with her derringer.

I raised my gun and took aim at Cleo's legs but Holmes shot her first, knocking her down. I heard Holmes's voice. "The exit, Watson! Do not let him reach the stairway!"

The doorway to the stairs was nearly fifty feet behind me. I took a few steps back, trying to detect any sign of Worth in the darkness between the massive crates. But my attention was immediately drawn to where Lucy and Zoe now stood looking down on the wounded Cleo. Holmes's shot had struck her in the thigh. She lay on her side, knees drawn up to her chest, bleeding profusely from what I knew to be the femoral artery. Both her hands were bright red with her own blood as she vainly attempted to stanch the flow.

My gaze turned to Moran, who was on his hands and knees. Behind him, Johnny Rockefeller was getting to his feet. Above him, Holmes stood with the shotgun. Barely an inch separated the tip of the gun barrel from Moran's neck.

Holmes spoke. "One is dead, Moran. Two are wounded, perhaps mortally, unless they receive prompt medical attention. I have one loaded barrel remaining here, as you doubtless are aware. What is to be the outcome for you?"

"I shall never go back to Dartmoor," Moran snarled. Then he made a lunge for the shotgun, grasping at the barrel, pulling it forward so that Holmes's finger could not help but engage the trigger.

The resultant blast took Moran in the neck and must have severed his cervical spine. His arms fell away from the shotgun. His knees buckled. As the last reverberations of the gunshot faded, his face hit the concrete. Relief surged through me as I realized our old enemy would threaten us no more.

But in the next instant there was movement at my right. From between two tall rows of crates the twisted figure of Adam Worth burst from the shadows. He was running straight at Lucy, eyes gleaming with murderous determination. I saw a long knife clutched in his right fist. Instantly I realized his dreadful purpose. From the dark recess of his position, he had seen his own daughter shot down. The cruelest vengeance he could take would be to cause the death of Holmes's daughter in return.

I raised my shotgun. But to my horror, I saw I was too late. Worth had reached Lucy and I could not fire on him without hitting her.

Eyes blazing, Lucy spun away and dropped down, causing Worth's knife to swing harmlessly over her crouching form. And before Worth could gather himself for another blow, Holmes, holding his empty shotgun by the barrels, swung it club-like in a short, accurate arc, striking Worth on the side of his head directly beneath the temple.

Worth staggered. He tried to raise his knife, but it slipped from his fingers and clattered to the concrete. Then his legs gave way beneath him and he fell.

Blood continued to issue from Worth's shoulder wound, spreading in a dark pool beneath him. I realized his subclavian artery had been hit. With quick action I might be able to apply a pressure compress and save him.

Worth lay on his back, hands at his sides, eyes addled with shock but nonetheless burning with hate.

Holmes gestured toward Cleo, who now was also on her back. In her dark-stained uniform she lay motionless, mirroring the position of her father. But the rush of blood from her wound had stopped, and her skin had the white, waxy pallor of the lifeless.

"Mr. Worth," said Holmes coldly. "As you are probably aware, your daughter has died. So have Blake and Moran. Can you hear me?"

Worth nodded.

"Are you the last Moriarty?"

"I am," came the whispered reply.

"Dr. Watson can stop your bleeding and you may live to face trial. What is your wish?"

An oddly pious smile appeared on Worth's face. "I wish," he whispered, "that you would please come a little closer."

Then I saw Worth's hand emerging from his coat pocket, holding a revolver.

My reaction was instantaneous. Before I knew it, I had pulled both triggers, shooting from the hip. The recoil tore the weapon from my hands. The two loads of buckshot struck Worth in the face and chest, rolling him onto his side.

Worth's revolver fell to the concrete floor several yards from his body, as if it had been thrown away.

58. CACOPHONY

A few minutes later, Holmes had explained that unless we were willing to see Johnny, Lucy, and Zoe put through an ordeal at the hands of the investigative authorities, we would have to forgo the customary respects for the dead. The five of us stood together on the motorized platform lift. Holmes had lowered the platform to a level that enabled him to rest his arms on the concrete floor of the warehouse as he stood holding Worth's revolver. Carefully he took aim at the boxes of ammunition that lay amid four bodies and one disabled Maxim gun. Holmes, Johnny, and I had placed the bodies strategically, three of them close to the incendiary ammunition box, on the side that faced the windows. The fourth, Worth's, lay facedown atop the piled chains of bullets with their phosphorescent tips.

"Will the building burn?" asked Johnny.

"Brick walls, concrete floors, steel girders," Holmes replied. "A stray bullet may hit the roof. We are below the floor level, so we should be safe if we descend immediately after the ammunition catches fire. Now, all of you keep down."

He fired the revolver once, twice, three times. There came a sharp clatter of gunfire as the first phosphorous-tipped cartridges exploded, igniting others. As the wave of explosions grew in strength, Holmes flung the revolver toward the sound and into the darkness. He turned to the control lever of the motorized lift, pushing it forward so that the platform would descend. The noise of the electric motor beneath us was obliterated by an explosive cacophony of sound. Above us flickered tiny lightning flashes, intensifying into a brilliant glare. In less than a minute the light diminished to darkness, as if a firework rocket had exploded in its moment of glory and then faded.

59. AWAY

We reached the ground floor. To our left we could see the front door open to the electric lights on the quay outside. All of us were silent. Zoe was having difficulty walking and was leaning on Holmes's arm.

Lucy went ahead of us and looked outside the building. "No one is watching."

"We were never inside this building," Holmes said. "We know nothing about it. Nothing at all. Do you understand?"

Each of us nodded solemnly, as if we were making a sacred vow.

We walked in silence to where the lights were blazing at the edge of the quay. Holmes looked at his watch. "Six o'clock."

"Time for the performance to begin," said Zoe. She drew a deep breath and released Holmes's arm, standing up on her own. "Lucy, can you go on?"

"I can if you can."

Zoe turned to Holmes. "I can hardly believe I am free of that man. I am still in shock. I cannot find words strong enough to thank you."

"Your bravery tonight will remain always in my memory," said Holmes.

"When you left the *Corsair,* you looked like you could use some help," said Lucy. "So we followed you." Her hand touched her reticule. "I never thought I'd actually use my derringer."

Holmes said quietly, "Lucy, I owe you my life."

"Well, now I know I owe you *my* life," said Lucy, her eyes shining. "So I guess we're even."

We were about to cross the quay when from behind the wall of lights on the other side an agitated cry reached us. It was Lestrade's voice, harsh and shrill with alarm. "Hold your fire, all you men! Hold your fire! That's Sherlock Holmes!"

60. AN EXPLANATION FOR THE COMMISSIONER

On the *Corsair*, the Commissioner and Carte each smiled broadly as Holmes told them it was safe to go forward with the night's performance. Carte shook Holmes's hand vigorously, then bustled off inside the theater tent. The Commissioner immediately gave a signal to one of his men, who flashed his pocket lantern at one of the soldiers lined up along the quay below us. A series of flashes went down the line. Within a matter of seconds we saw an answering flash of light emanating from the *White Star*.

"But you left us for a time there," the Commissioner said.

"A last-minute worry of mine. Nothing has come of it."

The Commissioner nodded, averting his gaze from the bloodstains on Holmes's coat. He pointed upward and away from the ship, in the direction of the warehouses. "I noticed lights in that window over there. On the top floor. I thought I heard gunfire."

Holmes shrugged. "Possibly an industrial accident of some sort. They may have been storing fireworks for Guy Fawkes Night. You know how lax these fellows in the shipping warehouses can be."

61. WHAT THE PAPERS SAID

Lucy's performance that night was a triumph, though it went unreported in the newspapers due to the confidential nature of the venue. Nor did the papers mention Cettie Rockefeller's reaction to the enthusiastic outbursts of applause from young Johnny after each of Lucy's solos, or his departure the following day to resume his college studies in America. Likewise unreported was the transport of four unidentified bodies aboard the *HMS Daring* to Southampton and into the Channel for burial at sea. However, following a series of late-night telephone conversations between Mycroft and certain newspaper editors, the early Wednesday editions did carry front-page accounts of the arrival from America of Rockefeller, Carnegie, and Morgan, and their respective entourages, here in London to discuss strategic business relationships with senior officials of Her Majesty's government.

62. A BANKER APPEARS

Just after nine o'clock the next morning, Holmes and I stood with Mycroft and Sir Michael Hicks Beach, Chancellor of the Exchequer, outside the entrance to Prussia House, barely a stone's throw from the Diogenes Club on the other side of Waterloo Place. The building was an imposing white limestone structure that housed, behind its classic Greek columns and pediments, the embassy of the German Empire. Sir Michael, sharp-featured, alert-eyed, and with magnificent black whiskers that rivaled the Prime Minister's, nodded toward a small, gray-bearded man, who shuffled unobtrusively toward the doorway. Mycroft nodded in return and removed his hat.

From the shadows of the building Lestrade and three of his men emerged and surrounded the new arrival. After a brief conversation, the small, gray-bearded man handed an envelope to Lestrade, who looked inside it, nodded, and handed it over to Sir Michael. At this, the gray-bearded man took to his heels as if the Devil himself were after him.

"Holmes, why not arrest him?" I asked.

"His trial would reveal too much to the public," Holmes replied.

"Here, gentlemen," said Sir Michael, briefly opening the envelope for us to have a glimpse before tucking it into his inside coat pocket. "In our modern financial times, this is what one million pounds looks like."

"He knew he had to return the money," said Holmes as we watched the gray-bearded man disappear into the crowds along Waterloo Place, heading for Pall Mall. "Now that the newspapers have made clear that the conference is proceeding, the Germans will know that Worth's scheme has failed. The Kaiser's men will insist on repayment of their million-pound success fee. Our gray-bearded, treasonous banker came here to make that repayment. But since these bearer bonds are now in our possession, he is now one million pounds short."

"He is now fleeing for his life," said Mycroft. "When the Kaiser's men find him, our government will save the expense of a trial."

"And a hangman," said Holmes.

63. NUMBER 10 DOWNING STREET

"Her Majesty's government is in your debt for the sum of one million pounds, Mr. Holmes," said the Prime Minister, a few minutes later at Number 10 Downing Street, where we had accompanied Sir Michael, at his insistence, to present the envelope containing the bearer bonds. "It is hard for me to imagine a more satisfactory conclusion to this most stressful affair. Goschen and Lansdowne are on their way to the *Corsair* for what I hope will be a fruitful series of discussions. Morgan and Rockefeller propose that you be given a handsome and generous reward."

"Please present them with my sincere compliments and ask if they would instead kindly make a handsome and generous concession in the negotiations."

Lord Salisbury paused. "You will have no trouble about the Official Secrets Act, Mr. Holmes. I told Halsbury that I shall require his resignation if he so much as mentions it in connection with the way you have handled this delicate matter. However, there is just one point on which I should like some clarification," he said. "This Adam Worth person that we have heard so much about. Has he been apprehended?"

"He will not trouble England, Prime Minister. I can assure you of that."

"And the escaped convict, the disgraced Colonel Sebastian Moran?"

"The same applies to him."

Lord Salisbury gave Holmes a long, appraising look and then a smile. "That's all right, then." He handed the envelope back to Sir Michael. "Get this into the treasury right away. We can purchase more artillery to use against those rebellious Boers."

And with a subsequent smile, handshake, and nod to each of us, we were dismissed.

64. HOLMES ADMITS A POSSIBILITY

We returned to Baker Street by cab. On the way, Holmes remarked, "A most satisfactory diagnosis, Dr. Watson."

"I beg your pardon?"

"What you wrote in that notebook forced upon you by Mr. Worth. I could not help reading the words as I burned the pages last night. Worth was indeed a dangerous madman. It was more than courageous of you to goad him the way you did, simply because you refused to put my reputation at risk. You were risking your life."

"Your reputation is an inspiration to millions. And when Worth was about to shoot me, you put your own life at risk. You never gave up."

Holmes gave a sigh. "Each of us acted in haste last night, without pausing to analyze the probabilities of success. For my part, I am forced to admit the possibility that I have grown soft and emotional, and that I may have lost my capacity for intellectual rigor. I wonder if that is because Miss James and Miss Rosario have entered my life. I wonder how I shall continue to function."

I was about to offer reassurance and support. Then I saw the twinkle in Holmes's eye. "You're having me on, aren't you?"

"Quite possibly, Watson."

I could not refrain from asking, "All right, but then what really are your plans regarding Miss James and Miss Rosario? Yesterday they both talked of going to Rome, and I strongly suspect it was you who made the arrangements with Mr. D'Oyly Carte for them to do so."

Holmes turned up an empty palm.

I pressed the point. I needed to know. "Holmes, how do you see your future with those two ladies?"

"I propose to help them with whatever enterprises they wish to undertake," Holmes replied. "It remains only to determine what those enterprises may be." He gave one of his little half smiles. "And that inquiry may take some time."

65. A VIOLIN BRINGS US TOGETHER

Zoe's Stradivarius was found that afternoon by the police, in a connecting stairwell between Worth's two flats at 198 Piccadilly. When I heard the news, I wondered how that valuable instrument had figured into Worth's plan. I envisioned him taunting Zoe with the threat of its destruction in an effort to manipulate Holmes.

"Or he may simply have planned to sell it," Holmes replied when I relayed my thoughts. "Fortunately, Mr. Worth is no longer able to tell us his true motives."

The next afternoon Holmes and I brought the violin to Zoe's flat. We found Lucy with Zoe, helping her pack for the journey to Rome.

Zoe opened the violin case and showed us the beautiful instrument inside. "I am so glad I did not lose this," she said, looking first at Holmes, and then at Lucy. "It brought us together."

"Twenty-one years ago," Holmes said.

Zoe said, "I have always wanted to tell you. When you spoke of Linton Hill I was certain that you knew. But as I said in that awful warehouse, I was ashamed of not telling you, so I ran away. I am glad you deduced the truth."

"So am I."

Lucy looked at Holmes. "I felt a connection when we first met. And so did you."

"I made observations and deductions," he said.

Lucy said, "But how did you *know*?"

"After I saw the registry of your birth, it was merely simple arithmetic," Holmes said. "You were born January seventh, 1875. You weighed eight pounds, seven ounces, which is quite a robust weight. We know the period of human gestation is nine months. So it would have been impossible for your conception to have occurred barely more than six months previously, at the time when I was away for school vacation during the early summer, and when Professor Moriarty falsely told his brother he had fathered you. Also, I knew where Zoe and I had been in the springtime of 1874."

He looked at Zoe for a moment and then went on quickly, "As I said, the calculation is a simple one."

"Oh, of course," Lucy replied. "Quite elementary."

66. INSOMNIA REVISITED

Zoe and Lucy departed Saturday on the Dover Express, on their way to Calais and then Rome.

Holmes and I were at Charing Cross Station to see them off. He embraced them warmly, as did I. Then he assisted each of the ladies in turn, lifting her by the hand as she stepped up from the railway platform into the first-class carriage. Lucy seemed amused and delighted at this, while Zoe accepted the gesture with a graceful smile.

We have had cheerful letters from each of them on several occasions during the five months that have passed since their departure. The most recent from Zoe came with the news that she had reconciled with her parents and that they had welcomed Lucy as their granddaughter. Zoe also mentioned that she would be remaining in Rome for a time because her mother was in failing health and needed care. Holmes accepted this news with equanimity.

Then yesterday we received a wire from Lucy. The troupe concluded its last performance in Italy and she was returning to London.

Last night, for the first time in five months, I was awakened by the sound of Holmes pottering about in his rooms below me. This morning I came down to breakfast and noticed that his papers, no longer strewn in their usual cascade, were now organized in neat stacks around our sitting room. In the adjacent space that had once been my bedchamber, his laboratory instruments and glassware shone with cleanliness.

At the breakfast table, Holmes informed me that he had made arrangements with Mrs. Hudson to make available a spare suite of rooms at the back of our building, in the event Lucy should need an accommodation for a few months.

"Or," Holmes added with a casual shrug, "perhaps longer."

I shall set these pages aside now, without recording any of my imaginings or hopes of what may transpire. I well know that it is a capital mistake to speculate until one is in full possession of the facts.

HISTORICAL NOTES

This is a work of fiction, and the author makes no claim whatsoever that any historical locations or historical figures who appear in this story were even remotely connected with the adventures recounted herein. However . . .

1. The design and location of the Diogenes Club in this story are based on The Athenaeum, a gentlemen's club in Pall Mall founded in 1824, active today, and thought by some to be the model for the Diogenes Club that appears in the original Sherlock Holmes stories created by Sir Arthur Conan Doyle.

2. The office of the registrar general of births, marriages, and deaths was located in Somerset House in 1895, but it was relocated nearly a century later. Due to its spectacular architecture, Somerset House has been used as a location for many film and television entertainments, including several involving Sherlock Holmes.

3. The Bank of England continues in full operation at One Threadneedle Street. No gold has ever been stolen from the Bank since its inception in 1654.

4. The Savoy Theatre and Savoy Hotel continue to operate adjacent to one another in the Strand, city of Westminster, London. *The Mikado* continues to be performed in hundreds of theaters throughout the world.

5. The Royal Navy converted from coal to oil, though the conversion was not complete until the end of the Great War.

6. John D. Rockefeller Sr. retired from business in 1897. In 1911 the United States government broke up the Standard Oil Trust. The move made Rockefeller the world's first billionaire, and, adjusting for inflation, the wealthiest man of all time. He gave nearly all of the money to charities and to his children before he passed away at age 97.

7. John D. Rockefeller Jr. married Abby Aldrich, the daughter of Senator Nelson Aldrich of Providence, Rhode Island, and devoted his working life to philanthropy. Their union provided Rockefeller Sr. with six grandchildren, five of whom went on to lives of significant fame and responsibility.

8. The *Corsair* was purchased by the US government in 1898 and served in the Spanish-American War as the USS *Gloucester*.

9. In 1902 Morgan formed the International Mercantile Marine, a shipping trust that included Rockefeller's American railway interests and, after a meeting with Kaiser Wilhelm on a new *Corsair*, the German Hamburg-Amerika Steamship Line. Morgan balanced his activity between business and philanthropic interests until his death in 1913.

10. Adam Worth was an American criminal who with his brother formed a successful crime network in London during the Victorian era. Sir Arthur Conan Doyle is thought to have used Worth as a model for his fictional Professor Moriarty and may have modeled the foiled bank robbery described in "The Red-Headed League" on Worth's successful robbery of the Boylston National Bank of Boston. Worth owned an estate in

Clapham Common, a flat at 198 Piccadilly, and a yacht called the *Shamrock*.

11. Watson never published a reference to Zoe Rosario or Lucy James. In "The Adventure of the Illustrious Client" he refers to Colonel Sebastian Moran as still being alive in 1902, which may have been a deliberate attempt to conceal the circumstances of Moran's death.

12. Sherlock Holmes continued to serve his country and other illustrious clients. His death has not been recorded, and there is speculation that he discovered a means of extending life through his researches on the properties of royal jelly, as recorded in his *Practical Handbook of Bee Culture, with Some Observations on the Segregation of the Queen.*

13. Lucy James will return.

ACKNOWLEDGMENTS

This book owes a great deal to the editorial wisdom and guidance of Thomas & Mercer's Kjersti Egerdahl, Girl Friday Productions' Jenna Free, Cathy Yardley, Anna Elliot, and especially my wonderful wife, Pamela Veley. I'm also grateful for the support and encouragement of Garner Simmons, Dan Matos, and also June Grube, who gave me the benefit of her fabulous proofreading skills. I also extend my warmest thanks to Todd A. Johnson of TAJ Design, Inc. for his creative cover, and especially to the remarkably talented Jacob Thompson for bringing these words to brilliant life in the audio version of this book, available on Audible.com.

ABOUT THE AUTHOR

 Charles Veley is an avid fan of Sherlock Holmes and Gilbert & Sullivan. He wrote *The Pirates of Finance*, a new musical in the G&S tradition, which won an award at the New York Musical Theatre Festival in 2013. His books include *Children of the Dark*, *Play to Live*, *Night Whispers*, and *Catching Up*.